MATTEO

THE DIMAGGIO CRIME FAMILY BOOK ONE

T. PRICETON

Book Cover by AK Cover Designs
Developmental Editing by Memos in the Margins
Line and Copy Editing by Dee's Notes: Editing and Proofreading Services

First Edition 2024

This one goes out to anyone who thinks their words on a piece of paper aren't good enough for others to read. Go ahead and publish that book. You won't regret it.

CONTENT WARNING

Please note this book contains explicit scenes of sex and violence, and is meant for a mature audience only.

The following is a list of content warnings: kidnapping, extortion, mentions death of parents, mentions sex/human trafficking, mentions drug trafficking, mentions weapons trafficking, gun violence, explicit scenes of murder, pruning shears violence, knife violence, unprotected sex, swallowing of bodily fluids, light sexual choking.

PROLOGUE

LUXTYN

"What do you want to watch tonight, sweetie? A rom-com or one of those reality TV shows?" my mom asks as she makes herself comfortable on the couch and scrolls through Netflix.

"I'm thinking tonight's more of a trashy reality TV show kind of night," I say while pouring the microwavable popcorn into a bowl for us to share.

I walk around the counter and take a seat on the couch, and my mom puts on our most recent bingeable show. "So how was work today?"

"Not too bad," she says before clearing her throat and adding, "I just . . . well, I have to head to New York City on Friday for a client. There's an event she has to attend, and she asked me to do her hair for it."

My jaw drops and I gasp in excitement, but when I take in the apprehension in her voice and the rigidness in her body, my brows furrow. "That's awesome, Mom, but why do I feel like I'm far more excited for you than you are for yourself?"

She slides her gaze over to me and gives me a tight smile. "Oh, no, it's very exciting. I just don't want to leave you, is all."

"Mom, I'm going to be twenty-three soon. I think I can handle being on my own for a few days," I say, chuckling.

That straight-lined smile of hers ticks up slightly, and she gives my forearm a light squeeze. "I know, sweetie."

She averts her attention back to the TV, and I study her for a moment. She's not angry about going to New York City, but she seems . . . nervous? That doesn't make any sense, though. Is she really that worried about leaving me alone for a few days? This would be our first time apart for that long, but that's not something I've even thought twice about.

"I promise I'll be okay while you're gone, Mom."

"Of course, Lux. I know you'll be just fine."

Her smile brightens this time, but not to its full extent. There's still something off about it, like she's holding something back.

"Mom—" She reaches for my arm and gives it another small squeeze.

"You know me. I'm just a little overprotective." Averting her attention back to the TV, she pops some popcorn into her mouth, silently telling me this conversation is over.

While I'm wondering what else could be the issue, I decide to ignore it but can't keep from laughing. "I like how your job lets you travel to new places while both of mine just leave me smelling like beer and food by the end of my shifts."

"You know, you don't need to work both of those jobs if you don't want to. We're doing just fine, you and I. Overworking yourself isn't a necessity."

I shake my head. "I really don't mind. You know I go stir-crazy if I don't keep myself busy. Besides, I only work at the restaurant a few days a week." I give her a relaxed shrug. "The extra cash is nice."

"Well, if you ever decide you want to take a break, just know that we'll be okay if you do. Good things are happening, and I have a feeling we'll have more than enough money to get by, okay?"

"I know. Promise," I say with a smile even though I'm not sure what she means. I do well with my tips, and my mom does well with hairdressing, but "more than enough money to get by" seems like a stretch.

It's always just been my mom and me my entire life. She was raised in the foster system, and my dad ran out on us before I was born, so we're the only family each other have. It's one of the reasons we're so close.

My mom has spent most of my life supporting us on her own, so maybe me working two jobs is my way of trying to give back and lighten the load she's carried for the both of us.

I take in her perfectly styled dark waves that come down just past her shoulders, and the smile on her face shifts to a frown, giving me the sense she's lost in her own thoughts. It reestablishes my suspicions that there's something else bothering her about New York City. I just don't know what it could be . . .

1

LUXTYN

"Luxtyn, I need four tequila shots with this beer order."

I glance up, brushing a dark strand behind my ear, and make eye contact with Macie, who's leaning over the counter at the opposite end of the bar. She's holding up her order ticket with the fake smile I've grown accustomed to over the past few months.

A *please* would be nice, but for her to use actual pleasantries around me would probably require a knife to her throat or a gun to her head—something dramatic like that.

Giving her an equally fake smile that will leave me with crow's feet at far too young of an age if I continue charading it around for people like her, I say, "No problem," as I head in her direction.

I pull the ticket from between her freshly manicured nails, then read the order.

Four Corona Lights and four Patrons.

Rolling my eyes, I hold up the paper between my fingers.

"You realize I can read, right?" She's wearing the same crimson lipstick I've seen her wear five days a week since my mom and I moved here three months ago.

Without a hiccup in her expression, she continues with her annoyingly condescending tone. "I figured I'd tell you too. You know, just in case."

Picking up her notepad and shoving it into the back pocket of her Daisy Dukes, she turns to walk away from the counter but, of course, has to add one last snide remark.

"I wanted to make sure there wouldn't be any excuses if there's a mistake." She gives me a patronizing wink before taking off toward a table full of male patrons with a sway in her step.

That girl irks me.

Grabbing four shot glasses, I line them up on the bar top and pour the tequila in each before grabbing the beers and popping off the caps.

You'd think with the way she acts that I'd be notorious at Snide's Dive Bar for messing up drinks all night, but nope. Macie's just a bitch. Your typical small-town, lived here my entire life so don't try to show me up kind of bitch.

I've come across several Macies in my life, so I'm used to her bad attitude. It's annoying but not something I need nor have the energy to combat.

Grabbing a circular serving tray, I load the drinks and bring it over to the side of the bar where servers pick up their orders.

Macie's still flirting her way through the four-top of preppy-looking guys wearing their pastel-colored polos, khaki chino shorts, and Sperry's. The go-to attire for this small coastal town in Florida.

I smirk while placing her order ticket on the tray. I've never served Corona or tequila shots without lime, but Little Miss

Efficient didn't write it on the order ticket, so I guess no lime it is. *Two can play petty, bitch.*

As Macie makes her way back toward me, my phone vibrates in my back pocket, and I know it's my mom calling from New York.

I pull my phone out of my back pocket and answer it. "Hey, Mom, hold on a sec," I say while ducking under the bar.

I walk down the hall, making my way to the kitchen when Macie's shrill of a voice comes from behind me. "Hey! You forgot the lime for these drinks, Luxtyn!"

As I peer over my shoulder, I take in her narrowed gaze and scrunched nose. *Poor Macie has to get her own limes. What ever will she do?*

"Maybe you should've left *explicit* directions if you didn't want any *mistakes* to happen with your order," I shout back at her with a shrug before pushing the kitchen doors open. "I'm not a mind reader, *Mace*."

I giggle to myself because I know how much she hates when I call her that. Which, in my defense, isn't very often, but she's pissing me off today, so I might as well poke the bear while I can.

"That's not my name!" The swoosh of the swinging doors drowns out her shriek.

I roll my eyes as I weave my way through the kitchen, doing my best to stay out of the cooks' ways as I head toward the back door.

Stepping outside, I breathe in the slight breeze from the ocean. You can practically taste the salt from the sea. I take a seat on the bench and bring my phone back to my ear. "Sorry about that, Mom. I just needed to get somewhere quiet."

"Oh, you don't have to worry about that, Lux. I know you're working tonight, but I wanted to chat before it gets too late. How's the bar?" she asks in her normal chipper tone.

"Not too bad. Still early, so it's not quite busy yet. Did you make it to New York okay?"

There's a brief pause before she answers. "Yes, I've just been relaxing in the hotel room."

"I'm glad you made it safely. Maybe if you get the opportunity to go back I can come with you. Or hey, maybe that'll end up being our next home for a few years." I laugh.

My mom and I have moved around a lot throughout my life, and when I say a lot, I mean like every few years.

I know it seems weird, chaotic even, but when you know nothing else, it's really just a way of life. I think my body has adjusted to wanting to be in a different place every few years, because sometimes when we get to the latter end of the three-year residency period, I get the itch to just leave. You could say I have quite the nomad's soul.

When I was younger, I used to question my mom, asking her why she was always moving us around, but she would never give me a solid explanation. Always brushing me off, telling me she was ready for a new adventure. I know my mom well, though, and that was never the *real* reason.

Something must've happened, but I gave up on pushing it a while back. If she's not telling me, then she has a good reason.

I know my mom's only ever had our best interests in mind. Some people might call me naive, but they don't know the relationship we have. There's none like it. She's always been there for me, like I'll always be there for her.

"Oh, I don't think so, Lux," she blurts. "It's far too crowded here. We do much better in smaller towns." She quickly changes the subject. "So, tell me, is that Macie girl still giving you a hard time?"

I chuckle because I know she heard us through the phone just minutes ago. "Oh, you know, she's just acting like her typical self. Nothing I can't handle, though."

I hear the grin spread across her face as she says, "That's my girl. Don't allow anyone to treat you like they're better than you."

"You've taught me well, Mom."

And she has. Ever since I was a little kid, Mom has always instilled the importance of having confidence in myself.

"The strength of a woman comes from her confidence within, and it's my job as your mother to teach you and make you see the worth you have."

"You've grown into quite the remarkable young woman. I couldn't have asked for a better daughter."

"Oh no. I know that voice, Mom."

She sounds like she just got done watching one of those welcome home videos you see on social media when a parent deployed comes home and surprises their child at school or somewhere public and unsuspecting. Those videos get her every time. She cries. Sobs, really, and right now she sounds like she just got done watching a long line of welcome home videos.

"Oh, hush, I'm fine," she says unconvincingly. "I'm just so proud of you, Lux. And I'm honored to be your momma."

"Mom, what's with the emotions? I haven't done anything for you to be *that* proud of," I mumble.

"Hey, you're strong, and that's a trait some can only aspire to have."

While rolling my eyes, I'm startled when the back door is thrown open. Sitting up straighter, I glance over and see it's Kelly, one of the other bartenders and Macie's best friend.

I give her a small smile before a muffled voice in the background, followed by my mom's gasp comes through the phone.

"Mom, are—"

The faint sound of a man's voice mixed with some shuffling, sounds over the line before my Mom's voice comes through an octave higher. "Angelo?"

"Mom? Are you okay?" I ask, bringing myself to the edge of the bench. My heart rate elevates when she doesn't respond right away.

"Mom!" I hiss out, trying to get her attention while also attempting to keep from drawing unwanted attention from Kelly, but she eyes me warily over the screen of her phone.

"I-I have to go, sweetie," my mom finally says, but her stammer, along with the sudden worried tone, has me on edge. Saying bye isn't something I'm inclined to do right now.

"Mom, what's going on? I heard a voice in the background, and now you sound worried. Are you okay?"

"Oh, yes, I'm fine," she replies, hastily brushing me off and forcing her voice back to normal. But I know when something is off.

"Mom—"

"Sweetie, I have to get going, but I'll talk to you tomorrow, okay?"

"But—"

"I love you. Text me when you get home from work tonight so I know you made it back to the apartment safely."

Sighing, I begrudgingly say, "Okay. I love you, too. I'll talk to you later, alright?"

"I look forward to it. Bye, sweetie."

"Bye, Mom."

Hanging up is difficult to do when there's a sinking feeling in the pit of my stomach telling me something was off with that conversation. My mom might have tried to act like it was nothing, but I know her well enough to know that something is up.

"Luxtyn!"

Snapping my gaze toward the sound of my name, I see Monique, my boss, poking her head out the backdoor. "There are drink orders piling up on the bar. I need you back inside now!" Glancing at my coworker, she adds, "You too, Kelly!" before disappearing back inside.

I can't shake the feeling that something is off, so I glance down at my phone, noting the time, and begin counting down the hours until I can talk to my mom again. I just need confirmation she's okay.

2

MATTEO

"Have you spoken to Mancini about the impending nuptials?" my younger brother, Enzo, asks over the pounding bass of the music at Fierce, a high-end nightclub I own in the heart of New York City.

"He rescheduled that meeting to Sunday," I say as a group of ladies led by a familiar-looking blonde with long pin-straight hair, and even longer legs, make their way toward our VIP lounge.

"Incoming, Boss," my guard, Rocco, says, nodding to the entrance of the room that is now occupied by the three girls. They're each wearing the same style dress, just in different colors. Short enough that they barely cover the curve of their asses, and tight enough that their tits nearly pop up over the edge of their tops.

Gianni, who's standing guard at the entrance of the squared-off room, glances back at me for confirmation, to which I give a slight nod, signaling him to allow the girls in.

The cushion of the black velvet couch sinks when my brother leans over, lowering his voice so only I can hear him.

"You're entertaining this?" Enzo scoffs. I'm sure he recognizes the blonde who hasn't taken her eyes off me since she got up here, just like every other time she's been at my club for the past month.

Angling my head toward my brother, I smirk as the blonde makes herself comfortable between Rocco and I while her friends flank him and my brother's sides.

"Thanks for letting us join you," the blonde next to me squeals, making me regret this decision. But there's a purpose for her tonight, and until that purpose is fulfilled, I'm stuck with her.

Glancing over, I take in her bright-blue eyes and red lipstick. It could've been worse. At least the girl *is* hot—when she doesn't speak.

"I'm Ashley." Her hand slides up my thigh, and I instinctively grab her wrist. She's more eager than I anticipated, but I guess that's to be expected coming from a girl who eye-fucks me every chance she gets.

Her eyes widen as she tenses, so I loosen my grip on her and extend my other arm around her shoulder while caressing her fingers on my leg. If I'm going to lead the girl on, the least I can do is not be a complete dick about it.

She relaxes into me, and her overly sweet perfume assaults my nostrils. *Great, just what I need. To smell like a damn stripper.*

"What's your name?" she asks, pressing her fake tits into my side. I'm not an idiot; she's been asking around about me and knows I own this club. I can't stand when they act dumb, but it's almost 11:00 p.m., so I'll entertain this for a couple more minutes.

"Matteo."

"Matteo," she purrs as her glistening eyes dart to my lips. Why do women make it so damn easy?

"I have to admit, I've noticed you around." She bats her fake lashes at me.

Look at that. Honesty. Say it ain't so.

"Have you now?" I ask, disengaged.

Before she continues, I feel Rocco's eyes shift toward me, likely trying to get my attention, which means someone else has finally found their way to our lounge.

Right on time.

"Yeah, I was hoping you'd—"

"What exactly is going on here?" a nagging voice interrupts from across the room.

I side-eye the source of the noise. "Giuliana," I acknowledge, my tone reflecting my relaxed demeanor. I feel my brother's gaze settle on my face as he puts together why I've chosen to entertain these girls tonight out of all nights.

Giuliana looks cute in her tight little black dress with her pin-straight dark-brown hair hanging down just past her shoulders. I'll even go as far as to say she's hot, but this thing about her irritates the hell out of me, and if I'm going to be stuck with her attached to my name the rest of my life, it's about time she understands where she stands.

"Who is this *whore* that's saddled up next to you with her talons glued to where they don't belong, Matteo?" she sneers, crossing her arms and giving each of her friends who flanked her sides a smirk.

Ashley caresses my inner thigh, clueless to what she's become a part of, and while I'd feel bad for her . . . well, I just don't. Sympathy isn't a trait I possess for meaningless women.

Nodding toward Ashley, I give Giuliana the introduction she asked for. "Ashley, Giuliana, Giuliana, Ashley."

Giuliana's dark eyes snap to Ashley's before she puts on a pristine smile, like a trained pageant queen. She glides toward us and extends her hand to Ashley. "Nice to meet you, *hun*."

Ashley stiffens next to me, surely not expecting Giuliana's one-eighty. Too bad for her it's all a ploy. She lifts her hand from my thigh and goes to shake Giuliana's.

Foolish girl.

Before Ashley can reciprocate the fake pleasantries, Giuliana takes her hand and jerks her out of her seat. She stumbles over her five-inch heels, falling to the floor. Yanking her up, Giuliana pulls Ashley toward her while I remain seated, intrigued in seeing what Giuliana thinks she can do in this situation.

"Listen here, you twat. Matteo is *my* fiancé. So unless you want me to arrange your sudden disappearance, I highly recommend you keep your trashy ass hands off him. Got it?" she snaps.

Giuliana and I have grown up in the same crime-ridden life, her father being the head of one of the four crime families in New York, so violence is something she's used to. She's only twenty-two, seven years younger than me, and was never my first choice for marriage, but her family has control of one of the two ports in the city, which is something I need.

Her father and I are signing a contract that will give me control of his port upon our marriage as long as I give him seventy-five percent of the proceeds. It's a fucking greedy ass deal, but I don't need the money. I need to control who has access to the port. Having control of both ports in the city is crucial.

"I-I didn't realize he was engaged," Ashley says. The poor girl seems to have lost her confidence just as quickly as she lost her balance when she was yanked up by Giuliana.

"That's because I'm not," I interrupt, my gaze placed firmly on Giuliana's. The flame in her eyes she had moments ago has extinguished.

"As of right now, you and I are not engaged, Giuliana, and

even if we were, you must be confused as to how this marriage is going to work."

Her eyes widen. "Matteo—"

I hold up my hand, silencing her.

"If you think you have any say in what I do, you're sorely mistaken, so I highly recommend you let go of Ashley and take yourself *the fuck* away from me before I decide to find another bride."

The meaningless threat lingers in the air as I glance back at Ashley and give her a grin that immediately relaxes her. She returns it with that same glisten in her eyes she had before we were interrupted.

"Someone more accommodating maybe," I add with a smirk before returning my attention back to Giuliana whose lip is curled and eyebrows are drawn close together.

She reluctantly releases Ashley's hand and steps back. "I apologize, Matteo," she says, her tone soft, no longer displaying that edge she had upon walking in here. She eyes me, waiting to see if I'll say anything else.

I don't.

When she finally realizes I'm done speaking to her, she turns to her friends and nods toward the door, exiting without another word.

Ashley returns to her seat next to me on the couch, placing her hand back on my thigh as if it never left, and I let her.

"Well, that was quite the show," Enzo says from next to me with a dark chuckle. "So what do you want to do now?"

"I'm not quite sure what *you're* going to do," I say as I rest my arm over the back of the couch, "but I'm going to take Ashley here back to my office and let her suck my dick."

Her eyes gleam at the excitement of finally getting what she's wanted for the past month. It's predictable. Boring. But it'll get the job done.

"I need to prove a point to Giuliana, and I'm going to use Ashley to prove that point. You don't have a problem with that, do you, Ashley?"

Her smile widens as she responds all too eagerly. "Not at all."

I prefer a chase, something that gets the blood pumping, but I can't remember the last time I felt that way regarding a woman. I enjoy sex like any other guy, but the push and pull makes it a little more exciting for me. It's always the same old thing—easy, and that gets boring real fucking fast.

"And what is that point exactly?" Enzo asks, pulling me out of my thoughts. I turn my attention back to him with Ashley's brunette little friend still glued to his side.

"That *no one* dictates my life. Her father and I might be signing a contract that involves us getting married, but she's fucking delusional if she thinks I'm going to allow her to have any say in this marriage of convenience."

Chuckling, Enzo shakes his head as he twirls his index finger in the air. "So, that's what this was all about. You're asserting your dominance."

He posed it as a statement and not so much a question, which requires only a slight nod of my head, confirming the accusation.

"This engagement is about to become a whole lot more real, so I needed Giuliana to understand that she's nothing but a business transaction to me. A means to an end. She needs to understand the role she's going to be playing in my life."

Standing from the couch, I pull Ashley up with me and glance back at my brother who looks awfully comfortable for someone who didn't want to entertain these women not too long ago. "I refuse to deal with a *wife* who thinks she's anything more to me than a name on a piece of paper when we have far bigger issues to work out with this merger."

Enzo raises his hands. "Hey, you know I'm here for the bigger picture."

After saying our goodbyes, I lead Ashley and I toward my office, and just as I predicted, Giuliana's eyes are glued on me from her VIP table in the corner.

I knew she wouldn't leave the club unless I ordered her to, and that would've defeated the purpose of allowing her to show up here tonight. I *want* her to see me bring Ashley into my office. I *want* her to know she'll be getting me off tonight. Because the sooner she understands this upcoming marriage between us means nothing, the better it'll be for both of us.

3

LUXTYN

I woke up this morning with that sinking feeling still in the pit of my stomach. When I texted my mom last night letting her know I got home from work, she never responded. Then I texted and called while I was at my day job, serving the breakfast and lunch crowds at a local diner, but she still hasn't responded.

She could be busy working. Maybe her client has her doing other things, but it's unlike her to not answer me.

I'm getting ready for my job at the bar when I decide to just call her repeatedly until she answers the phone. That seems like an annoying enough thing to do to elicit a response.

Pulling out my phone, I click on my mom's number, but instead of the dial tone taking over the speaker, it goes straight to voicemail.

Voicemail.

She never turns her phone off, not even at night.

I try it again in hopes that maybe it's a technological issue that has rectified itself in the past few seconds, but no, voicemail again. How the hell am I supposed to go to work when I don't know what's going on with my mom?

Glancing in my bathroom mirror, I tell myself to relax and that I'm just being paranoid. My mom is busy working and lost service. Everything is fine. I look down at my phone, willing it to light up with my mom's picture, but it doesn't.

"Don't worry, Lux," I mumble to my reflection in the mirror. "I'm sure she'll text while I'm at work, and that'll prove I'm just acting like a crazy person."

As soon as I get to work, I'm distracted the entire time, constantly checking to see if she's called or texted.

"Are you okay, Luxtyn?" someone asks while my head is buried in my phone.

I glance up to Kelly pouring a slew of beers from the tap. She's eyeing the phone in my hand before I shove it in my back pocket. "Yeah, everything's fine." I point to the row of pint glasses she has lined up on the counter, waiting to be filled. "Do you need help with those?"

"Actually, yeah," she says, tucking some strands of shoulder length golden blonde hair behind her ear. "If you could grab eight chilled tequila shots for this order, I'd appreciate it. Macie has that large group of guys over there who apparently came out to get shitfaced," she says as she nods toward a group of guys that Macie's busy entertaining.

"Yeah, I can do that." I line up eight shot glasses and pour the tequila in the shaker with some ice.

I'm putting the filled shot glasses on a tray when Kelly comes up beside me, placing her first tray of beers on the counter next to the shots. "You seem distracted tonight."

I shake my head. "Everything's good."

Even though Kelly and Macie are best friends, Kelly's always been cordial. Even so, I've never been one to open up to people, so we've never gotten to know each other.

"You've been checking your phone a lot tonight. Are you expecting a call or something?"

She's trying to be nice and make conversation, but opening up to her about my mom is the last thing I want to do. So instead of telling her about my concerns, I lie. "The Yankees and the Rays are playing tonight. I'm a huge Rays fan, so I've been stalking the game."

Turning around, I walk down to the other end of the bar before Kelly can negate what I'm saying because I have *no* idea if the Yankees and the Rays are playing tonight. I don't even know if baseball games are on this late, but that was the only thing I could think of. I pray I got the hint across that I don't want to talk and she leaves me alone for the rest of the night.

Thankfully, Kelly does just that, only occasionally speaking to me when she needs assistance with an order here and there. And Macie surprisingly does the same. I'm not sure if Kelly said something to her when they wandered off on their break earlier, but it's not important. Right now, I need to figure out what's going on with my mom because I know something is wrong.

4

MATTEO

"Hey, Boss. Mancini just arrived with one of his men. They're sending them up now," Rocco alerts to me as I sit at my desk in the office of my penthouse going over the numbers from the last load of guns we received.

Weapons trafficking is the number one way my family makes money, which is why port access is highly sought after by the crime families of New York.

Drawing my attention to Rocco, I nod to him.

"Mancini never sent over a copy of the contract beforehand?" Enzo asks as he sits in one of the two black leather chairs positioned across the desk from mine.

"Nope. He said something about wanting to go over it in person." Having the time to go over a contract before the meeting is preferable, but I intend to have two signatures on that document before Mancini walks out the door today. So if he needs to go over it in person, then that's what we'll do.

"You sure you don't want our lawyer to look it over before you sign it?"

"That's not necessary. You know the faster we get this done, the better. The only way I can get control of his port is with a wedding ring on Giuliana's finger."

"Besides," I continue as I lean back in my oversized chair, "it's not going to be a complex contract. Just our names, a few terms, and a couple of signatures."

Rocco exits the room to meet Mancini at the elevator, leaving Enzo and me by ourselves. "You ready for this, then?" he asks, raising a brow at me as if he thinks I don't know what I'm getting myself into.

"You know this is the life we lead, Enzo. Arranged marriages are a staple in our world. At least I'm able to make a strategic move and pick a wife that will benefit us. This gets us that much closer to taking down Giuseppe Silvestri and stripping his family of their power before we get rid of him. The alliance between them and the Mancinis has been going on for far too long."

"As long as you think marriage to Giuliana for the rest of your life is worth it."

"Of course it's worth it. Giuliana might think this marriage is going to be more than a contractual agreement between her father and me, but it won't take me long to show her how our lives are going to be."

Enzo nods. "And you used that chick as an example last night."

Chuckling to myself, I rest my elbows on the arm rests of my chair and interlock my fingers in front of me. "Yep, and I'll do it again to prove to her she has zero say in what I do. Our lives are not to be interconnected. The port is all that matters. She can continue living her life the way she sees fit, and I'll continue living my life the way I see fit."

Shaking his head, Enzo narrows his gaze on me. "I don't understand how it can be this easy. Silvestri and Mancini have been in an alliance since Silvestri's sister was married off to Mancini. Why would he allow Mancini to join forces with us? He has to know our plan is to cut his ties with the port."

"Giuseppe Silvestri still sees me as a young, naive leader. One that won't retaliate for what he did to our parents." Which makes sense, considering I haven't retaliated in the three years since he ordered the hit on them. But what I have planned for the Silvestri family is more than death.

"If he thinks we've aligned ourselves with Mancini, then he'll think he's just gotten access to our port. The man is power hungry. Power in our world is what's important, Enzo. It'll blind even our worst enemies."

"So, when you marry Giuliana, where will she live? Here or at our family home?"

My penthouse is in the heart of the city. It's where I spend time when I need to take care of business here. Our family home, where our parents raised us, is located forty minutes out of the city, secluded on several acres of land. We're selective about who we bring there, and I don't plan on starting with Giuliana.

"She can continue living with her father for all I care."

"So, you're not planning on having any kind of relationship with her?"

"That's correct. It'll be a lot easier if we keep our lives separate."

Enzo studies me quietly for a minute. "You shouldn't have to marry someone you want nothing to do with. We can figure out another way to dismantle the Silvestri family."

Raising my eyebrow at him, I silence his doubts. "Getting married means nothing, Enzo. It's simply a business transaction. I'll continue to live my life the way I'm doing now, and Giuliana has free rein to do the same."

Our attention is pulled to the door when a knock sounds on the hard oak. My eyes flicker back to Enzo's. "You ready?"

He nods. "I'm taking your lead, Teo."

"Come in," I say just before Rocco enters the room with Mancini in a tailored light-gray suit, holding a black briefcase down by his side. His salt-and-pepper strands are slicked back, and his matching goatee is perfectly trimmed. I quickly glance behind him to spot Fausto following him.

Interesting.

Fausto is an old family friend of Mancini's, his consigliere. He's someone who advises him on affairs in our world, but not someone who typically accompanies him to meetings. That spot is usually held by Mauricio, his underboss. Right-hand man. What Enzo is to me.

"Matteo, thank you for having us," says the man who's led the Mancini family for over two decades now. "Forgive me for the last-minute change the other day. An emergency came up. You understand."

Standing, I gesture to the empty chair next to Enzo. "Of course. Please, take a seat."

We both take our seats while Fausto remains standing by the door next to Rocco.

"No Mauricio today?" I bring my attention back to Mancini who pauses for a moment before responding.

"Not today," he answers tightly, as if trying to dissuade me from asking further questions. It'll work for now, but I make a mental note of it. "Are you ready to go over the contract?" he asks as he hands me the document from his briefcase.

"I am," I say, taking the contract from him. "I must say, this is the first time I've ever received a hand-delivered document."

There are only three reasons someone would hand deliver a contract: one, they have zero access to technology, two, they're hiding that document from someone with access to said technology, or three, they trust no one.

Mancini laughs, responding without a beat of hesitation as he takes out a copy for himself. "Call me old school."

I let out a light chuckle. "You might be old, Mancini, but you're not *that* old." I furrow my brows. "So, tell me. What's *really* going on here?"

I feel my brother's eyes boring into me.

Mancini's gaze remains on mine as he sits back in his seat, crossing one leg over the other. "I came here to sign a contract, Matteo, not to participate in an inquisition."

"And I'm here to make sure I know exactly what I'm marrying into." My tone is stern, rigid.

After a few tense moments of what feels like a showdown between us, he finally relents with a smile on his face. "Of course, Matteo. Please . . ." He holds out his hand for me to proceed. "Continue."

I clench my teeth slightly, making sure it's undetectable but enough for me to refrain from saying what I want to say to this man.

Bringing my gaze down to the document, I study it. "Is everything in the contract as we discussed?" Everything should be straightforward. There's not much to contracts like these. You have the name of the couple to be wed and the conditions. No need for wasted words for such an easy arrangement.

"I am a man of my word, Matteo."

I'm silent for a few more moments while I scan the contract until a name pops up that I don't recognize. Heat floods my face as I take in the abrupt change Mancini tried to sneak in on me. "I just have one question, then." Snapping my gaze to his, I can already tell he knows exactly what I'm referring to. "Who the hell is Luxtyn Stockwell, and why the fuck am I marrying her instead of your daughter?"

5

MATTEO

"Ahh shit," Enzo mutters under his breath as he readjusts his position, now sitting up tall in his seat, waiting for my signal to get rid of the old man.

"Let me explain before you go on the offense," Mancini says, holding up his hands, his bushy brows raised to his hairline.

"Please do." I lean back in my chair and continue to hold Mancini's gaze. If this bastard thinks he can pull one over on me, he has another thing coming. I'll fucking kill him now and figure out another plan to take down the Silvestris later.

"Matteo, you and I are not enemies. I'm here to help you, but I need your help in return."

I notice Enzo's knee bouncing out of the corner of my eye, but I stay focused on Mancini, trying to figure out what the hell he's talking about.

"There's a girl. A girl I need you to protect."

"Does she happen to go by the name Luxtyn Stockwell?" I mock.

The relaxed and confident Mancini that walked into my office not so long ago has disappeared and has been replaced with a much more serious, might I even say, concerned Mancini. His body tightens, the tension prominent in his demeanor. Whoever this girl is, she must be important, but what the hell does he expect me to do? I can't marry some insignificant no-name. And why the hell would I even care to help this girl?

"Luxtyn Stockwell is the daughter of an old friend of mine." He clears his throat and runs a hand over his goatee. "And possibly mine, as well."

"Oh fuck," Enzo mumbles. *Right fucking there with you, brother.*

With a sigh, Mancini continues. "I do not have confirmation that she is my blood. It's just a suspicion. One I believe to be accurate."

"So what the hell is the purpose of this?" Enzo spits out. His outburst is unprofessional, but I would also like to know the answer to his question.

Mancini slowly tilts his head toward Enzo and looks between the two of us before settling his eyes on me. Raising a brow, I encourage him to answer the question.

He lets out a long breath before speaking again. "The reason I wasn't able to meet the other night is because I met up with a woman I fell in love with over twenty years ago." He pauses, the frown on his face lengthening. "And I was informed yesterday that she disappeared."

"Excuse me?" Not exactly what I was expecting to hear. What the hell has he gotten himself into?

Releasing a long, drawn-out breath, Mancini stretches his neck from side to side, the joints cracking. I rest my elbows on my desk and clasp my hands together as I wait, eager to hear what he has to say.

"Before my marriage to Elena was arranged by our fathers, I fell in love with a woman. She wasn't from our world. She was innocent. Pure. Undeserving of the dark lives we lead, but that didn't keep me from falling in love with her."

Mancini stares at my desk, and a slight smile forms on his face while he speaks about her, giving him a sort of boyish charm.

"I ended things with her upon the announcement of Elena's and my engagement," he says, the smile falling off his face. "I knew if our fathers found out about her, they would have her killed."

Releasing a shaky breath, he continues. "She tried reaching out to me a few times, but I cut off ties with her completely. I didn't want to risk anything happening to her because of my own selfishness of wanting to see her again. I did, however, send one of my men." He nods to Fausto.

"One of my most trustworthy men. One I knew wasn't under my father's thumb or the influence of the Silvestris. I bought her a condo where she lived for a couple of years so I knew exactly where to send him."

He speaks of the Silvestris as if he doesn't like them, but that doesn't make sense. They've been in business together for over two decades. Why would he do that if he didn't want the alliance?

Mancini shifts as he glances down, switching which leg is crossed over the other. Once he brings his gaze back up to mine, the slight glisten in his eyes doesn't go unnoticed. He must've truly cared about this woman. Enough to get choked up, which is not what I was expecting.

"I told him to tell her whatever he needed to, to get her to move. I didn't care what it was, I just needed her to get out of New York City . . . and she did. I had Fausto keep tabs on her condo in case she ever decided to come back. Twenty-three years later, she's made her appearance again." He pauses, and his Adam's apple bobs when he swallows hard. "And I made the mistake of meeting up with her."

So, he blames himself for her disappearance.

"There are things you don't know, Matteo. Things I don't have time to explain. Things I *can't* explain. But I need you to do something I know you'd never expect to have to do. Something men in our world *don't* do easily."

"Spit it out, Mancini." I'm growing impatient, especially when whatever he has to say affects me.

"I need you to trust me."

Enzo bursts out laughing as my glare hardens on Mancini. "Well, he wasn't wrong when he prefaced *that* statement," he mutters before silencing himself again.

"Upon learning about Char's disappearance, I did some research. I know she has a daughter. A *twenty-two-year-old* daughter named Luxtyn Stockwell."

I shrug. "Could be a coincidence."

"I doubt that. The timing lines up perfectly. Char wasn't with anyone else while she was with me."

Smirking, I say, "Maybe you weren't cutting it for her, Mancini."

"The girl is mine, DiMaggio, and I need you to protect her." His hands form fists on the arm rests.

"Oh, hell, here we go," Enzo grumbles.

"The contract says—"

"Oh, fuck the contract," Enzo belts out before turning his attention to me and lowering his voice. "This is a damn joke, Teo. We can figure something else out. We don't need Mancini."

There is no other choice. I have to marry a Mancini. Everything we've actively worked toward since I took over after our parents' murders is finally coming to fruition. *This* will not deter me.

Mancini's forehead creases as he fidgets with his fingers.

I peer into his sunken-in dark eyes, as if he's had no sleep in days. He really believes what he's saying is true, but why does she need protection, and why does he need it from me?

"I'm going to need physical evidence that this girl you speak of is yours."

"Teo," Enzo warns, as if that'll deter me from doing what I need to do for our family.

"Done," Mancini responds.

"And I need you to tell me why this supposed daughter of yours needs protecting, and who from."

Mancini takes a few moments to respond. "The Silvestris will come after her once they find out Luxtyn's name is on that contract, and when they do, they'll kill her, just like they planned on doing to you once you wed Giuliana if you didn't give them access to your port."

Ahh, so they were going to kill me. They're fucking naive if they didn't think we hadn't thought of that already. We would've been prepared. We *will* be prepared.

"So you expect me to believe after all these years of being in bed with the Silvestris, that you're just willing to throw them under the bus? All over a girl you don't even have confirmation of whether she's yours or not?"

"Yes."

"And why do you think I'd believe a damn word you're saying, Mancini?"

"Because I've failed my daughter and I've failed the love of my life thinking I was protecting them. The Silvestris can't have control anymore. *None* of us can let them have control anymore. I'm here to attempt to right my wrongs, and that starts with you."

I take a moment to consider my options. I can either tell Mancini to fuck off and try and figure out another way to take down Silvestri, or I can sign my name on the line of this contract and get the justice my parents deserve.

This is the most rash decision I've ever made, but I know what I need to do. I'm not doing this for myself. I'm doing this for my parents. For my family.

I pick up my black and gold Montblanc pen and sign my name on the line, sealing my fate, before sliding it over to Mancini.

Mancini's eyes widen as he takes in my signature, but he quickly signs above my name before sliding the document back to my side of the desk.

"So, tell me, Mancini. What exactly is it you need me to do?"

6

LUXTYN

It's been two days since I've heard from my mom. She was supposed to get back from her business trip yesterday, but she never showed up. I tracked her phone using the *Find My* app, and after doing a quick *Google* search, I determined her last known location was at a condo where I'm assuming her client is staying.

I don't fucking know.

When I called the police, they were useless, repeatedly transferring me from officer to officer, and by the time I got to a detective, he told me he would work on it and get back to me. The way he brushed me off infuriated me and left me with no other choice but to go to New York myself and figure out what's going on.

I hopped on the first available flight to New York City, and now three hours later, I'm in the most chaotic airport ever, which is only escalating the anxiety I've been experiencing for the last few days.

After retrieving my checked bag, I follow the signs to the

rideshare area. According to the app, my driver should be here in five minutes in a silver Ford Fusion.

With my duffle bag hanging off my shoulder, I exit the terminal, taking in the sea of people working their way to their transportation. Out of habit, I grab my pocketknife from the side of my duffle bag and slip it into my purse. My mom always taught me to carry it on me, and now that I'm in a city I know nothing about, I'm more inclined to have it on me at all times.

I'm waiting by one of the several passenger pickup lanes when my phone dings.

Your Uber has been canceled.

"What the hell?" I mutter. Who cancels an Uber when they're a few minutes away?

I let out an annoyed sigh as I start to order another ride before I'm interrupted.

"Are you in need of a ride, ma'am?" I turn toward the voice and pinpoint a tall man in a dark expensive-looking suit standing only a few feet away.

Eyeing him suspiciously, I ask, "Are you an Uber driver?"

"I am."

I glance around with narrowed eyes at all of the people squeezing by one another as they make their way through the crowds, and notice a taxi driver only ten feet away, calling out to a passerby, asking if they need a lift somewhere. *I guess approaching customers for rides is normal here.*

I bring my attention back to the driver. "Which car is yours?"

"The G-Wagon," he says, pointing behind him to the blacked-out Mercedes Benz I know I can't afford to take.

"Yeah, I'm going to have to politely decline. Uber Black isn't in my budget. Thanks, though."

I turn my attention back to my phone so I can continue ordering another ride when the man speaks again. "The person

I was picking up canceled, so I'm just heading back into the city. If you're headed toward the Upper East Side, I can bring you at the same price as a regular vehicle since I'm heading that way anyway."

I raise a brow and study him. He seems friendly enough with that pearly white smile he's worn ever since he came up to me. He's attractive with his freshly shaved face and his clean-cut hair style that's faded on the sides and styled longer up top. This *would* be a lot more convenient than having to order another ride.

"I have an address, but this is my first time here, so I'm not sure if it's in your direction."

"What's the address?" he asks.

I flash my phone to him, showing him the address of my mom's last known location. "Is this the Upper East Side?"

He takes a small step toward me, as if he's trying not to invade my personal space, and peers at my phone. "Lucky for you, it is," he responds without a hitch in his smile. He turns and holds his arm out toward the G-Wagon. "Shall we?"

Making my way to the back passenger door, he holds out his hand. "I can put your bag in the back."

I offer him an appreciative smile and a thank you before handing him the heavy duffle bag, which he takes effortlessly.

He holds the door open for me while I step up into the SUV and slide onto the black leather seat. I plop my purse onto my lap.

Upon shutting the door, the locks click, which sends a sense of eeriness through me, straightening my spine.

Relax, Lux. Cars lock. Totally normal.

"You should really be more aware of your surroundings," a smooth, deep voice says from beside me, causing me to shriek and my hand to fly up to my racing heart.

"Oh my gosh. I-I'm sorry. I didn't see you there."

"I'd say that's obvious," he grumbles.

Okay, asshole.

"Look, I didn't realize this Uber was already taken." I grab my purse and sling the strap over my shoulder. "I'm more than happy to order another one." As I go to unlock the door, the driver slides into his seat, but to my annoyance, this car is apparently too high-tech for me and I can't figure out how to unlock it.

The driver slides into his seat. "Can you unlock the door, please?" I call out to him. "I didn't realize you were already taking someone. I can just order another ride."

"No can do, pretty lady," the driver says with a chipper attitude before making eye contact with the other passenger in the rearview mirror. "We good?" he asks.

I finally take in the man who was crammed so far in the corner of the vehicle just moments before. Now that he's leaning forward slightly, the terminal lights peering in through the window allows me to get a better look at him, and *holy crap*. He might have no manners, but he's by far the most attractive man I've ever seen.

His thick dark hair is styled back, putting his loose waves on display, and it makes me want to comb my fingers through it. His facial hair is well kept and his dark eyes are, well, they're dark.

Menacing, actually.

A spark of annoyance seems to pass through them when he nods to the driver, which pulls me out of my distracted state of mind as the car begins to move.

"Could you please let me out of the car, sir?" I call out to the driver once more, which is proving to be useless, as he ignores me. Pulling on the door handle again, I look for the lock button. My heart rate picks up and my palms begin to sweat as I realize the situation I've gotten myself in.

"You might as well stop trying to open the door. No matter what you do, it won't work," says the man next to me. The sinking feeling in my gut lights up with fury.

Turning back to the man, I ask, "What is this? A kidnapping?"

Is this what happened to my mom? Is this sort of thing common in New York City?

"Call it what you want," he says with a shrug. It's like he does this every single day. It doesn't even seem to affect him.

Think, Lux, think.

"Aww, c'mon, Matteo. Give the girl a break. Can't you tell you're scaring her?" the driver says before giving me a wink in the rearview mirror.

Is this a damn joke?

"Is that true, Little Lux. Am I scaring you?" the passenger asks in a condescending tone.

My eyes snap to his, narrowing in on him as he says my nickname that only my mom uses. "How the hell do you know my name?"

"I know a lot more about you than you think," he responds before gazing out the tinted window.

That's it? That's all he's going to say?

Taking a deep breath, I try to relax my nerves and calm the racing thump in my chest. Panicking will not get me anywhere in this situation. The only thing I can think to do is call the police, so I slowly reach for my phone in my purse, trying to be discreet.

Feeling around, I brush across my pocketknife and slip it into the sleeve of my sweatshirt. I silently send a thank you to my mom for always telling me to keep it on me at all times.

"You take your phone out and I take it away. Actually . . ." Matteo says before yanking my purse off my lap.

"Hey!" I shriek as I throw myself across the back seat,

finding myself in his lap as I try to retrieve my purse. When I think I have a chance at pulling it out of his grasp, he manhandles me like some brute, overpowering me with his massive size, then spins my body around and slams my back against his chest. He wraps his arms around me, holding me in place, pinning my arms to my sides. The cool metal of the pocketknife presses into my forearm.

"Is this really necessary?" I exclaim, frustrated at how easy it was for him to treat me like a rag doll. "You realize this is kidnapping, right?" I attempt to wiggle myself free from him, but it proves to be useless, as his hold only tightens.

"Keep wiggling like that and you're going to have a bigger issue to deal with than finding your mom," he whispers in my ear. The heat of his breath sends a wave of goose bumps along my skin. His threat doesn't come across as intimidating, though. It comes across . . . suggestively?

The driver glances at us in the rearview mirror and smirks at our compromising position. Heat rises through my cheeks, not because I'm blushing, but because I'm pissed.

His arms loosen ever so slightly around me, so, catching him off guard, I rear my elbow back and jam it into his ribcage. I might not carry a torch to him in size, and that hit might've not had tremendous power behind it, but the shock factor takes him by surprise, causing him to release me as he grunts out a curse.

I roll off him back to my seat and lean as close to the door as I can, putting as much distance between us as possible. "How the hell do you know about my mom?"

The driver laughs while Matteo rights himself. "Fuck off, Enzo," he mutters.

Matteo and Enzo. Got it. I'm reporting these assholes as soon as I figure out how to get the hell out of here.

"What did you guys do to her? Kidnap her like you're

kidnapping me?" I struggle to keep my voice from cracking with each octave.

"We're not kidnapping you, Luxtyn," Enzo says. I meet his gaze in the mirror before he brings his attention back to the dark road.

"No, let her think we're kidnapping her. A little fear might do her some good," Matteo snaps.

I glance between the two men; Enzo has a charismatic smile painted on his face, and the annoyingly ruggedly handsome one to my left has a look of annoyance prominent on his features as his mouth forms a straight line and his eyes harden into a glare.

I settle my gaze on Matteo. "I'd say locking me in this vehicle and not allowing me to leave is the definition of kidnapping. And you know my mom is missing. What kind of fucked-up situation is this?"

"So much for waiting for her dad, huh?" Enzo mutters.

My dad?

What the hell?

"One of you better start talking right now or I'll . . . I'll . . ."

"You'll what?" Matteo grinds out. "You have no leverage here. You're stuck in a car with no way out, and even if there was a way out, what're you going to do? Jump out of a moving vehicle onto a heavily populated interstate?"

He's right. I have no plan. He has my phone and my wallet. He's locked me in this damn car. Even if I could open the door, I'd just get hit by another car and die.

"Just calm the fuck down. We're almost to my penthouse, and when we get there, your dear ol' dad can break the exciting news to you."

I scoff. "You clearly have me mistaken for someone else. I don't have a dad."

Matteo clenches his jaw, something I'm surprised I can

even notice through the shadow of his stubble and the dark of the night. "Everyone has a dad. How do you think you were brought into this world?"

I grind my teeth. *This patronizing asshole.*

"Just because you don't know who he is, doesn't mean he doesn't exist," he adds. "Now put your damn seatbelt on and keep quiet. You're giving me a headache."

He settles in his seat, takes his phone out, and types away on it, ignoring me, which only infuriates me more.

I don't know what the hell he's talking about when it comes to my dad, but he mentioned my mom, and if I want to find her, I need to do what he says and zip my lips for once. Allowing myself to get kidnapped by these guys might've been a terrible idea, but it also might get me a step closer to finding her.

7

MATTEO

For a small little thing, Luxtyn sure has some power behind her jabs. Or maybe it's because she caught me off guard, but either way, my ribs are still feeling the aftermath of her bony elbow.

Luxtyn Stockwell isn't anything like I expected. Mancini gave us a copy of her photo ID so Enzo could intercept her at the airport after we had our tech guy hack into the rideshare app and cancel her ride, but that picture doesn't do her justice.

She's beautiful, with her nearly jet-black hair that contrasts with her porcelain complexion, looking like it hasn't seen the light of day.

Her eyes, though. Her eyes are dark brown, nearly black, similar to mine. Her high cheekbones and full lips fill out her face, and the lack of makeup gives her a young vibrancy.

Having lived in the city my entire life, I'm used to women dressed to the nines with their hair and makeup done twenty-four seven. Luxtyn's minimalist look is . . . refreshing.

Now, her attitude. Her attitude is something I could do without. Add in the theatrics, and there's the reason for the throbbing pain in my head. Yes, Enzo and I kidnapped her, but fuck. If I was going to kill her, I would've done it already.

At least the girl isn't completely naive.

It's reassuring that her guard immediately went up with us, and that her fight-or-flight response is more on the fight side. Luxtyn didn't grow up in this world, and being the wife to the don of one of New York's largest crime syndicates is no place for a dumb, naive little girl.

Luckily for me, the remainder of the car ride is quiet. Luxtyn hasn't said a word, which I didn't think would be possible for her. If I had to guess, I'd say her sudden compliance has something to do with what I said about her mom while her tight little ass was perched on my lap.

I didn't think Mancini's plan for me to wed Luxtyn would work, at least not willingly by her, but I've quickly learned I can use her mom as a form of leverage. They must be close if she's willing to let herself get "kidnapped."

Luxtyn continues staring out the window as Enzo parks the SUV in my private parking garage beneath my forty-two floor residential building. My penthouse takes up the top two floors of this building while the remaining residences are occupied by people of all trades, including many whom work for me.

"The door's unlocked for you now," I say while I open mine, but before I get out of the car, I glance at her over my shoulder, and our gazes meet. "And don't try running. You're in a closed-off parking garage, one you need more than a key to get out of, so don't try anything stupid. I'm really not in the mood."

She mutters something under her breath that sounds an awful lot like "dick" as I climb out of the SUV, and the corners of my mouth rise at the brazenness of it. Enzo smirks while waiting to shut the door behind me.

"What?" I snap, pasting a scowl back on my face.

He gives me a cocky shrug. "Oh, nothing." I know he wants to say something, but I'm not in the mood to decipher the meaning behind his smug attitude. He shoves my door shut before adding, "Don't think I don't see what's going on here."

"I thought you said it was nothing? Nothing means you have no opinion on anything, Enzo."

Luxtyn climbs out as I make it around the SUV. I brace myself for her to start running, but she surprises me and does the opposite. After shutting the door, she stands there and stares at me. Unmoving. Not even blinking, which leaves me feeling uneasy. This is a stark shift from the girl who threw her body over mine in a failed attempt to get her bag back.

Ignoring her, I turn around and lead the way to the private elevator that goes directly to the penthouse. But before I make it three steps, a sharp pain on the lower side of my back erupts. "What the fuck?" I shout.

My words bounce off the concrete walls as I whip around in time to see Luxtyn attempt to jump on me while screaming, "Tell me what you know about my mom, you asshole!"

Enzo pulls her arms behind her back and snakes his through them, holding her in place. My gaze is pulled to the floor where a fucking pocketknife with a shiny coat of blood is now lying on the ground between us.

Did she just fucking stab me?

"Tell me what you know!" she yells again.

I eye her up and down and take in her heaving, perky-as-hell breasts as she attempts to break free from Enzo.

The fact this woman stabbed me in the back and I'm still checking her out tells me there's something seriously fucking wrong with me. I barely pay attention to the females that throw themselves at me every night at the club, yet here I am checking out one who tried to fucking kill me. With my back turned, nonetheless. Fucking ridiculous.

After picking up the pocketknife off the ground, I inspect the thick red liquid that now coats the tip of the blade. Enzo's bark of laughter draws my attention back to him and the new thorn in my side. Or should I say my back.

Yeah, keep laughing, douche.

I shoot him a glare before drawing it to Luxtyn. She has a gleam in her eye and her chin raised high, looking like she enjoyed stabbing me a little too much.

I wipe the front and back of the blade on the sleeve of my charcoal-gray Armani suit jacket, which must now be thrown out, thanks to the outrageously bold move on Luxtyn's part.

"This was one of my favorite suits, Little Lux. What're you going to do about that?"

"I don't really care, and stop calling me that." She seethes. "Tell me what you know about my mom, or you can just go fuck yourself."

"You really think stabbing and cussing out the people who kidnapped you and hold the fate of your mother's life in their hands is a smart idea?" I might be falsely leading her to believe I have her mother, but I don't really fucking care. I'm not above using her mother against her. Not when it comes to getting what I want. What I need. And *she* is what I need to take down the Silvestris.

The fire burning behind her eyes extinguishes as the presumed threat of harming her mother lingers in the air between us. Her shoulders drop as Enzo continues to keep a firm grasp on her.

"Are you calm now?" I ask.

"You're not going to hurt her, are you?" While I should probably feel bad for making her think I have her mother, I don't. I don't know where she is. Hell, I don't even have confirmation that she's alive, but I need Luxtyn to chill the fuck out.

"If you keep making stupid decisions like stabbing me, there's no telling what will happen to your mother." I ignore my brother's disapproving gaze as I spin on my heel, making my way back toward the private elevator.

She might think I have her mother locked up in some grungy basement, and that's fine. That was my intention. The only problem is, why's there a little voice in the back of my head that disagrees with what I'm doing?

8

LUXTYN

I stabbed a man.

It's not something I've ever done before, but it's something I'd do again in a heartbeat to save my mom. Clearly Matteo makes the calls between him and Enzo, which is why I stabbed him.

If these assholes think I'll roll over and just let them kidnap me, they're sorely mistaken. I might be asking for my death sentence, but something tells me they're not going to kill me. I mean, I stabbed him for crying out loud. If they were going to kill me, they would've done it by now.

"Do you think you can keep your hands to yourself?" Enzo asks from behind me.

"Sure," I offer and he chuckles at my nonchalant response before releasing his hold on me.

"I'm watching you now, Luxtyn," he says before he nudges me, silently telling me to follow Matteo to the elevators.

After some high-tech elevator technology scans Matteo's hands and eyes, the doors open for the three of us to step inside the small space. After what feels like the longest minute of my life, it dings, letting us off at the top floor.

I follow Matteo off the elevator, which opens into a grand foyer with high ceilings. I'm sure my mouth falls open at the sight of the extravagant entryway. The walls are black with doors that have geometric windowpanes and gold accents. Walking around the corner, he leads us through a massive living room with floor-to-ceiling windows that overlooks the city lights.

The luxurious view matches the interior design, with lots of black features paired with the high contrasting gold accents. You'd think the black would be too overpowering for the space, but with the sleek marble floors and the ivory furniture, it gives it an art deco feel with lots of natural sunlight being cast in through the windows.

I study Matteo's broad back as he leads us down a hallway lined with minimalist textured art pieces hanging on the walls. If it weren't for the inch-long tear in his suit jacket, you'd never know I stabbed the man. He continues to walk with perfect posture, shoulders set back, head held high, not even a hitch in his step. It's unsettling how unfazed he is by it.

"I'll meet you both back here. Rocco texted me on our way back that Doc was waiting on us, so I'm going to have him patch me up real quick and make sure no vital organs were damaged during my assault," he grumbles before stopping at a door and turning back around to narrow his gaze on me.

"Don't let her out of your sight." He glances up at Enzo, who is directly behind me. "And maybe check her for any other weapons. I'd prefer *not* getting stabbed again," he adds before turning to walk down the hall.

"C'mon, you little spitfire. Let's get you inside before the boss gets too mad," he says with a playful tone before pushing the door open and gesturing for me to walk in.

The office conveys a similar black, gold, and ivory theme, except this room has a chevron designed light hardwood floor.

"Now, Luxtyn, I'd really appreciate it if you'd make this easy and be honest with me. Do you have any more weapons hiding somewhere, or do I need to strip search you?"

Whipping around, the color drains from my face. He can't be serious . . .

Raising a brow at me, Enzo chuckles. "My brother might not be too happy with me if I do that, so how about you save me from that potential disaster and tell me the truth?"

So they're brothers. Makes sense with how similar they look.

"No," I blurt. "I don't have any other weapons on me. *Your boss* took the only one I had."

Enzo tracks his gaze up and down my body, as if he's trying to see if I'm hiding anything beneath my leggings, boots, and plain black sweatshirt.

"Where did you even get that pocketknife?"

"My mom gave it to me when I was fifteen. She told me to carry it with me everywhere. I checked my bag so I would have it with me here. You never know what kind of situation you could get yourself in." *Obviously.*

Enzo laughs, displaying that friendly smile that fooled me into putting myself in this dire situation. "I like you, Luxtyn. Keep up that strong-willed personality and you'll do just fine here."

"What does that mean?" I ask, taking a few steps toward him. I should get as far away from my kidnappers as possible, but I'm still not convinced these guys want to hurt me. So that begs the question. "Why would you guys kidnap my mom?"

Enzo's smile vanishes from his face, and I swear a look of sympathy flashes through his eyes. "Everything will be explained to you shortly."

"Just tell me now. How can you play coy with me? What

did me or my mom ever do to you guys?" My voice grows louder with each question until I'm screaming at him. "Why would you take her?"

Matteo appears in the doorway behind Enzo wearing a pair of dark pants and a white button-up, no jacket, with the first few buttons undone, giving me a glimpse of his smooth tan chest with dark ink peeking through. His sleeves are rolled up, revealing his muscular forearms branded with the same dark ink.

Tattoos.

Great.

That just adds to his overall appeal, which irritates me because the last thing I need to be feeling is any attraction to my kidnapper. I must be disturbed.

"We haven't taken your mother," he says as Enzo steps to the side, leaving nothing but tension filled space in between his brother and I.

"Bullshit," I say, staying rooted in place. "You already told me you did, so don't lie to me now."

Matteo takes a few steps into the room, easily closing the distance between us. I have to crane my neck to keep my gaze on his.

"I told you that we hold the fate of your mother in our hands. *You* made the assumption that we have her and *that* assumption is incorrect."

He stalks around me, like I'm nothing but a measly construction cone in his way, causing me to whip around. I follow him while he makes his way around his desk, then takes a relaxed seat in his black leather chair. "What the hell is wrong with you?" I ask, stopping in front of his desk.

His lip curls into a smirk. "Sit down."

"I don't take orders from you," I snap.

"Sit. Down," he commands. "Or you won't get any information out of me." He raises a brow, waiting to see how I proceed, and as much as I don't want to submit to him and don't trust a word he says, I reluctantly take a seat in the chair next to his brother. What other choice do I have? I have to play along. For now, at least.

Matteo sits up in his seat, setting his forearms on the desk. "Your father just got here. My head of security is bringing him up. Once you speak to him about everything that's going on, we can talk about your mother's whereabouts."

Exasperated with this dad storyline, I slam my hands on his desk. "I don't have a dad here, okay? You have the wrong person."

"Luxtyn?" A low, yet soft voice comes from behind me. I turn in my seat just as an older gentleman makes his way into the room.

He's wearing an expensive-looking navy-blue suit with a white button-up underneath. His slicked-back hair is mostly silver with darker strands sprinkled throughout, and his goatee beard is freshly trimmed. The slight creases in his forehead and on the outer corners of his eyes have me guessing he's in his fifties.

I narrow my eyes on him. "Who are you?"

"Come on in, Mancini," Matteo says from behind me. The older man's soft eyes remain on mine as he proceeds forward. The addition of another man to this kidnapping should alarm me, but there's a vulnerability in his eyes.

What the hell is going on?

"You look just like her," he says softly as he continues to stare at me.

Matteo clears his throat, making me realize he's stepped out from behind his desk and is standing next to me. "Maybe you should introduce yourself. She's been quite the headache since I retrieved her from the airport for you, so I'd appreciate it if we could get this show on the road. Doc is here and ready to take your DNA samples."

"Excuse me?" I peer up at Matteo. "I'm not giving you any DNA." What the hell is going on here? Nothing is making sense, and this is a waste of time when I could be going to the police about my mom.

Matteo looks down his nose at me, like I'm some petulant child he doesn't want to deal with. "Relax. I'm not trying to clone you or whatever dramatic situation you've drawn up in that mind of yours. The DNA sample is just to prove whether you two are related."

"You two," I repeat, glancing back at the older gentleman. "As in him and I?" I point between the two of us.

"That's right, Luxtyn," the older man says. "I knew your mother, Char . . . or Charlotte." He chuckles to himself. "I used to call her Char back when I knew her. I'm not sure if she still goes by that."

She does, but that's beside the point. Who the hell is this guy?

"I know this is going to be difficult to hear, but I believe I'm your father, Luxtyn." He takes another step closer as I rise out of my chair, not sure how to respond. Not sure how to *react*. "My name's Angelo Mancini."

Angelo Mancini.

That name.

Why does it sound so familiar?

Wait . . .

Angelo . . .

Heat floods my face as recognition hits me.

I know that name.

9

MATTEO

Luxtyn lunges toward Mancini so fast I almost miss it. I wrap my arms around her while Enzo leaps from his chair, prepared to help where needed, but I nod to him, letting him know I have it handled.

"You!" she screams at Mancini while trying to tear herself out of my grasp. I try not to tighten my grip on her, in fear that I'll hurt her unintentionally, so I let her thrash in my arms.

"What did you do to my mother?" she screams, and her hair whips me in the face, showering me with her sweet scent.

I shouldn't be thinking about her intoxicating aroma, especially at this moment, yet I can't help but notice the citrus and vanilla scents emanating from her, blending to create an enticingly sweet but not overpowering fragrance.

Get it the fuck together, Teo.

I release a nearly undetectable groan, trying to rein in that ridiculous thought and keep my body from reacting to Luxtyn squirming in my arms.

Enzo gives me one of his shit-eating grins, surely reading my mind, which is not what I need right now.

She is a means to an end.

A business transaction.

Exactly what Giuliana was going to be.

And that's it.

Mancini holds up his hands, with his eyes wide and locked in on Luxtyn. "That's why I'm here. I don't know where she is, but I think I know who took her."

"Liar! You're the one who took her! I know you did!" Luxtyn sinks her sharp nails into my forearms in an attempt to break free from me.

Oh, my Little Lux. You stabbed me. It'll take a lot more than that to get out of my grasp.

"One of the last conversations I had with her! On the phone!" Her words come out in pants. "I *heard* you!"

Ahh, I see where the confusion lies, and while I don't blame the girl for thinking Mancini took her mother, especially after hearing him while she was on the phone with her, there's no way Mancini took her mother. He wouldn't have made this agreement with me if he had.

Lowering my head, I whisper in her ear, "Relax, Little Lux," and to my surprise, after a few seconds and a few deep breaths, she slackens and loosens her grip on my forearms, leaving behind a trail of ten crescent-shaped marks in them.

I keep a hold of her, even though she's stopped thrashing around, and her breathing begins to even out. "That's my good girl," I whisper. Although, I don't know why I said *my*, as if she's *mine*.

She's a means to an end, Teo. Fucking remember that.

"I suggest you explain to Luxtyn why she heard you on the phone with her mother. I'll only hold her off for so long, Mancini."

His desperate gaze bounces from me to her. "It's true. I did see your mother. The night before she disappeared. But I promise you, Luxtyn, I had nothing to do with her disappearance."

"Well, not intentionally at least," I mumble, which causes her to stiffen and straighten her spine. *Whoops.* "Listen to what he has to say, Luxtyn."

"I do believe I know who was behind her disappearance, though, and I'm here to offer my help. If you'll let me." He gives Luxtyn a pleading gaze with desperate puppy dog eyes that actually make me feel an inkling of pity for the man.

"I'm going to let you go. Can you remain calm, Little Lux?" I whisper, and the soft strands that have fallen over her ear sway with each word I breathe out. I'm not sure why I keep calling her *Little Lux* like it's some cute fucking petname I've made for her, and it's not something I want to figure out right now.

She nods. "Use your words, sweet girl." Again with the fucking petnames, but I can't help it when she responds so perfectly to me.

"Yes, Matteo," she breathes out. The way she says my name, it's as if I commanded it out of her. Well, hell, I did, didn't I? My dick jolts awake. *As if containing it from the excitement it felt while she was rubbing up against it in a feat of anger just moments ago wasn't enough.*

I release her but remain rooted in place behind her in case she decides to change her mind. *Or is it because I enjoy being near her?* Nope. Not the latter.

"Start talking, *Angelo*," Luxtyn spits out, which has me biting back a grin. She's not afraid. An admirable trait.

Dropping his hands to his side, Mancini explains the torrid love affair he had with her mother and how he pushed her away out of fear of harm coming her way if he continued having her in his life. How he never knew about Luxtyn's existence, and how he believes the Silvestris are behind her disappearance, which is new information to me.

Is that why Mauricio hasn't been with him lately?

Mauricio being Mancini's underboss means he's the one who takes over if anything were to happen to him. A stipulation I had Mancini add to the contract we signed gives me full control of the Mancini family upon his death or retirement. It's another reason I was so motivated to sign that contract the other day.

Mauricio used to be Giuseppe Silvestri's underboss, but when Angelo Mancini married Elena Silvestri, he started working for him instead.

I don't know the details of the marriage contract, but it doesn't take a genius to figure out why Mauricio started working for Mancini. It was just another power move for Giuseppe Silvestri. Having one of his own men on the inside of the Mancini family.

I wouldn't put it past the Silvestris to be behind her mother's disappearance, but what exactly would their plan be for her?

10

LUXTYN

I listen intently as Angelo tells me about his relationship with my mother, the reason he abandoned us, and his speculations on her disappearance. He's still speaking, but the only thing shouting through my mind as my brain processes this information is, *What the fuck*?

Angelo stops speaking and stares at me like a deer in headlights. "Oh, I'm sorry. Did I just say that out loud?" I say deadpan. Enzo chuckles under his breath from my side.

"Luxtyn, I realize this is a lot to take in."

"Oh, do you now?" I snap at Angelo. "Well, as long as you're understanding, that's all that really matters, right?"

"Luxtyn—" Angelo attempts again.

I hold my finger in the air. "So, let me get this straight. You led my mom on, *knowing* you'd have to get married to someone else—"

"It just happened."

"I'm not done speaking. You've done enough talking, and I kept my mouth shut. Now it's my turn to speak and your turn to listen. Are you capable of that?" I pause, waiting for his answer, which he gives with a defeated sigh and a slight nod.

"Maybe we should take a seat," Matteo chimes in from behind me. I glance over my shoulder and see he's gesturing to the sitting area by the fireplace.

Enzo leads the way and takes a seat on the ivory sofa while I take a seat in the armchair. Angelo sits across from me in the loveseat while Matteo shares the sofa with his brother. A matching ivory ottoman in the middle of the space separates us all.

"So, you had one of your friends scare my mom into leaving New York City. Then after all these years she comes back here for work, and now she's missing because of you?"

"Maybe I haven't done the best job at explaining this," Angelo states.

No shit, Sherlock.

"Your mom wasn't here for work. She was here to meet with a realtor about selling her condo. The one I bought for her all those years ago. I believe Mauricio found out that I met up with her and informed Giuseppe."

I eye Matteo who nods to Angelo as if this is all starting to make sense to him.

"I'm clearly missing something here," I say. "I don't know who these people are you're talking about, but I'm having a hard time understanding why anyone would care if you met up with your ex."

Enzo frowns as if to silently tell me I'm not going to like what I'm about to hear next, while Matteo stares at me with a blank expression before speaking. "Your father is the don of an Italian crime syndicate. Giuseppe Silvestri runs another Italian crime syndicate. The two of them formed an alliance when your father married Giuseppe's sister. Your mother is a problem for him because without the marriage of his sister and your father, they wouldn't have access to your father's port. A port Giuseppe uses to traffic drugs, weapons, pretty much anything you can think of. A port that make him a lot of fucking money."

My mouth falls open as Matteo continues. "Your father rekindling a relationship with your mother threatens their alliance, which threatens their income, and *that* is not something they can allow to happen."

My brain is reeling, and my breathing picks up as I begin to spiral, trying to wrap my mind around all of this information.

Italian crime syndicate.

Trafficking.

Don?

I take a few deep breaths and shake myself out of it, trying to focus so I can get some answers, knowing my mom's life depends on how I handle this. "Italian crime syndicate. What exactly do you mean by that?"

"Matteo . . ." Angelo warns.

"Remember whose house you're in, Mancini." The threat is low, but it comes across loud and clear, which sends a shudder through me as Angelo concedes.

Turning back toward me, Matteo answers my question as if I asked him something simple and not life changing at all. "Mafia. Your father is a Mafia boss."

Sighing, Angelo waits for my reaction, which I'm sure isn't one he'd expect as I bring my gaze back to him and break out into a fit of laughter.

Keeled over, I try to rein it in, but this is just too damn ridiculous. I wrap my arms around my stomach as my abs contract repeatedly from the motion. "I'm sorry, I'm sorry." I laugh, waving my hands in front of me. "This is just absolutely ridiculous. Did my mom set you guys up to this?"

Shaking my head, I continue to laugh. "Okay, I get it. This

is some big elaborate joke on me. C'mon, where is she? I can't believe she got you guys to do this. I wouldn't have stabbed someone had I known this was all a joke."

Angelo tilts his head, studying me. "You stabbed someone?"

Ignoring him, I bring my attention back to Matteo. "Did you tell her I stabbed you? She's going to die when she hears that."

Matteo watches me in bewilderment as I continue to cackle. Once I've finally gotten control, he questions me. "Are you done now?"

Rolling my eyes, I say, "Yes, but seriously. Where's my mom? Is she watching through some hidden camera?"

Standing up, I walk over to the bookshelf next to the fireplace and inspect the books to see if I can find a blinking red light hidden somewhere. This is the only explanation for this scenario because I refuse to believe this bullshit is real.

"She stabbed you?" Angelo says from behind me. He doesn't sound upset, though. He sounds . . . proud? "She really is my daughter, huh, Matteo?"

When I whip around, Angelo's wearing a beaming smile. "Wipe that smirk off your face. The only reason I know how to sink a knife into someone is because my mom taught me how to defend myself. *Not* because of you."

"She stabbed me in the back while I was walking away from her," Matteo mumbles while Enzo covers his mouth with his fist, stifling a laugh.

"Besides, you're not my dad." I cross my arms over my chest. "Now, tell me where she is. This isn't funny anymore."

"Luxtyn, I assure you this is not a joke," Angelo says as he stands. He holds his hand up to me like I'm an animal ready to attack and he's doing his best to keep me at bay. I roll my eyes at the theatrics.

"You really want me to believe you're a Mafia boss?"

"It's not a matter of wanting you to believe me. It's the truth, and the sooner you come to terms with it, the better." Angelo's voice comes across with an air of superiority, and I don't like it.

My eyes narrow and I crinkle my brows as I drop my arms to my side, clenching my fists. "Where do you get off bossing me around like that?"

His dark eyes soften and he's back to holding his hands up in defense. "I understand this is a lot, but your mother's life is in danger. The sooner you come to terms with who you are and what's going on here, the faster we can work at finding her."

"Fine. You're in the *Mafia*. And what about you?" My eyes flicker to Matteo's, and I'm immediately annoyed at how relaxed he looks. "You are too? What, you work for Angelo or something?"

He releases an amused scoff. "The fuck I do."

That was expected. The way Angelo recoiled when Matteo reminded him of whose house he's in already answered that question for me. I just wanted to hit a nerve. "Then what's your role in all of this?"

Something flashes through Matteo's eyes, but before he can answer, Enzo speaks. "Maybe we should hold off on bombarding her with more information. She looks like she's on the verge of overloading. You're going to end up causing her to pass out from overstimulation."

That doesn't deter him as he stands from the couch and stalks over until he's directly in front of me, enveloping my senses in woody, earthy tones that contain a hint of spice. I would be intoxicated by it if I wasn't in this ridiculous situation. "Your father and I made a business deal," he says low, almost like a growl. "I get control of his port as long as I hold up my end of the bargain."

"Matteo, I really think this should wait."

Matteo holds his hand up to his brother, silencing him, while his eyes remain glued on mine. I want to look away, but it's as if those dark-brown irises have captured me, locking me in place, making it impossible to look away. I want to ask him what his end of the bargain is, but I can't seem to formulate the words.

"Go ahead. Ask me what my part of the deal is," he urges, reading my mind.

"W-what is it?" My voice comes out barely above a whisper.

Matteo smiles something fierce. Something wicked. Putting his perfectly straight white teeth on display. I'd swoon over it if I knew no better. Whatever his part of the deal is, I'm not going to like it.

"You and I, Little Lux. We're getting married."

11

MATTEO

Luxtyn takes no more than two seconds to process what I said before attempting a right hook to my face, but knowing my girl here likes to play dirty with knives and shit, I'm a lot more on guard with her than I was before.

I catch her small fist in the air and give it a light squeeze, encouraging her to put it down. She finally does, then pulls her hand away from me and backs away, never taking her eyes off mine. The frustration wafts off her in waves.

"What the hell are you talking about?" she bites out. "We're *not* getting married."

Raising a brow, I take a few predatory steps toward her, causing her to fall back into an armchair. I lean over her, placing a hand on each arm rest, caging her in. "Yes, we are. Because if you don't, you'll end up dead, and you really will never see your mother again."

Luxtyn raises a brow, and it's a shock when she doesn't attempt to knee me in the balls while the threat to her life lingers in the air. "So, you're going to kill me if I don't marry you? I didn't realize you were so desperate to have a woman by your side," she says. "Why do I even need you? Angelo can just help me find my mom."

"Your dad can't even trust the people closest to him. What makes you think he can find your mother on his own? You need resources, not to mention protection once they discover who you are. Two things I can easily provide."

I continue to hover over her in the chair, not because I think she'll run away, but because I relish being in her space. This girl might actually make having a wife . . . exciting.

There's a thought I never thought I'd have.

"The police . . . the police can help me. I'll just go to them," she says. The girl is eager to find a way out of this situation, but unfortunately for her, there aren't any other ways.

"There are corrupt police all over this city, Luxtyn. You're more than welcome to try that, but you'll just put a bright-red fucking target on your back. You have ties to the Mafia now. They won't be able to do shit for you."

Her face pales, the pink from the fire in her cheeks disappearing as she takes in what I'm saying.

"Doctor," she says as if she just remembered. "You said there's a doctor here?"

"I did."

"Bring him in. If everything you guys are saying is true, then I need confirmation that Angelo is my dad. I . . . I need to know the truth," she says softly. "Until then, this isn't getting us anywhere."

I study her face. She doesn't want to believe any of this is true, but she's beginning to realize I'm her only hope at finding her mother. Standing tall, I turn to Enzo. "Bring in Doc."

I resume my seat on the sofa while she repositions herself in the armchair, looking flustered.

Doc comes in with his bag and promptly gets to retrieving

the blood samples with no questions from Luxtyn, who continues to shoot me glares throughout the entire process. Unfortunately for her, that doesn't bother me.

Doc finishes packing up the samples and turns to me before leaving. "I should have the results back to you by tomorrow."

"Tomorrow isn't good enough," I say.

The wrinkles in Doc's forehead form as his bushy gray eyebrows rise. "The lab is already closed for the night, Mr. DiMaggio."

Eyeing him, I ask, "Do I pay you generously?"

He nods. "Yes, sir."

"Do I not provide you with state-of-the-art machinery to use to your liking?"

"You do, sir."

"Then you can do your job and get those lab results rushed, correct?"

The older gentleman's shoulders sag, realizing he doesn't have a choice in the matter. "Of course, sir. I just had some plans tonight with my wife, but I can cancel them and work on these samples. I'll get you the results later tonight."

"Good answer."

A scoff comes from Luxtyn, causing me to snap my gaze to hers. "Did you have something to add, Luxtyn?"

Sitting up in her seat, she narrows her gaze on me in a challenging way. "You don't have to be a dick. He said he has plans with his wife and that he'd get you the test results by tomorrow. The difference between tonight and tomorrow is minuscule, don't you think?"

"Well, I don't know, Luxtyn. The difference between tonight and tomorrow when it comes to your mother's kidnapping must be pretty minuscule too, then, huh?"

Her face blanches and the cockiness she had when she

called me a dick dissipates. She throws herself back in her seat and crosses her arms, bringing her attention down to the floor as she sulks.

She makes it too easy.

Glancing back at Doc, I say with finality, "Tonight." He nods before exiting.

"I have to get going," Mancini says as he brings his attention back to us after having his head buried in his phone for the past few minutes. "Elena and Giuliana want to have dinner tonight. They've been inquiring about the contract."

"Are you going to tell them the contract is no longer valid between Giuliana and I?"

Mancini nods, but I disagree with that decision. "And you're confident there won't be any repercussions from you telling them?"

"Elena and Giuliana are innocent people, Matteo. They're just two women who wound up stuck in the Mafia world due to their fathers. That's not something that should be held against them."

"Elena is Giuseppe's sister. You're naive to think there won't be any consequences to going behind her back and taking Giuliana off the contract. Hell, I wouldn't be surprised if Elena's the one who's behind Luxtyn's mother's disappearance."

Mancini steps toward me, baring his teeth. "Don't bring them into this, Matteo," he snarls. "They know nothing about Char. Don't blame them for having a shitty family."

Stupid fool. If the Silvestris *are* behind the kidnapping, then he's blind if he thinks there's zero chance Elena knows about it.

"Who are Elena and Giuliana?" Luxtyn's small voice comes from the side.

Mancini's expression softens immediately.

"Elena is my wife, and Giuliana is my daughter. Your half sister."

Luxtyn's expression remains neutral, which is impressive given everything she's learned today. Add in a half sister she knew nothing about and I'd say it's a miracle she hasn't passed out from system overload like Enzo said she might. She's stronger than any of us give her credit for.

"Maybe you can come to dinner and meet them soon," Mancini suggests.

"Over my dead body," I interject. "She's not going near any Silvestri, and you're dumber than I thought if you think I'll throw her to that feral daughter of yours." The possessiveness in my tone shocks me as much as everyone else in the room. Well, except for Enzo. Enzo remains seated next to me, annoyingly quiet and with that stupid ass grin he's held on his face ever since we picked her up at the airport.

"DiMaggio . . ." Mancini says my last name in a threatening tone and steps toward me, causing me to leap to my feet.

Enzo quickly does the same, intercepting our potentially explosive blow as he places a hand on my chest and pushes me back. "Let's all calm down, okay? We can talk about meetups after the DNA test comes back."

"We're not talking about any fucking meetups. She's not meeting Mancini's family. End of story."

"*She* can speak for herself," Luxtyn says, causing me to dart my eyes in her direction. My anger starts taking over and my breaths become shallow as my heart rate increases. "And if I decide to meet Elena and Giuliana, then that's exactly what it'll be. *My* decision. *You* are not the boss of me."

"You're going to be my wife. Therefore, you *will* listen to me," I grind out.

Luxtyn huffs a laugh as she stands from her chair. "You're in for a rude awakening if you think I'll let you walk all over me like that, *Teo*." My nickname on her lips sounds so good that I surprisingly relax the slightest bit, even with Luxtyn disregarding her safety. "You might be able to use my mom against me right now, but make no mistake, I am my own woman. If you can't seem to wrap your mind around that, then this *marriage* isn't going to work."

Walking over to Luxtyn, I say, "Oh, this marriage *will* work. You just wait and see." Her eyes shift from left to right as she gazes into my eyes.

"Luxtyn, I hate to do this to you, but I have to leave," Mancini says, causing me to turn back to him. "As soon as the DNA results are in, please let me know, Matteo." He glances around me, back to Luxtyn. "I already know the answer in my heart, but I know you need the physical proof."

Scoffing, I roll my eyes at how endearing he's being and cross my arms over my chest. "Rocco will see you out," I say loud enough for Rocco to hurry into the office and lead him out.

Once they've left the room, I turn my attention back to Luxtyn who's fidgeting with the cuff of her sweatshirt and biting the inside of her cheek like there's something she's keeping herself from saying. "What?" I snap.

She swallows hard before speaking. "I need to ask you a question. As much as I don't like you, you seem to be the only one that's honest and doesn't beat around the bush with me."

I cock my head and raise a brow, intrigued to hear what her question is. She straightens her back, almost as if she's preparing herself for my answer while still fidgeting with the cuff of her sweatshirt.

"What are the chances my mom is still alive?"

Her voice is soft, and I see the vulnerability in her eyes. It nearly makes me falter. She's scared, and while I'm not here to be the girl's hero, it unravels something in me. Some protective instinct like I experienced when Mancini made the dumb suggestion of having her meet Elena and Giuliana. It's not something I've ever experienced with a woman. It makes me feel vulnerable, and I don't like it. I don't like it one fucking bit.

"The probability of your mother being alive is high."

A glimmer of hope lights up her eyes. "How do you know?"

"If she were dead, Silvestri would've already sent her body to your dad."

Luxtyn swallows hard, I'm sure imagining what it would be like to see the dead body of her mother. It's a terrible feeling. One I know all too much about.

"What makes you say that?" she asks.

I turn away from her, brushing a hand through my hair. The flashback of seeing my parents' dead bodies running through my mind. "Because Silvestri likes to do things a certain way. If he had your mother and killed her, he would've had her body dropped off at Mancini's doorstep as proof that he holds all of the power."

Her eyes widen and her jaw drops. "That's sick."

"That's the life we come from, Luxtyn," I bark out. "Bodies send a message, and Giuseppe Silvestri loves sending very direct messages. If he felt Mancini was going behind his back with a woman who could sabotage their alliance, you bet your ass he's going to shove it down his throat that he took her away from him."

She winces at the rigidness of my voice, but she needs to understand this is the world she lives in now.

"Do you think they've hurt her?" Her quavering voice tells me she doesn't want to know the answer to that question.

I let out a deep breath, thinking about how I want to

respond to that. "Do you really want me to answer that question?"

Her hands tremble as she drops her gaze to the floor, which makes me regret my honesty with her, but if I were in her shoes, I'd want to know the facts, as well.

"I'll take that as your answer," she says quietly, her words squeezing my heart.

There's something about this girl. Something that brings out an empathic side of me. Or maybe it's just pity. Whatever the fuck it is, I need it to stop. I need to put some space between us to figure out what the hell is going on in my head and how the hell I get it to stop. It's only been a few fucking hours and my mind is already being messed with when it comes to her.

"C'mon. I'll show you to your room, and if you're hungry, I can order you some dinner."

She snaps her head up. "Excuse me?"

"Which part of that didn't you understand?" I ask, my face expressionless.

She narrows her eyes and snaps her hands to her hips. "First of all, you're an asshole, and secondly, I'm not staying here."

A smirk plays out on my face that I try to hide but fail so miserably at. "My end of the deal I made with your father was to protect you. If Mancini does tell Elena and Giuliana about you tonight, you're going to need someone looking out for you sooner than I thought. So, you'll be staying here for the duration."

She rolls her eyes and opens her mouth to speak but hesitates slightly before doing so. "Is there even any point to arguing with you about this?" She sounds tired, surely from how her life has done a one-eighty in the past few hours.

My response is quick and easy. "No." I turn back to my brother before she gets her second wind and puts up another fight with me. "Enzo, I'm not going to make it to the club tonight. Think you can handle it?"

"Hah, oh yes. Whatever will I do without you, Almighty Teo?"

I ignore him and breeze past Luxtyn before ordering her to follow me down the hall to one of the five master suites I have in this penthouse. Instinctively, I bring her to the one across the hall from mine. The reason which I don't care to dive into right now.

I open the door, and an automatic light illuminates the open room with its own private bathroom. Luxtyn slowly moves into the space, making it seem even more grand than I previously thought, as her small body stands so out of place in it.

I give her a minute to take in her surroundings before asking, "Are you hungry?"

Turning around to face me, she shakes her head. "No, thanks. I'm pretty exhausted, so I think I'm going to take a nap. Will you wake me when you get the results, please?"

While I don't like that she's skipping dinner, I can always order her something when she wakes up later. I give her a small nod before closing the door to give her time to come to terms with her new life. Because even though I'm not the nicest guy on the planet, I can only imagine what she's going through right now.

The girl's entire life got turned upside down between finding out her father is in the Mafia to having her hand be forced into a marriage with another asshole in the Mafia. And something tells me it's not going to get much easier from here.

12

LUXTYN

I give myself a tour of the room, which is bigger than any of the apartments my mom and I have lived in. It's complete with a master bath, walk-in shower, Jacuzzi, and walk-in closet.

After nosing around, I finally find the remote that closes the shades. It's already dark out, but there's something about being in a fishbowl with floor-to-ceiling windows. I don't like it, probably because I've seen *The Glass House* far too many times to count. It's one of my mom's favorites, and somehow she always convinces me to watch it with her.

I climb onto the bed and lie down, letting my body sink into the cloudlike mattress, exhausted from everything that I've learned today. How have I gone my entire life not knowing who my dad is and now I learn he's in the Mafia?

If it's true and he is my dad, I can't say I blame my mom for taking me away from him when she did. If kidnapping and killing people is what these Mafia people do, I want nothing to do with them.

My mind races as I wonder how long it'll take for the doctor to get the DNA results back. Even though I can't seem to shut my brain off, my eyelids still grow heavy, closing on their own as I'm pulled into a deep sleep. I end up in a slumber I had no idea I could have in a moment like this.

13

LUXTYN

"Luxtyn. Hey, Luxtyn." The voice comes through like it's far off in the distance, so I ignore it.

"Luxtyn. Hey. Wake up."

Wait. Where am I?

Cracking my eyes open, my early morning blurry vision attempts to remedy itself as it focuses on a body standing over me. "What the hell?" I bolt straight up and wipe the sleep from my eyes, forcing them to focus on the body again.

"Morning, sleeping beauty."

Oh hell.

My memory of yesterday comes flooding back. So it wasn't just an awful nightmare. I'm really stuck in this Mafia world. "Hi, Enzo," I groan as he hands me a cup of coffee. He's wearing a navy-blue suit and a white shirt. If I didn't know any better, I'd think he's a well-respected businessman heading off to work.

I take a sip and relish in its sweet taste. "How did you know how I like my coffee?"

"I didn't know for sure, but I'm good at reading people.

It's a skill we're taught from a young age. I take it I nailed it, then?"

I take another sip, determining it's the best coffee I've ever had. "It's okay," I say, which causes him to chuckle. I'm sure the satiated look on my face as I take each sip tells him he did better than nail it.

"Wait, what time is it?" I ask, frantically looking around for a clock.

"It's 7:00 a.m. I would've let you sleep in, but we need to get our day started."

I rub my head as I still attempt to wake up. "I thought Matteo was going to let me know when the DNA results came back. I told him to wake me if I was sleeping."

"He did try to wake you, but you're an extremely heavy sleeper. Has anyone ever told you that? You could probably be kidnapped, and you would have no idea because you'd sleep through the entire thing."

I narrow my gaze on him.

His lips curve into a smirk. "Too soon for a kidnapping joke?"

"Way too soon," I grumble, taking another sip.

While I feel numb to having a father figure in my life and hate that my hand is being forced in marriage, I desperately need to find my mom. It's something I'm prepared to do anything for, and I don't have much time.

This whole Mafia business is still unbelievable, and while I'm not completely sold on it, the only thing that matters is finding my mom. So if I have to go along with this stupid marriage until I find her, then so be it. I'll get a divorce after. We just have to get to her before anything bad happens.

The panic at the thought of not finding my mom soon must consume my face because Enzo pulls me out of my daze by placing a comforting hand on my shoulder and says, "Hey, are you okay?"

"Yeah, I'm fine," I say, shaking him off.

As if he can read my mind, he softens his voice and says, "Everything will work out. Teo might come off as—"

"A dick?" I offer.

He chuckles under his breath. "Not many people can call him that without repercussions."

"My repercussion is being extorted by your brother to marry him so he can have access to whatever port you guys want. Why is he so desperate to get access to that, anyway?"

He opens his mouth to answer the question but quickly shuts it.

What was he about to say?

"Come on," he says, ignoring my question. "We need to get you up and going. Fortunately for you, Matteo assigned me as your personal guard." Enzo pulls on the lapels of his suit jacket, like he's impressed with himself for being assigned to watch me all day.

"I'm sure you have better things to do," I grumble, swinging my legs over the side of the bed and placing my empty coffee mug on the nightstand. The bed frame is set so high I can barely reach the floor with the tips of my toes.

"Better things to do than keep my brother's most prized possession in safe hands?"

That causes a cackle from me. "I highly doubt I'm your brother's most prized possession," I quip while I hop off the bed and walk around Enzo to where my duffle bag was dropped off at some point.

Digging through it, I notice my phone wasn't dropped off with it. I let out a sigh before turning on my heel to look at Enzo. "Am I ever going to get my phone back?"

"In due time. The boss has to make sure he can trust you

before returning it. We wouldn't want you doing something silly like calling the police. Although, they wouldn't be able to help you, anyway. New York City's law enforcement is full of crooked cops, and if the wrong one hears you asking around about your mom, that could end very badly for both of you."

My stomach drops and the feeling makes me feel immediately nauseous. "And what if I miss a call from my mom?"

"We're monitoring your phone. So far, no one has called or texted you."

I let out a huff as I fold my arms across my chest, immediately feeling violated at the lack of privacy.

"I'll let you get ready," he says, giving the outfit that I'm still wearing from yesterday a once-over. He turns to exit the room, but I stop him before he's able to because I have one last question. One that will affect my future from here on out.

"Did the test results come in?" My heart pounds at an alarmingly fast rate while I wait to hear his response. Do I want to be related to Angelo? If I am, then that means I'm permanently tied to the Mafia. I don't even understand what that means. But if I'm not, what does that mean for me finding my mom? Will they still help me?

Enzo glances over his shoulder, and instead of giving me his usual cocky smile, his mouth sets in a straight line. "Yeah. You're a Mancini now, Luxtyn," he says before walking out the door and closing it behind him.

I sulk down into the chair, squishing my duffle bag in the process. The room spins as I take in the realization that Angelo Mancini is my dad and I will have to marry Matteo to find my mom. The information I've been given in the past twenty-four hours hits me. This isn't anything I expected when I got on that flight to New York City. How the hell did this happen?

14

MATTEO

The crack of splintering bone echoes in the room as I land a powerful jab to Francesco's nose, causing blood to spill from his nostrils. It drips down, and the stain grows, ruining his crisp white shirt. I lower myself down to his level where he sits on a cheap metal chair in my makeshift interrogation cell in the basement of Fierce. Rocco pulls Francesco up by the nape of his neck so he's forced to look into my eyes. His long dark hair shields his face from me, but he groans in pain. "What made you think you could steal from me, Francesco?"

Francesco is a young associate under one of my capos. Typically, I would have my capo handle this, but I was feeling a little restless this morning, like there was too much energy running through me. Energy I needed to burn off. I tried letting out some punches on the bag back at the gym I have in my penthouse, but that only increased my adrenaline. So when my capo informed me that one of his associates was getting a little greedy, I decided to take matters into my own hands.

"I-I don't know what you're t-talking about, B-boss."

How is this guy even an associate? He's weak. I'll be able to break him in no time.

"Okay, Francesco. I see how it's going to go." After pushing myself to my feet, I walk over to the tray of toys I had Rocco set out for me prior to bringing Francesco down here. I pick up the pruning shears and stalk back over to the pathetic excuse of a man who's now dripping blood onto my shiny concrete floors.

I twirl the shears in my hands as I give Francesco a maniacal look, my gaze sharp on his. His eyes widen as they bounce back and forth between me and the shears. "I really didn't want to have to get bloody this early in the morning, but you give me no choice."

Rocco slams his hand on one of Francesco's. It might already be strapped to the metal armrest, but cutting someone's finger off is a nuisance when they're constantly moving.

"No, no, no!" Francesco screeches as he realizes what I'm about to do. "Please, it wasn't me. I promise! I would never steal from you, Matteo! I swear it!"

That's a lie.

He fidgets and struggles to keep eye contact with me, and before he knows what's happened, I slide one blade of the pruning shears underneath his pointer finger, right at the knuckle that's closest to his fingertip, and clamp down. I slice right through the skin and bones, and the blood spurts in multiple directions. His howl bounces off the soundproof walls.

I lift his middle finger, prepared to do the same thing until he cries out, "Stop! Please, stop! I admit it, I admit it! I saved some of the cash!"

There we go.

"Now, that wasn't so hard, was it?" I ask in a condescending tone while Francesco continues to weep in front of me. *Pathetic.* "What did you need the money for, Francesco?"

He whimpers as he answers, "Drugs."

Ding, ding, ding.

This fucking waste decided to steal from me because he needed money for drugs, something I already had my suspicions of when my capo reached out to me about him. Fucking pathetic.

He groans when I put my weight on his knee to push myself up to my feet. It doesn't help that I took a hammer to the spot before I broke his nose. "See what happens when you're honest with me, Francesco? Now had you been honest with me sooner, it could've saved you from a lot of unnecessary pain."

Rocco releases Francesco's hand and backs away from him, knowing what's going to happen next. I pull the Glock from the waistband of the back of my pants and shoot Francesco in the middle of his forehead. His body goes limp before the smoke from the pistol can dissipate in the air.

I pull my handkerchief out and start wiping off the blood that splattered on my gun. "Clean this up," I say to Rocco. "Dump his body where no one will find it."

He gets to work without a falter in his step. He's one of my best, aside from my brother, that is. But since I've reassigned him to watch Luxtyn, Rocco will need to pick up a lot of the slack.

With it being 8:30 a.m., the club is empty, but Enzo and Luxtyn should be arriving soon, and I need to change before she sees the blood on my shirt, so I head up to my office. It's not something I should care about since this is the life she'll soon be married into, but a part of me still wants to shelter her from the worst of it.

I've changed my pants and am sliding my arms through my

fresh white shirt when a pulling sensation comes from the stab wound in my back and sends a small trigger of pain to the surrounding area. It's nowhere near the worst I've had, but it's enough to remind me that my soon-to-be-wife stabbed me.

Someone clearing their throat at my door catches my attention, causing me to turn around and come face-to-face with Luxtyn, whose eyes widen and mouth drops as she takes in my bare torso.

Has she never seen a half-naked man before?

Enzo stands behind her, giving me that stupid ass smirk again. "Did we come at a bad time, Boss?"

"Perfect timing," I grunt out as I button up my shirt while keeping my gaze on Luxtyn who's still rooted in place at my office door. She hasn't looked me in the eye since I turned around, as she kept her eyes on my exposed chest and abs the whole time. It has me grinning like a damn fool.

"I was just taking care of some business," I say, bringing my attention back to Enzo's. "Rocco's downstairs. Why don't you go help him."

Enzo's shit-eating grin gets bigger as he wiggles his brows before stepping back. "Sure thing, Boss."

"Come in and sit." I gesture to the seat across from my desk. Luxtyn finally brings her gaze up to mine, and I give her a knowing smirk.

I know exactly what you've been staring at, Little Lux.

She shuffles into my office and takes the seat opposite me. I study her for a few moments, waiting to see if she'll tell me that Enzo already broke the exciting news to her about being Mancini's daughter, but all she says is, "So . . ."

"So . . ." I repeat.

She fidgets while gazing around my office. There's not much to it. Not even a piece of art on the walls. Enzo and I share this office, as I don't use it often, so we've never done much with it. The dark interior with red accents was his idea. I'm more of a gold guy myself, but the red goes with the theme of the club, so it only made sense.

She finally brings her attention back to me. "Why didn't you wake me up last night when the DNA results came back?"

"You're a heavy sleeper. Impossible to wake up." Leaning back in my chair, I lace my fingers together as I position them over my stomach. I could've woken her up, but she was exhausted, and seeing her lying in bed so innocently did something to me I've been doing my best to bury.

"Well . . . now what happens?"

"That's entirely dependent on you." Kind of. Even if she said no to marrying me, I'd just use her mother to coerce her. She's already proven multiple times that she's her weak spot.

She tilts her head before shaking it. "I don't want to marry you," she says firmly, which makes me laugh. *I thought we were past this.*

"So you've said," I respond nonchalantly.

She narrows her gaze, and it's the cutest fucking thing I've ever seen. Irritating Luxtyn Stockwell might be my new favorite hobby.

"You think this is funny?" She clenches her jaw. "You're messing with people's lives." Her voice gets louder. "What the hell is wrong with you?"

Sitting up, I ground my elbows into the black wooden desk. "You need a favor from me, correct?" She doesn't answer, but it was a rhetorical question, as we both know the answer. "Well, I need a favor from you. Favors go both ways, Little Lux."

She remains silent, the words lingering between us. She's wearing another variation of the same thing she wore yesterday—a sweatshirt and leggings. Her hair's pulled up into a messy bun and still wet from her shower.

I wonder what her body looks like underneath that sweatshirt.

I already know how delicious her curves are in those skintight leggings, but what about those perky tits of hers. What do they look like when they're not being overshadowed by a hoodie?

"Fine, I'll marry you so you can control the stupid port, but as soon as we find my mom, we're getting divorced."

That's cute. She thinks divorce is an option.

I shake my head. "No divorce, sweetheart."

Rolling her eyes at me, she sighs. "Is there something in the contract that says we have to be stuck together for the rest of our lives?"

No, but now that she brings it up, I should've put that verbiage in there.

"If we're not married, then I don't get your father's port. Marriage equals port access. No marriage equals no port access."

"This is fucking ridiculous," Luxtyn spits out as she slams her hands on the edge of the desk. "What if I can convince Angelo to let you have control of the port upon our divorce?"

Shaking my head again, I say, "Nope. That will not do. You want me to help you find your mother, then you're going to have to stay married to me. There is no other option for you, Luxtyn."

"I can just ask Angelo to help me. He's the only one that *wants* to help me. I don't need you."

"We've gone over this. Angelo is too close to it. Why do you think he asked me to assist him with this?"

She sits there contemplating her options, which shouldn't take long since she has none. "And what if you can't find my mom? Then this *arrangement* is only beneficial to you."

I see. She's worried I won't hold up my end of the deal.

Well, fortunately for her, I'm a man of my word. I already have people combing the streets to see if they can find any intel about a woman who's been taken by Silvestri. "I assure you, I will find your mother. You have my word."

She ponders it for a few more minutes, then her face falls flat for a brief moment before she lifts her chin and looks me square in the eye. "Fine. I'll do it. I'll marry you, Matteo."

A smile of satisfaction forms on my face before we're interrupted by a knock on my door. "Hello, Matteo," says an older gentleman. "Are you ready for me?"

Bringing my attention to the man who's been in my life for as long as I can remember, I say, "Yes. Please come in."

Luxtyn glances over her shoulder before bringing her attention back to me. Her eyebrows are raised and a slight frown forms on her face. "What's going on?" she asks.

"What's going on, my lovely fiancée, is that we're getting married. Right now." I gesture to the older gentleman who's married everyone in our family for the past couple of decades now. "Meet Father Barone. Father Barone, meet my soon-to-be-wife, Luxtyn Stockwell."

15

LUXTYN

"We're getting married *now*?" I'm dumbfounded. He already coordinated having the officiant here because he knew my only option was to say yes to him. I can't stand the arrogance of this man, yet here I am, signing my life over to him.

"No time like the present," he says as he rises from his seat. "Besides, I won't help you find your mother until you sign your name on that marriage license. I assumed you'd want to get this done as soon as possible. Was I wrong in that assumption?" He cocks a brow at me, waiting for my answer.

I glance back at Father Barone who looks uncomfortable over our disagreement. I wonder if he'll help me . . .

In one last ditch effort to get out of this situation, I say, "Father Barone, isn't it against your religion to force someone into marriage?"

"Yes, dear, it is."

"Maybe you can talk some sense into my *fiancé*, then."

Father Barone looks from me to Matteo before Matteo

speaks. "Father Barone, please excuse my *fiancée*. It seems she's lost her manners."

He gives Matteo a small smile.

You have got to be kidding me.

"Father Barone, I just want to let you know that if you follow through with this coerced marriage, you'll be responsible for fraud in the Catholic church. Are you sure you're okay with going to hell?" I snap at him, but it doesn't seem to faze him.

"I'm sure you and Matteo will live a long, happy life together, Luxtyn." He says it with so much confidence, like he truly believes that. Bringing his attention back to Matteo, he asks, "Now, where would you like the ceremony to take place?"

"Here is fine," Matteo says.

I look around the office space and take in the black walls and red velvet furniture. All it needs is a pole and it would pass as a private room in a strip club. "How romantic," I mutter.

"Is this not to your liking, sweetheart?"

Rolling my eyes, I turn back to Matteo and respond with little to no enthusiasm. "It's perfect. Everything is just perfect." There's no point in fighting the inevitable. As long as he holds up his end of the bargain, it doesn't matter where we get married.

This whole thing is ironic, really. I never pictured myself getting married. It's not something I ever thought was in the cards for me. I've never had a boyfriend. Hell, I don't even like forming platonic friendships with people. It's always been my mom and me, which I've been content with. Sure, I've had sex, but emotions and feelings were never something I brought to the table. There was never a point to setting down roots when I knew I'd be leaving soon. But as I take in the reality of my situation, it dawns on me that this will be the only time I ever get married, and it's not what I expected at all.

As Matteo stares at me, there's a flash of something in his eyes. Is it sympathy? Does he actually feel bad for me? I might've just met Matteo, but he doesn't seem like the type to show people sympathy. And he's especially not going to show someone like me, someone who's just a means to an end for him, sympathy.

Matteo addresses Father Barone once more. "Enzo should be up any minute. We can do this wherever you see fit, Father Barone."

He nods as he finds a spot by the far wall with a large window overlooking the dance floor.

His timing impeccable, Enzo strolls into the office wearing a different suit than before, an all-black suit with a black shirt instead of a navy-blue one. "Alright," he says, clasping his hands, then rubbing them together. "Who's ready to have the most romantic wedding of the season?"

I roll my eyes but can't keep the smirk from spreading on my face as I try to contain a laugh. His humor is the only thing that's going to get me through this, because honestly, it's amazing I can even find any at a time like this.

Matteo narrows his gaze on me and lets out a huff before stalking around his desk and extending his hand to me. After placing mine in his, he helps me out of my seat, and when I think he's going to release it, he doesn't. He keeps a soft, yet firm grip on it as he leads me toward Enzo and Father Barone. I'm not sure how to feel about it.

"You changed for the occasion?" I ask Enzo as Matteo stops in front of Father Barone, taking both of my hands into his as we face each other.

He and Matteo exchange knowing glances, like they're in on a secret about Enzo's suit choices that no one else knows about. "I had to dress in my big brother's favorite color for the most important day of his life," Enzo says while slapping Matteo on his shoulder.

Most important day of his life my ass.

"You can just skip through all of the filler stuff and go straight to the vows," Matteo tells Father Barone, who gives him a slight nod.

"Aww, looks like big bro here is overly eager to get to the grand finale."

Crinkling my brows, I ask, "What grand finale?" Matteo wants to get this over with as much as I do. There's no point in elongating something that doesn't matter to either of us.

The gleam in Enzo's eyes tells me I'm not going to like his answer. With a waggle of his brows, he says, *"You may now kiss the bride."*

My gaze shoots to Matteo, who's watching me with an unreadable expression. I never thought about the kiss. Hell, I never thought about anything of the physical nature. *Oh my gosh.* Does he expect me to kiss him? Wait . . . does he expect me to have *sex* with him?

"I don't think we need to do all of that," I blurt. "Let's just sign the marriage license and call it a day."

Matteo ignores me by turning his attention back to Father Barone and nodding for him to begin.

Surely, he agrees with me. This isn't a conventional marriage. There will be no kissing. There will definitely be no sex. We're just two people coexisting to get what we want.

I'm barely paying attention as my thoughts ricochet off the walls of my brain when Matteo gives my hands a slight squeeze.

I look between him and Father Barone, who's giving me the same expectant look, like they're both waiting on me for something. "I'm sorry, what?"

"It's your turn to repeat your vows after me," Father Barone says.

"Matteo can go first," I scramble out, not ready to take the plunge yet.

"Matteo has already recited his vows."

He did?

"Um, yeah, okay." It feels like an out-of-body experience, my mouth moving on autopilot as it recites the words back to Matteo. I want to tell myself to run, to get the hell out of there, but I can't. I have to do this for my mom.

"We're ready for the rings," Father Barone says, addressing Enzo who pulls two bands from the front pocket of his suit jacket. When the hell did they get those?

Matteo slides the dainty silver, diamond encrusted wedding band over my ring finger while repeating the words Father Barone says. It's a beautiful, simple wedding band, and because it's skinny, it doesn't overwhelm my slender fingers.

Father Barone hands me Matteo's ring and leads me in another declaration while I slide the plain silver wedding band over his finger. His knuckles are red, and a couple of them have fresh cuts as if he's been pounding into a cinder block. *Where the hell did he get those from?*

"In the sight of God and this witness, I now pronounce you husband and wife!" Father Barone says with enthusiasm. "You may now kiss the bride!"

Even though I know Matteo has no interest in kissing me, I can't help but feel the slight flutter in my heart at the thought of him doing it. It's not what I want. It's not what either of us want, and yet my body still reacts to the idea of it.

Matteo's gaze falls to my lips, causing me to lick them. Everything from there seems to happen in slow motion as he pulls me to him and wraps his strong arms around me.

Before I have time to react, he leans down and captures my lips with his in what surprises me to be a soft but firm kiss. The warmth that spreads through me as he moves his lips across mine cannot be contained while I slowly melt into him.

Instinctively, I lock my hands around his neck as I rise up on my tippy toes. A low groan emanates from deep within his chest, a chest I regrettably haven't stopped thinking about since walking in on him changing earlier.

Before the kiss can go any further, Matteo pulls back, and the rejection leaves me feeling incomplete. But why? I don't even know him. I don't even *like* him. Or am I just trying to convince myself of that?

Matteo's fixed gaze has me questioning everything. His eyes are nearly black now, as his pupils have dilated, almost excluding the irises from his eyes completely. He has me pulled into him so closely, I can feel the rise and fall of his chest as he heaves for breath.

I study him, waiting for his next move when he pulls away, releasing me. He runs a hand through his hair before dismissing Father Barone. Turning back to me, he says, "I have to get going. I'm going to be late for a meeting."

I'm sorry, what?

"You're leaving?" I hate that my voice comes out more desperate than I intended it to, but I'm not sure how to take that kiss. How *I* reacted. How *he* reacted.

"Yes," he says, making his way to his desk. I follow on his heels, brushing past an amused Enzo.

"Where are you going?" I ask him.

Sliding on his suit jacket, he turns around and snaps at me. "I didn't realize I had to inform you of my whereabouts."

"That's not how I meant it," I snap back.

He stalks around the desk and stops in front of me, making me crane my neck to hold eye contact with him. "This is nothing but a contract being fulfilled. You're a business transaction, Luxtyn. Nothing else. Where I go—what I do—it doesn't concern you."

His face is expressionless even though something passes through his eyes as he speaks those words. It doesn't matter, though, because he's right. I *am* nothing but a business transaction to him. Like he's nothing but a business transaction to me. I'd be smart to remember that.

I step back. "You're right," I say, my eyes remain fixed on his. "I held up my end of the deal, so now it's time for you to hold up yours."

Matteo clenches his jaw before squaring his shoulders. He straightens his black suit jacket and buttons it. "I told you I'm a man of my word."

He stalks toward the door but glances back at me one last time. "I'll update you when I know more. Until then, Enzo will be your direct contact should you need anything."

Before I can argue, he exits the office, leaving me alone with Enzo. Did he just force me to marry him and then pawn me off onto his brother? I shake my head. Fine. If that's how he wants this marriage to go, then fine. A business transaction it is.

Enzo places a soft hand on my shoulder, but I can't bring myself to look at him. "C'mon," he says. I note the hint of sympathy in his tone. "I'll take you back to the penthouse."

I just nod as I think about how this morning went. I can't believe I was stupid enough to think for a second this could ever be anything more than what he told me it was. If that's how he wants to treat me, then fine, but he better remember he's nothing but the same to me.

16

LUXTYN

Enzo and I make it back to Matteo's penthouse in silence, and I'm thankful for that. I didn't want to listen to anything he had to say about Matteo and me getting married or that stupid kiss we shared.

"Are you hungry?" Enzo asks as we walk off the elevator.

"Not really, but I could use some water. Possibly another coffee." I'm still full from the breakfast he ordered earlier. He didn't know what I liked, so he got every breakfast item you could think of. Pastries, eggs, bacon, sausage , bagels, fruit, yogurt, granola. And being that I'm an exceptional guest, I ate a little of everything. My stomach is still paying for that decision.

"Follow me to the kitchen," he says as he leads me down the hall to the open room I got acquainted with earlier. Black cabinets with gold hardware line the walls, but the main attraction is the oversized marble island that sits in the middle of the brightly lit room.

Enzo grabs a bottle of water from the fridge and hands it to me before preparing my coffee.

"You don't have to make my coffee, you know. I'm perfectly capable of doing it myself."

He turns the stove on to heat up the kettle before taking out the french press. Smirking, he asks, "Do you know how to use a french press?"

"I can figure it out."

Pushing the contraption over to me, he responds, "Oh, I would love to see that."

Rolling my eyes, I take the top off and am about to ask him where the coffee is, but he beats me to it, dropping the bag of whole beans in front of me.

These people grind their own coffee beans?

Sighing, I place my hands on the edge of the cool counter. "Okay, can you please show me how to use the french press? I'd like to learn so I don't have to ask you every single time I want a coffee."

He chuckles before giving me one of those endearing smiles of his. *Why can't Matteo be more like his little brother?*

"What're you thinking about?" Enzo asks as he takes the coffee beans and walks over to the grinder.

Following him, I brush him off with my response. "Nothing."

He shows me how to load the coffee beans and where the start button is. "I might not know you too well yet, but I can tell something's off."

"Well, I was kidnapped, found out my estranged dad is in the Mafia, and forced into a marriage with an asshole who is also in the Mafia all in twenty-four hours. I apologize if I'm acting . . . *off*."

"Damn. When you put it that way, your life definitely sucks right about now."

I want to be irritated, but his playful tone makes me sputter out a laugh.

"I don't know what the hell I'm doing, Enzo. I came here to find my mom and ended up slamming face-first into a whole other world. One that I don't understand and don't *want* to understand."

Enzo gives me a sympathetic look, his dark-brown eyes, so similar to his brother's, softening. "Look, I can't lie and say I know what you're going through, but try to think of the positives. Think of the things that'll get you through the day."

I scoff. "Yeah, like what? I don't exactly have much going for me right now. I don't even know what I'm supposed to do with my day-to-day life anymore."

"Your mom is the reason you came out here, so that's what you focus on. Forget about the other stuff for now. Focus on holding onto finding your mom."

"I want to help find her, but I have no idea where to start. I know Matteo said he's going to help me, but who knows if he was being honest about that."

"Matteo never goes back on his word, Luxtyn. He told you he would help you find your mom. He will. *We* will."

I try to take Enzo's reassurance and use it to calm my nerves, but it's not working. "So, what do I do in the meantime?" I ask him.

"Just try and do your best to not drive yourself insane with finding your mom. Let us handle it. We have the resources. We'll figure it out."

I scoff. "You're kidding, right? That's your advice? To not worry about finding my mom? My best friend?"

Hell, my only friend.

"There's nothing you can do to help right now, Luxtyn. We need to keep you safe."

My shoulders slump and I drop my head as this helpless feeling washes over me. I didn't have much of a plan when coming here. I figured I'd go to the condo and if I wasn't able to figure anything out from there, then I would go to the police.

I glance back up at Enzo who's watching me as if he's studying me. Maybe waiting for me to have a meltdown, which I'm surprised I haven't done so yet. "And you guys are *sure* we can't go to the cops?"

He shakes his head. "If you talk to the police, that information could easily wind up in the wrong hands. You can't trust all of them."

"And why should I trust you and Matteo?"

Enzo offers an effortless shrug. "Because who else do you have?"

"Is that supposed to be helpful?"

"No. It's just a fact. You have no one else out here," he says as he pours my freshly pressed coffee into a black ceramic mug. "We're not the bad guys. Teo . . . he might come off as—"

"An arrogant prick?" I offer.

He gives a breathy laugh. "Yes, but he's not all that bad. You just have to break through that outer shell of his."

"I'd really rather not," I say as I add the creamer and sugar to my coffee.

Enzo eyes me while I take a sip of the delicious brew. "What?" I ask as I pull the cup away from my lips.

"You two have your stubbornness in common, that's for sure."

I roll my eyes and continue to take small sips, enjoying the hot liquid with hints of vanilla.

"Just hang in there, okay, Lux? I think you'd be surprised at the kind of person Teo can be."

I chuckle under my breath. *Yeah, okay. We'll see about that.*

17

MATTEO

It's been three days since I left Luxtyn at the club after forcing her into marrying me, which means it's been exactly three days since I last spoke to her. I've been avoiding her, throwing myself into work, just so I have an excuse not to go back to the penthouse and be around her during the day. That sure as hell didn't keep me from sneaking into her room late at night just to watch her sleep, though. Like a fucking creep. The need to be close to her was strong. To see her even though she wouldn't see me. To make sure she was okay.

I'm fucking pathetic.

One kiss. It took one kiss to turn me into a starved man.

But that kiss. That kiss was *not* what I expected. The way Luxtyn so effortlessly melted into me as if we were becoming one. And her lips. So soft and plump, ready for the taking. I struggled to keep myself from begging for more access. It took everything in me to pull away from her.

As much as I've tried focusing on work, Luxtyn continues popping up in my mind. It's as if she's embedded herself deep inside me. What is it about this woman that has me so mesmerized? After everything she's been through, with her mom disappearing to finding out she's the daughter of a Mafia don. Then to be forced into marrying me. The strength she's shown. That sharp tongue of hers. The boldness of stabbing me in the back. It's impressive. *Very fucking impressive.*

I've holed myself up in my office at Fierce, not even working. Just sitting here staring off into space, not getting shit done. The ding of my phone grabs my attention.

Enzo: If you don't come back to this penthouse soon, I'm going to lose it.

Me: What, you can't handle my new wife?

Enzo: Oh, I didn't realize you wanted me to handle her. In that case . . .

Pressing the call button next to Enzo's name, I bring my phone up to my ear. He picks up after the first ring, but I speak before he can say anything. "You put your hands on my wife, and I'll fucking end you."

"Okay, first of all, I'm offended you've taken the side of a woman you haven't even known for a week over me. And secondly, I'm just messing with you, big brother."

"What do you want?" I snap.

"Uh, well, *you* called me. Or did you already forget that in your old age?"

I rest my elbows on my desk and let out an exasperated sigh while I splay my fingers across my forehead, rubbing my temples. "I'm only three years older than you, Enzo."

"Yeah, whatever. You need to come to the penthouse. Your wife is getting very antsy. She's bordering on stir-crazy at this point."

"It's been three days."

"Yes, three days of just being around me. And while I know I'm great company, she wants to be proactive with finding her mom."

"Have you not relayed the information to her that I gave you about her mother's situation?"

I've paid off some gang members to start threatening low-level associates in the Silvestri family to see if they've heard anything through the grapevines about the disappearance of a woman. None of them have turned up anything, which is fucking frustrating.

Sending my men after high-level Silvestri men is not an option, though. Unless I want to increase the possibility of Giuseppe discovering I'm behind it. That would start a war, and that's not something I can do right now. My plan to take him down is more strategic than just killing him. I want to strip him of his power. Take away what he and his family have built until there's nothing left. Then after he's witnessed the downfall of his empire, *that's* when I'll kill him. Knowing he's leaving this world with his legacy in shambles will be the best form of revenge for killing my parents.

"Of course I told her. But keep in mind you haven't given me much *to* tell her. She's worried sick *and* she's bored. So all she does everyday is worry to the point where it's beginning to drive *me* crazy."

"Sounds like you're not doing a good enough job at entertaining her, then," I grumble as I pull a report of Fierce's numbers last night, something that the distraction at the forefront of my brain kept me from completing over an hour ago.

Enzo's voice gets low and cocky. "Oh, I can entertain her. You say the word, Teo, and I'll happily oblige."

"Enzo, how many jokes are you going to make about having sex with my *wife?*" I growl out.

"Enough to make you be a damn *husband* and get your ass

back to the penthouse instead of hiding from *your wife* because you realized you're not as cold and heartless as you thought you were," he says before hanging up on me.

I hold out my phone and stare at it, shocked. *Did he just fucking hang up on me?* My phone dings, indicating a message came through.

Enzo: I hope my theatrics got across the gravity of the situation. And don't worry, I promise to keep my hands to myself.

Another message comes through before I can type out a response.

Enzo: Unless you don't get back to the penthouse immediately. Then these hands are going to be all sorts of loosey-fucking-goosey.

"This fucking idiot," I breathe out while shaking my head as I type out a quick response.

Me: I'll be there in an hour.

Enzo: It's about damn time.

Finding Luxtyn's mother has proven to be more difficult than I anticipated, but Giuseppe Silvestri is a cocky son of a bitch. Keeping his mouth shut about a kidnapping goes against his MO. It wouldn't be unheard of for lower-level associates to hear about the dealings of the higher-ups by chance of it all.

Leaning back in my chair, I let out a long sigh as I angle my head back to rest on the headrest. I still need to figure out what I'm going to tell Luxtyn, because I have nothing, and it doesn't make sense.

Giuseppe would be the only one interested in taking her mother. If he killed her, he would've sent proof of that to Mancini. He hasn't done that, so what is his plan?

The pressure starts to get to me as I rack my brain, trying to figure this out. Because If I don't soon, I fear Luxtyn will end up with the same unfortunate hand I was dealt.

18

MATTEO

The elevator dings, letting me off on the main level of my penthouse. I've been here more in the last week than I have in the past month combined.

I typically stay at my family's secluded estate, which sits on sixteen acres of land located outside the city. It's large enough to hold my family home, a pool with a pool house, and a gym, while still being small enough to keep secure. The concrete wall perimeter around the entire property, twenty-four-seven surveillance, along with several armed guards on at all times makes sure no one can get in or out of the property without my knowing.

Voices come from the living room as I make my way down the hall. Rounding the corner, I see Enzo and Luxtyn on the couch.

"I don't know, Enzo," she says. Her shoulders sag and her gaze drops to her fidgeting fingers in her lap. I can hear the defeat in her tone from here and it does things to my heart that it really fucking shouldn't, but I'm beginning to figure out that when it comes to Luxtyn, my mind and body will act on their own volition.

"What if we don't find her?" she asks.

Enzo slides his arm around her on the back of the couch in a comforting way. I swear she leans into him slightly, and that's when I see red.

"What the fuck is going on in here?" I demand. This doesn't look like she's going stir-crazy. This looks like my brother's going to be fucking slaughtered for touching my wife.

Enzo glances up. "Well, look who's finally back," he says with a hint of a smirk drawing up on his face. He leans back into the couch looking comfortable as fuck.

Luxtyn's gaze shoots to mine, and there's a slight ease in my chest at the innocent sight of her. Her face is void of any makeup and her dark hair is pulled up on top of her head in a messy bun. However, that innocent look on her face quickly disappears and is replaced with a scowl as she jumps to her feet, and stomps toward me.

"Where the hell have you been?" she demands. "You force me to marry you and then leave for three days and give me *nothing* about my mom?"

Just when I think she's going to stop in front of me, she doesn't. She barrels into me, shoving me with all her strength. It doesn't sway me in the slightest, but I commend her on her effort.

"What is *wrong* with you?" She shoves me again, but I remain rooted in place, which seems to irritate her more.

"You said you'd hold up your end of the deal, so what's going on?" She attempts to shove me once more, but this time I take her small delicate wrists in my hands and pull her close to my chest.

It's not until now I realize the "outfit" she has on, which

immediately has me in a damn rage. "What the *fuck* are you wearing?"

The little minx gives me a sly smile like she just remembered. "You haven't let me leave this place, so I'm wearing my comfy clothes."

Her *comfy clothes* consist of a baggy shirt I know for damn sure is Enzo's, short ass shorts I can only see because she has Enzo's shirt tied up in the corner, and no fucking bra. Her nipples brush against me when her chest rises and falls, nearly in sync with mine. And hell, it feels so damn good.

"Besides, it was warmer out today than it has been, so my usual sweatshirt and leggings were out of the question. It was hot."

"If you're hot, put on the damn air conditioning," I grind out. She's been prancing around in this getup all day with Enzo here? I'm going to fucking kill him.

"Enzo knows how to control the thermostat. Don't you, Enzo?" I call out from over Luxtyn's head, but my eyes remain glued to hers.

"Sorry. Must've forgotten," Enzo calls out from the couch. I snap my gaze to his, and he's smiling. *Definitely going to kill him.*

"And why the fuck are you wearing Enzo's shirt?" My voice is harsh, but Luxtyn doesn't show if it's affected her. In fact, she seems happy. As if she finds enjoyment in getting under my skin.

"I *was* wearing mine originally, but I spilled my coffee on it this morning, and since I didn't bring a surplus of clothes with me to NYC in the first place, Enzo was generous enough to lend me his for the time being while I wash my stuff."

She gives me a sardonic smile as she wiggles to free herself from my grasp. I let her struggle for a few moments, relishing the way her body feels as it rubs up against mine.

"This'll be the last time you ever have another man's shirt on. You need something to wear, Little Lux, you come to me." Her breath catches in her throat as she stops moving and her eyes stare up into mine. I drop my gaze to her lips, and her delicious pink tongue darts out to moisten them.

She falters slightly but attempts to pull the shirt down as if it'll cover anything with it tied at her hip. I rake my gaze down her frame, taking in her toned legs. Legs I've been fantasizing about having wrapped around me.

"So," she says, pulling me from my intrusive thoughts. "Do you have anything on my mom?"

I let out a sigh. "Nothing other than what Enzo told you."

"You said you would help me find her."

"I know."

"Then why haven't you figured anything out?" she yells. Stepping back, she lets out a long breath as if she's trying to calm herself down. "Put yourself in my shoes. If your mom was missing, wouldn't it drive you crazy? Wouldn't you want to do everything in your power to get her back?"

Yes. Not being there to help my parents is something I regret every single day.

The sadness washes over her face as her eyes grow glossy. "Can I at least help? Please. I want to help. I *need* to help."

Nothing but silence encompasses the air around us as I contemplate my options. Running a hand through my hair, I finally speak. "I'm not sure why it's been this difficult to find your mother. Silvestri can be cocky, and he can be messy. If he's the one who kidnapped her, I should've heard about it by now with the tactics I've been using."

"Okay . . . so, what does that mean?"

"You don't think Silvestri's behind taking Lux's mom?" Enzo asks as he pushes himself up off the couch and walks over to us.

When the fuck did he start calling her Lux?

The way he says her name is so . . . comfortable. Like they're best friends who've known each other for years. I don't fucking like it.

I shake my head. "Not exactly. Mancini's theory with Mauricio behind it is strong. I need to gain access to Mauricio, but if I do, that'll put us in the limelight and has the potential to start a war."

Silence fills the air once more. "What if I do it?" Luxtyn asks. "What if I can get close to Mauricio?"

"Absolutely fucking not," I say at the same time Enzo responds, "The fuck, no."

Luxtyn bounces her gaze from mine to his and back to mine again. "Fine. That would probably be too obvious anyway, but what about Elena and Giuliana?"

"Another terrible idea," I say while Enzo asks, "Are you insane?" at the same time as me.

Rolling her eyes, she continues. "Angelo brought up wanting me to meet them." She points at me. "You even said you wouldn't be surprised if Elena knows something about my mom's disappearance. I think I should go and see if I can figure anything out."

"No," I say with finality.

She lets out a frustrated breath and mutters, "So ridiculous." She folds her arms across her chest, causing her shirt to ride up and her tits to lift.

Fuck this.

I stalk over to the couch and pull the throw blanket off it, tossing it to her. Her eyebrows furrow as she barely catches it at the last second. "Wrap it around your body," I order, answering her unspoken question.

"I'm not cold."

I close the distance between us and lean down, inhaling the

delicious sweet scent of her body wash. "Either you wrap this blanket around your body *now*, or I'll bend you over the back of this couch and give my brother an even bigger show than you already have."

A spark flares in her eyes before a smirk pulls at the corner of her lips. "What makes you think I wouldn't like that?"

She pushes the blanket into my chest as she walks away. "I'm going to go to the bathroom. When I get back, I expect you guys to have a real plan for finding my mom, and if you don't." She pauses as she glances over her shoulder, her eyes focused on mine. "We're going with my plan."

Turning back around, she saunters out of the room, and I drop my gaze to that tight ass of hers. Round and perky, just waiting to be spanked. Waiting to have my teeth sunk into it.

Fucking hell.

Enzo's voice pulls me out of my daze. "Man. I bet you guys are going to have some fucking fantastic sex."

"Why does my wife feel comfortable enough around you to be prancing around in nothing but her underwear and *your* shirt?"

"Would you rather I have her walk around with *no* shirt on?" Before I can answer with what would've been wrapping him up in a chokehold, Enzo holds up his pointer finger. "And one, she wasn't in her underwear. She was in a T-shirt and shorts." Adding another finger, he continues. "And two, Lux and I are practically best friends now. I've been the girl's only human interaction in three days. *Three days, Teo.*"

"You say it like it's been a fucking month," I say, bored. Three days is not that long. "Besides, you could've taken her somewhere. *You* both decided not to leave the penthouse."

"Oh, I've tried. *Trust me.* She hasn't wanted to go anywhere because all she's been thinking about is her mom. Do you know how often that girl paces? She could break a damn world record for it."

He lets out a sigh. "The point is, you can't keep ignoring the girl. I know finding her mom is proving to be more difficult than you anticipated, but you can't keep coming home at one in the morning just to be a fucking creeper and check in on her while she's sleeping, then leave by five. What's the point of even coming here at that point? You might as well stay away."

I *should* stay away, and if I was smart, I would, but every night I come back to the penthouse late and find myself drawn to Luxtyn's room, spurring a feeling inside of me that I never thought I'd experience in my life. Her dark hair sprawled across her pillow has been incinerated into my brain. Knowing I get to come home to the same image, it's fucking pathetic and it's ruining me, slowly chipping away at the stone wall I've built around my heart.

My phone rings, so I pull it out of my back pocket and see it's Mancini. I've been dodging his calls the past few days. He's been wanting to see Luxtyn, but the idea still doesn't sit well with me. We might be working together, but the protective instinct that comes out of me when it comes to her is overpowering anything else. She's mine, and I'll keep her safe. Even if that means needing to keep her away from her father and his family.

"Let me get this real quick," I say, bringing the phone up to my ear. "Mancini."

"When are you going to let me see my daughter, Matteo?" He's irritated. Good. The old man waited nearly twenty-three years to have a relationship with her. He can wait a little longer.

"That depends. Have you figured out where her mother is?"

He clears his throat. "I haven't heard anything from Mauricio. I've had a few guys I trust keep their eyes and ears open, but that hasn't turned up anything. What about on your end?"

"Nothing," I say.

"I want to see my daughter, Matteo. We're having a family dinner at my house tonight. I would like for her to come." His tone has a hint of desperation, like he's been longing for this moment his entire life.

Luxtyn walks back into the living room, and I'm pleased to see she has a pair of leggings on this time. I'm *not* pleased to see she's still galavanting around fucking braless.

"She's busy. Maybe another time," I grind out before hanging up the phone and stuffing it into the pocket of my slacks.

Luxtyn slows her pace as she approaches, eyeing Enzo and me with a wrinkle in her brow. "Who was that?"

"No one."

She crosses her arms in front of her chest, pushing those tits up nice and high once again. She's far too much of a distraction for me.

"Obviously that's a lie. So who was it?"

"It's none of your business, Luxtyn."

"You were clearly speaking about me, so who was it?" Her eyes widen. "Angelo. It was Angelo, wasn't it? What did he want? Does he want to see me?"

Her excitement doesn't go unnoticed, and it kills me. Why doesn't she get this excited when it comes to me? Oh, right, because I'm a fucking asshole who's been trying to convince us both that I want nothing to do with her.

I should lie to her about it being Angelo, but my heart shatters thinking about doing that. I don't want her to see him, but I don't want her to think he doesn't want to see her. To feel rejected.

Isn't that what I've been doing, though? Rejecting her.

Our situation is different. This arrangement is a business transaction, but there's no rule that says we can't enjoy each other's company. Maybe I've been going about this all wrong, keeping her away as much as I have. Pushing her directly into my brother's hands. We'll be husband and wife for the rest of our lives and instead of embracing it, I've been avoiding it. That's all about to fucking change now.

"Yes, he was asking about seeing you," I say to her.

She drops her hands to her sides. "This is perfect. I can see if he wants to have that dinner with Elena and Giuliana."

"You're not going." She opens her mouth, surely to argue. "And that's the end of that," I say with finality. I go to walk past her, but just when I'm about to, she grabs ahold of my arm. Not too tight, but it still stops me.

She stares up at me with pleading eyes. "Please." The single word squeezes my chest so tightly it hurts. "Let me do something." She swallows deeply while she waits for my response.

I close my eyes and tilt my head up to the ceiling, letting out a long sigh. This is not what I want to do, but I say, "Fine," and the excitement on her face is immediate. A smile pulls at her lips, and I love that I put it there.

"Thank you, thank you!" she squeals before reaching up to place a light kiss on my cheek. The act was so innocent, so comfortable for her, she didn't even falter when she did it. "I'm going to go get changed," she adds before scurrying back down the hallway that leads to her room, leaving Enzo and me in silence.

The silence is broken a few seconds later when Enzo claps a hand down on my shoulder and says, "Well, looks like you're pussy whipped now," before walking off toward the kitchen with a stark laugh. And at this point, I can't deny it. But do I even want to?

19

LUXTYN

I was ready to go to battle with Matteo over this dinner with Angelo. He's basically locked me up in this penthouse to do nothing, and I can't take it anymore. If I can help figure out where my mom is, then I'll do it. Plus, a part of me wants to get to know Angelo, Elena, and Giuliana. I have a half sister I knew nothing about. An entire family I knew nothing about. It makes me wonder what exactly my mom was thinking when she kept me away from them.

I brought a limited amount of clothes to NYC, so I put on the nicest outfit I packed: a pair of high-waisted skinny jeans tucked into the black combat boots I wore on the plane ride here, paired with a simple white T-shirt that ends just above the waistline of my pants. Topping it off, I add my cropped black leather jacket. The sun has set, so I'm sure the cool spring weather will comb the air outside now.

Checking my reflection in the mirror, I take my hair out of its messy bun and run my fingers through it, pulling the kinks out. I'm fortunate enough that after a few tosses of my hair, its normally straight appearance has more volume and some waves to it after being up in a bun all day. After applying a touch of makeup—mascara, blush, and a cherry-tinted lip balm—I decide I'm ready to go.

I'm prepared to meet Enzo out in the living room to take me to Angelo's, but am surprised to find Matteo standing there with his face buried in his phone. He hasn't acknowledged my presence yet, so I take a moment to observe him.

He changed. He's now wearing a black button-up with the sleeves rolled up, exposing his inked forearms. The fitted shirt stretches around his tight muscles, showcasing his impressive arms. Arms I've pictured wrapped around me since our kiss a few days ago.

"Did you let Angelo know I'll be there for dinner?" I ask.

Matteo glances up from his phone and slowly rakes his eyes over me. Something flickers through them as he brings them up to meet mine. "I did," he answers. "He's expecting us soon."

I raise a brow. *"Us?"*

He tucks his phone in his pocket, his gaze remaining only on mine. "Enzo's been watching over you enough." He walks up and stops before me, causing me to angle my head back to keep eye contact with him. "I think it's time you and I start acting like husband and wife."

His words give me whiplash. "But I'm nothing but a *business transaction*, remember?" I say, throwing his words back at him. Words that hurt me more than I care to admit. I thought I could withstand being stuck in a marriage with a man I mean nothing to, but I'm not so sure now. Especially when that man is Matteo. An overbearing, insanely attractive, making me question everything that I know kind of man.

He stares into my eyes, and the sincerity behind them is clear. "I think you and I both know those were just words, Little Lux." He glances down at my lips, and I dart my tongue out to moisten them. "There's something about you. Something that draws me to you. Something that doesn't allow me to get you out of my head."

His eyes follow the path of my tongue, excitement and need radiating through them as he leans over and wraps his hand around the back of my head. My heart rate picks up and the rest happens in slow motion.

Matteo's lips brush over mine, and the taste of peppermint lingers as my body immediately reacts and I suck them into my mouth. A groan escapes him as I lightly tug his lips with my teeth, which has me wanting more of that feral sound.

I part my lips, eager to see if he'll continue and take from me what I'm willing to give him or pull away and leave me like he did last time.

His tongue slips into my mouth, and I let out a whimper at the heat that consumes me, our kiss instantly becoming more intense. Placing a rough hand on my waist, Matteo pivots us and pushes me up against the wall. It wasn't soft, but it was the way I needed it to be. I want to forget about the crap I have going on in my life and marinate in the arms of Matteo. *When did this happen?*

Locking his hands around my wrists, he brings them up above my head, trapping me against the wall as he spreads my legs with his knee. He leans into me, our kiss becoming more heated, like he needs this with every breath. Just like I do.

I arch my back off the wall to get closer to him when the clearing of someone's throat interrupts us. Matteo hesitantly pulls his lips off mine but doesn't look toward the sound. His nearly black lust-filled eyes stare down into mine as my hands remain pinned above my head.

A woman's voice breaks through our haze. "So this is what's kept you in the city this past week?"

My eyes widen as I take in the smooth, unfamiliar voice. She sounds young. I try to wiggle myself free from Matteo's hands, but he doesn't let me go. He hasn't moved. He continues to stare into my eyes as if the intruder hasn't made herself known.

"Matteo . . ." I whisper while I try to break free once more.

He closes his eyes as if he's in pain and mutters, "This isn't finished," before opening them and releasing his grip on my wrists.

The clink of heels on the marble floor sounds as the newcomer draws near us. I move to the side to glance around Matteo's hulking frame, and make eye contact with a stunning brunette, with her voluminous hair in perfect waves cascading over her shoulders. She's wearing a long-sleeved emerald-green dress that hugs her tall, slender body and ends right above her knee.

I snap my gaze back to Matteo's with wide eyes, which he takes in immediately. Spinning on his heel, he brings his attention to the gorgeous woman who could make supermodels feel inferior. I can't help but wonder who she is to Matteo. This self-doubt in me isn't a feeling I've ever felt before, and it's not one I want to get used to.

"Isabella, I had no idea you were coming here," Matteo says calmly.

She takes his extended hands I hadn't realized he'd given her and leans in to kiss both his cheeks. "Well, I haven't seen you all week, so I came to take you out to dinner," she says before bringing her gaze to mine. "But it seems you already have plans?" she asks, bouncing her gaze back to his.

"*You* were going to take *me* out to dinner?" Matteo asks, ignoring her question.

She gives him a soft, bubbly laugh. "Okay, fine. You were going to pay, but I was going to offer my amazing company. You've been texting every night letting me know you're not going to be home, so I decided to track you down myself."

Home.

They share a home?

Oh my gosh.

I didn't even think about the fact that Matteo could have a girlfriend. Why the hell didn't I think about that? Oh right, because there wasn't any time to think anything through before getting married. I internally cringe as I realize his girlfriend walked in on us full on face-fucking each other against a wall. My face heats with anger knowing that he put us in this situation. I refuse to be married to a cheater.

"I told you, I've been busy with some things," he says, not offering her many details.

"Oh, I see that," she sasses, raising her brow at him before turning to me with a warm smile. Extending her hand, she introduces herself to me with enthusiasm. "Hi, I'm Izzy."

I take her hand and give it a shake, returning the greeting. "Hi, I'm Lux." My nickname rolls off my tongue, which is surprising. It's not how I usually introduce myself to someone, especially the girlfriend of a guy I was just making out with. But her friendly demeanor has apparently rubbed off on me a bit.

"Oooh, Lux," she says, wiggling her brows at me. "Now that's a cool name. Very edgy. Is it short for something?"

"Luxtyn," I state, still unsure how I should act in this situation.

"Isabella," Matteo interrupts.

Izzy leans into me and gestures toward Matteo with her head. "This one has always called me by my full name. I tried getting him on board with Izzy, but he just won't do it. Tell me, does he call you Lux, or is it always *Luxtyn*?"

"He calls me Luxtyn." I pause as I consider that answer before adding, "Well, except for when he calls me Little Lux."

I have no idea why I told her that.

Izzy raises an impressed and perfectly arched brow at me. "Little Lux." She glances back at Matteo and says, "Nicknames, huh? What a cute little kink."

Matteo lets out a sigh. "Now that you've met my little sister, I think it's time for us to get going." He wraps a hand around my forearm and pulls me away.

Relief washes over me as I take in that information.

His sister.

Of course.

How stupid of me.

"Enzo's in his room. I'm sure he'll take you out to dinner, Isabella," Matteo yells back to her as he continues pulling me toward the elevator.

"Mm-hm, you two have fun now," she singsongs before her shoes click across the marble again and she calls out, "Oh, Vincenzo."

Matteo's fingers slide down my arm and enclose around my hand. He's being so affectionate, and I'm not sure what to take from it. It's messing with me, and I need answers.

Tugging on his hand, I bring him to a stop. "What are we doing?"

"I thought we were going to dinner at your father's house."

Father's house. That sounds so strange to hear.

Rolling my eyes, I say, "You know what I mean."

"I already told you. You're my wife. Going to dinner at your father's house seems like a husband-and-wife thing to do, don't you think?"

"You really want to start acting like husband and wife now?"

"Don't you think it would make it a bit more tolerable since we're going to be stuck together for the rest of our lives?"

I cock an eyebrow. "How romantic," I mutter before stepping around him so I can continue making my way toward the elevator, but before I'm able to, Matteo grabs a hold of my forearm, stopping me. I can feel his gaze on me, but I refuse to look at him.

"Is it romance you're after?" he teases.

My eyes remain locked on the elevator door as I say, "The only thing I'm after when it comes to you is finding my mom."

He chuckles softly. "That's not what your body was saying just a few moments ago."

I snap my head in his direction, narrowing my gaze on him. "Oh, good for you. You can play tonsil hockey like a champ."

He lets out a full laugh this time, and the sound is deep, vibrating through my bones. "Tonsil hockey, huh? Can't say that's been used to describe that sort of skill set of mine before."

The thought of him playing tonsil hockey with other women doesn't settle well with me, but I push that vicious green lady down as deep as I can. She's never been a part of my life before, yet she's already shown up twice tonight.

Ignoring his comment, I say, "We should probably get going. We're already running behind." I pull my arm from his grasp and make my way to the elevator with him on my heels.

"Aren't you forgetting something, dear wife?" Matteo calls out from behind me, but I ignore him as I press the down button and watch the doors open.

We step onto the car, and I feel Matteo's gaze on me. "What did I forget, Matteo?" I ask, keeping my focus on my reflection in the shiny metal door as it closes. I have nothing here, so I'm not sure what there is that I could've possibly forgotten. This is just another one of his stupid games, like playing into the whole being husband-and-wife thing.

I watch his reflection as he reaches into the pocket of his slacks and pulls something out. Turning to him, he holds the object up between his fingers, and I see it's a wedding band.

My wedding band. The last time I saw it was the morning he forced me to marry him. I took it off and left it on my nightstand and haven't thought about it since. When the hell did he get that?

"I know you haven't been wearing it."

"Well, there wasn't really anywhere *to* wear it."

"This is a symbol of our marriage. It represents the binding of our relationship. I would like for you to wear it at all times."

I almost roll my eyes at the statement, but then I notice the shiny metal band he has wrapped around his ring finger. *Does he wear his at all times?*

"I keep mine on, so keep yours on . . . please."

I think that's the first time I've heard him say *please*. The shock from it, along with his want for us to keep something so symbolic on at all times has me mute as he takes my hand and slides the ring on, like he did on our wedding day.

I drag my attention back to the elevator door when it dings. Matteo takes my hand into his as we walk off and guides me to the G-Wagon that's sitting there idling for us. Now, instead of thinking about the dinner, the only thing on my mind is the confusion at Matteo and his sudden change of heart when it comes to our marriage . . . and what that means for us.

20

MATTEO

After going through security, we pull up to Mancini's impressive estate, which has a grand three-tiered stone fountain in the middle of the circular driveway. I had Rocco drive us in case I need backup, so he'll wait in the SUV until we're ready to leave. Mancini and I might be working together, but it would be lazy of me to not practice the same level of security I would with anyone else.

I lace my fingers with Luxtyn's as I pull her out of the vehicle, then make our way up the steps to the front door. A man dressed in a butler's uniform greets us before we're able to knock, gesturing for us to come in.

Walking into the grand foyer, the butler takes our coats before showing us down the hallway lined with small marble statues on top of pedestals. I notice Luxtyn's hands tremble as we round the corner into the dining room, so I grab her hand with my own and give her a soft squeeze to remind her I'm here. She gives me a small smile in return.

"Ahh, you've arrived. Perfect timing. Dinner is just about ready to be served," Mancini says as he walks around the table to greet us. He takes my hand into his and gives me a firm handshake before embracing Luxtyn in a hug she wasn't prepared for. Her eyes widen over Mancini's shoulder, but she reciprocates the endearing act.

With his arm still placed firmly on her back, Mancini directs her toward Elena and Giuliana. I watch closely as the introductions are made.

"Elena, *il mio tesoro*, this is Luxtyn," he says before turning to Luxtyn. "Luxtyn, this is my wife, Elena, and our daughter, Giuliana."

Elena holds out her hand with a blank expression on her face. "Pleased to meet you, dear," she says, but her tone says the opposite.

Luxtyn puts on a smile and shakes her hand. "You too," she says, matching her unenthusiastic tone. Elena raises her drawn-on eyebrow in response. *She didn't like that, but I sure as hell did.*

Luxtyn turns her attention to Giuliana who's wearing high-waisted dark jeans, black thigh-high boots, and a tucked in, tight red shirt that has her cleavage on full display. She looks like she's about to have a night out in the city versus a quiet family dinner at home. The scowl that's pasted on her face as she takes in Luxtyn tells me we might be in for an interesting night.

"Giuliana, say hello to your new half sister." Elena gives her a small nudge, causing her to reluctantly step forward and extend her limp hand out in greeting. Luxtyn gives her a questionable shake before dropping it.

Giuliana slides her predator-like eyes over to me and a smile breaks free on her face as she rakes her gaze up and down my body. Pushing her shoulders back, she raises her chin, and a dark gleam springs from her eyes. "It's so nice to see you, as always, Matteo." The seductive tone in her voice doesn't go unnoticed by me.

Did her father not *inform her about the change in our contract? Or is she purposely being disrespectful?*

"Please, let's all take a seat," Mancini says as he makes his way to the head of the grand dark-oak table.

Giuliana gives me one last look, biting her lip with a mischievous smile. The desperation rolling off her has me immediately grateful we didn't end up stuck in a marriage.

Ignoring her, I turn to Luxtyn whose gaze is narrowed in on Giuliana, and I can't help but feel a sense of satisfaction at the jealousy she's displaying. I place my hand on the curve of her back, drawing her attention to me, and give her a reassuring smile.

When Giuliana realizes I'm not giving her the reaction she wants, she lets out a scoff before turning around to take her seat on one side of her father. Her mother takes the other, leaving the other head of the table and a seat next to Elena open for Luxtyn and me.

Leading her over to our seats, I slide out the tufted brown leather chair before Luxtyn has a chance to. "Let me get that for you," I say. She smiles and thanks me before taking her seat.

I take the spot next to her at the opposite end of the table as Mancini. An intricate crystal chandelier hanging from the two-toned coffered ceiling with branches extending and curving their way around each other to form an extravagant centerpiece is the only thing between us.

"Let's dig in," Mancini says after the server brings out our first course, a caprese salad. Only the occasional clanks of the silverware against the salad plates fill the air around us. I keep an eye on everyone as we continue eating our food in silence.

Mancini might not think Elena knows anything about Luxtyn's mother disappearing, but I'm not so convinced. If her brother is behind the abduction, then Elena must know something, but if she does, she's playing it off a lot better than I'd expected.

When Mancini introduced her to Luxtyn, I looked for a tell, any sway in her step or a falter in her expression, but there was nothing. Sure, she was cold, but Elena Mancini has never been known to have a charismatic personality. And even now, as we sit here, quietly enjoying our salads, Elena remains focused on the food in front of her. She's not giving me any kind of sign that she knows.

"So, Luxtyn, what have you been up to all week?" Mancini asks, finally breaking the silence.

She clears her throat and wipes her mouth with her napkin before speaking. "Oh, nothing much. Just been at the penthouse," she says as she brushes her hair behind her ear.

Mancini's eyes light up as he tracks the movement of her left hand, which reminds me, I never told him about us tying the knot. I've been so distracted with Luxtyn and her mother, that I haven't even clued him in on that important piece of information. The port that was so important to me, that's *still* important to me, has suddenly found itself knocked out of that number one spot on my list of priorities.

"Is that what I think it is?" Mancini asks, his eyes settled on her ring finger.

Luxtyn glances over at him and follows his line of sight to her wedding band. "Oh, yes," she says as she holds her hand up to him. "Matteo and I got married."

Giuliana drops her fork onto her salad plate with a loud *clank*. "Excuse me?" she shrieks, the pitch so high I'm surprised it didn't crack the glass in the chandelier.

I guess that answers the question of whether or not Angelo told them about the change in the contract.

"Angelo?" Elena questions.

"Daddy, the marriage was supposed to be between *me* and Matteo. Not *that.*" Giuliana gestures to my wife with a crinkle in her nose as if Luxtyn's nothing more than the dirt on the bottom of her Louboutins.

My jaw drops open as I go to step in, the anger consuming me at the disrespect Giuliana is showing Luxtyn, but before I'm able to, a soft, warm hand covers the fist I hadn't realized I'd formed on the table, almost immediately putting out the raging inferno. My gaze finds its way to Luxtyn, who's focused on Giuliana.

"The marriage that was supposed to be between you and Matteo was a business transaction. I'm sure Angelo can find you another one, but until then, you should probably learn to control those emotions of yours. Your future husband doesn't need a ticking time bomb attached to his name."

Giuliana's eyes widen and her mouth falls open as she lets out a frustrated gasp. She snaps her head to her father's. "Daddy, are you just going to let her speak to me like that?"

Mancini eyes me, and I raise my chin slightly, intrigued to hear how he responds. Because if it's not what I want to hear, I won't hesitate to hammer the nail in so Giuliana understands where she belongs.

"The contract has been signed, Giuliana. And I'd appreciate it if you and Luxtyn got along. She is your sister, after all, which means you need to treat her with the same respect you expect her to treat you with."

Giuliana lets out a huff as she folds her arms in front of her and throws herself back in her seat like a sulking child that didn't get her way.

Luxtyn starts to pull her hand from me, but I catch her fingers with mine, holding them. Not wanting to let them go.

Her eyes drift to mine, and I give her a wink. A small smile breaks out on her face, and my lips form the same, proud of my wife for sticking up for herself.

"I'm a little less than impressed with the lack of rock on your finger, but I'm glad to see the joining of our families finally," Mancini says, interrupting the moment.

With an unimpressed look, I bring my gaze up to his smirking one. "That wedding band on my wife's finger is a family heirloom. One that's been passed down for several decades now, the most recent inhabitant of it being my deceased mother."

A small gasp comes from Luxtyn as she learns the fate of my mother for the first time. It's not exactly how I imagined her finding out, but it was bound to come out at some point.

"It's worth far more than that overly lavish chandelier of yours," I say, raising my gaze up to the monstrosity above us before settling back on Mancini who looks like he's about to croak. He covers it up with a laugh before wiping his mouth with his napkin.

"I see . . . well, I just want the best for Luxtyn."

She gives my hand a firm squeeze, and I can tell by the look in her eyes that she's trying to silently console me for the death of my mother. It's a small gesture, but the fact she's giving it to me means more than she could know.

We all go back to eating, and the rest of the meal goes smoothly, with barely any conversation being had. The tension about our marriage remains stagnant in the air.

"Matteo, come join me for a nightcap, yes?" Mancini asks as we stand from the table.

"Of course," I say before turning my attention to Luxtyn. I pull her into me and whisper, "Are you okay with Elena and Giuliana while I speak with your father?"

"Yes. Will you ask him if he's heard anything about my mom though, please?"

"Of course." I lean down and place a light kiss on her cheek, which causes her to hiss a breath in. "I'll be back as soon as I can."

I follow Mancini to his study where the walls are lined with full bookcases. Closing the door behind me, I track his movements toward a small table that holds a crystal whiskey decanter set. Without glancing back at me, Mancini speaks. "Care for a drink, Matteo?"

He pours the amber liquid in a glass as I say, "Sure."

Grabbing both glasses, Mancini walks over and hands me one.

"So I see you've upheld your part of the contract." He stands there, swirling his glass in one hand while his other hand is shoved into the pocket of his charcoal slacks. "You haven't requested I uphold my end of the contract yet."

"I've been busy trying to locate your ex-lover." He winces upon hearing me describe her that way.

"Too busy to take control of my port?" Angelo tsks me, raising an eyebrow. "Wasn't that your plan this entire time? Take over the port so you can eliminate Giuseppe's access to it?"

Yes, but my priorities have shifted a bit.

"Luxtyn agreed to marry me because I promised I would help her find her mother. I'm surprised you wouldn't think that's important enough to be my top priority."

"Of course it's important. Just make sure you treat my daughter well, Matteo. Because I'll be here if you don't." He takes a sip from his glass, letting his threat hang in the air between us. He's lucky it regards my wife's safety, or I'd kill him right now with the gun strapped to the inside of my ankle.

"You have nothing to worry about when it comes to your daughter, Mancini. She's my wife, and I take care of what's mine. Very good care."

His jaw clenches, and I love that I struck a chord with him with my suggestive comment.

"We'll talk about your port after we find Luxtyn's mother. Finding her is the priority right now."

Mancini perks up. "Have you discovered anything of importance in regard to Char's disappearance?" His dark eyes lighten in anticipation.

I ignore him and walk over to the brown leather couch to take a seat. I hike my foot up, resting it on the opposite knee, and let my arm hang along the back of the couch.

"I have not," I answer, holding his gaze, and pause for a moment before continuing. "It's strange, actually. Silvestri isn't known for keeping secrets. Someone would've either heard about a woman getting kidnapped by now, or you would've heard from Silvestri in regard to her." Whether that be as a threat to keep Angelo in line or to show him what happens when Silvestri thinks he's going behind his back.

"It's a possibility," Mancini says, the intrigue lighting up his eyes even more. "What are you saying, Matteo?"

"I'm saying I've paid men to threaten and beat the shit out of people within the Silvestri organization. Yes, lower-level associates, but even low-level associates have ears. None of those men have brought any useful information to me."

"You paid your men to beat up Silvestri's men?" he asks, dumbfounded, as it's typically not a wise thing to do. It could start a war going after his men like that. Especially with no solid proof of a good reason to do so.

"Of course not. I hired some street gang members to do it." I take another sip of the whiskey and revel in the burn as it slides down my throat. "You and I both know I can't have my name tied to that."

Mancini takes a seat in the leather chair across from me and lets out a small sigh.

"I'm assuming you haven't heard anything from Silvestri?" I ask him. "What about Mauricio? What's he been up to these days if he's not following you around?"

"I have him busy doing menial tasks. Distracting him so he's not out doing more dirty work for Giuseppe."

"If he was out doing dirty work for him, wouldn't that be good for you? You could get an inside look at what Silvestri's doing. Maybe he'll slip up and give you some intel on Luxtyn's mother's kidnapping."

He shakes his head. "No, he's never that loose lipped around me. We need to do something more drastic. Too much time has passed since she's disappeared. There's no telling if she's even alive at this point."

"We both know that no body means she's still alive."

He downs the remainder of his drink. "Fine, she might still be alive, but that doesn't mean she's unharmed." He stands up and slams his glass down on the table before turning back to look at me. "You and I both know that Giuseppe Silvestri doesn't care what he does to people."

He's right. Her mother might not be dead, but she could be wishing she was, and we're not any closer to finding her than we were at the start of this. I can't be responsible for the death of my wife's mother. She doesn't deserve to feel the pain of losing a parent.

I have to figure this out quickly.

For Luxtyn.

I promised her I would find her mother, and I've always been a man of my word.

"I'll think of another plan," I say before downing the rest of my whiskey and standing.

Mancini holds out his hand to retrieve the empty glass. "Let me know what I can do to help."

"She's torn up about it. She might seem like she's holding it together, but that's because the hope of the search is distracting her. If we can't find her soon, or there isn't some kind of hope that she'll find her, I'm not sure what will happen with her."

Walking toward the door, I'm about to exit when Mancini calls out from behind me, halting my steps. "I'll see what I can find out on my end."

I give him a nod over my shoulder before pulling the door open to go find my wife.

21

LUXTYN

Matteo and I say our goodbyes and meet Rocco at the SUV.

"Back to the penthouse, Rocco," Matteo says.

"Yes, Boss," he says before driving back down the lit-up driveway to exit Mancini's estate.

Talking to—or I should say sitting with—Elena and Giuliana was nothing short of awkward and pointless in regard to finding anything out about my mom. I'm not quite sure why I thought that would work.

Giuliana sat there with a scowl on her face the entire time, holding back whatever it is she wanted to say while Elena didn't even acknowledge my presence. Conversation was not had with either of them, and after the disastrous dinner, it wasn't something I was begging for.

Matteo's face is void of expression as we silently make our way back to his penthouse. I'm dying to know if he got any information from Angelo, but he continues to sit there with his elbow propped up on the armrest attached to his door, resting his chin in his hand.

Nothing. He's giving me nothing.

What seems like an eternity passes by before he finally speaks. "I'm just waiting to see how long it takes before you crack and ask me about my conversation with your father."

The passing city lights allow me to see the smile break out on his face as he keeps his stare straight ahead at the back of Rocco's seat. *He's joking with me right now?*

Slowly, he turns his head, and his teeth are on display as he beams at me. *Oh my gosh, he* is *joking with me right now.*

"You think you're funny?" I ask, swatting him on the shoulder.

Enclosing his hand around mine, he drags the pad of his thumb along the lines of my palm, never taking his eyes off me. It feels intimate. Like he's searching my face for something.

"A genuine smile," he says softly.

"I'm sorry?" I ask, confused by his comment, which he subtly brushes off with a shake of his head.

"Are you going to ask me how the conversation went with your father?"

"You have me on the edge of my seat," I say deadpan.

He releases a long breath, which has my heart sinking into my gut. "He doesn't have anything at the moment."

Now it's my turn to let out a long, languid breath.

"But we're going to work together to figure out where she is. Between the two of us, we'll find her," he adds.

Tonight has turned out to be extremely unproductive. Just when I thought I might be able to help find my mom, I've proven to be useless. I have no idea why I was expecting to figure something out during this dinner, like I'm *Nancy Drew* cracking the clues to some easy case.

Staring out the window, I take in the lights of the passing

cars before Matteo squeezes my hand, gaining my attention again.

"I promise I'm going to come up with a plan. We *will* find her, Little Lux. And I'll go to the ends of the earth to dismantle the bodies of anyone involved in her disappearance." He raises my hand and places a tender kiss on my knuckles. His soft lips cause my heart to flutter. Setting my hand back down on his thigh, he continues to hold it as he brings his attention back to his phone.

"Were you able to talk to him about taking over control of his port?" I'm not sure why Matteo wants control of the port so badly, but that's the only reason he agreed to marry me. Knowing he used me to gain access to it doesn't settle well with me, but isn't that what I'm doing to him too? We're using each other.

Without lifting his head from his phone, he says, "I told him we'll talk about it after we find your mother." Drawing his head up, he turns to look at me. "I want to focus on that first. *That* is my priority."

His declaration takes my breath away. "Why are you suddenly making this your priority?" This feels like more than a business transaction. It feels like he could actually care about what happens to me and my mom.

"We're married, Little Lux. It's you and I, you got it? I know our vows were done under not so normal circumstances, but they're vows, nonetheless. I plan on taking them seriously, and I hope you do too." I swallow deeply and nod because my mouth can't seem to form words.

Rocco pulls into the parking garage of the penthouse. As Matteo and I walk hand in hand into the elevator, thoughts of what's going to happen once we get to our floor swirl in my mind. When we walk to our rooms, will Matteo come to mine? Am I expected to go to his? Am I overthinking this? He wants to act as husband and wife, so what does that mean exactly?

The ding of the elevator pulls me out of my spiraling thoughts. Stepping onto our floor, we walk down the hall toward our rooms. The thud of my heartbeat is synced with our footsteps as we get closer. It's as if it's happening in slow motion. But before a decision is made, the loud, yet comforting voice of Enzo interrupts us from the living room.

"So, how was dinner with the in-laws?" he calls out from the couch. Matteo brings us to a stop, but before he can respond, I blurt out an answer.

"Unproductive."

Enzo hops up to a seated position on the couch. "Mancini hasn't been able to figure anything out either?"

Matteo shakes his head. "Nothing."

"I had a few gang members shake up one of Silvestri's soldiers down off thirtieth like you asked to see if getting one of his made men to talk would be possible, but no luck. He says he has some information, though. Information we'd find interesting."

"What's a *made man*?" I ask, suddenly feeling ignorant as I listen to the terms they toss around when they talk about their world.

"It's a fully initiated member of the Mafia. They start as associates, but once they've been initiated, they become soldiers," Matteo answers.

"But not all associates become made men. Only the fancy ones," Enzo says with a wink.

I love his ability to lighten the mood.

"Enzo, I don't hear the movie starting. Why don't I hear the movie starting?" Izzy walks in wearing a matching light-pink silk short set with black piping lining the edges. Her face lights up as it settles on Matteo and me. "Oh perfect! You're both back, which means we need more popcorn," she says excitedly as she rushes over to Enzo and shoves the bowl of popcorn into his hands. She turns back to us. "We were just about to watch a rom-com. You can both join!"

Watching a rom-com. Like my mom and I would be doing right about now if we were back in our little apartment down in Florida. I try to brush that thought aside, knowing that I can't get lost in my emotions. I need to stay strong and hold onto any and all hope that we *will* find her.

"We're going to pass on the rom-com," Matteo says before directing his attention to Enzo. "But I *am* interested to hear what Silvestri's guy had to say."

"Oh, come on, Matteo. You never hang out with me. I came all the way into the city to spend time with my brothers. Plus, I want to get to know my new sister-in-law. Are you really going to deny me that?" Izzy pouts her lip and gives her brother puppy dog eyes that nearly have *me* caving.

"Another time, Isabella. It's already getting late, and I want to hear what information Enzo got today."

"Ugh. Fine. Well, if you're going to be lame and talk all business, at least let me hang out with Lux while you do it."

Matteo glances down at me. "Are you okay with that? I don't want to force you to entertain my sister. She can be . . ." He pauses as he ponders the right word to use.

"I can hear you," Izzy states, which doesn't faze him as he finishes his thought.

"A lot."

I giggle softly. "I don't mind." And I don't, which is a new feeling for me. Hanging out with people, making friends, it's never something I cared to do in the past, and yet here I am, more comfortable with these strangers that are now my family than I've ever been with anyone else.

Izzy claps as she prances up to me, then loops her arm

through mine. Matteo leans down, brushing his cheek against mine and whispers, "I'll be there in a few minutes." The hairs on the back of my neck rise as his warm breath dances across my skin. I give him a small smile before descending the hallway with Izzy intact.

Upon entering my room, Izzy jumps on my bed and makes herself comfortable among the ridiculous amounts of throw pillows.

"So, Lux, tell me"—Izzy lifts her brows in curiosity—"what did you have that my brother wanted *so* badly that he was willing to marry you?"

I nearly trip over myself as I shut the door. "Um . . ."

"Marriages in our world are purely transactional. They're only arranged to benefit both parties. Besides," she says with a shrug, "my brother has never been interested in love, so you must have something that he wants for you to get on his radar the way you did."

I guess that's true.

"It'll be the same for me," she continues. "One of these days, *I'll* be married off to someone to benefit our family. Just like it's always been done." She gives me an expectant look like I should know arranged marriages are common.

"And you're okay with that?" I ask as I climb up on the edge of the bed and lean over to untie my boots.

"I guess. I don't really have a choice."

I glance at her over my shoulder as she plays with the ends of her hair, which is still as perfect now as it was a few hours ago. Her somber eyes are focused on each strand as she runs her fingers through them.

"Arranged marriages seem like an outdated practice. Maybe you can fall in love with a really great guy and a marriage will naturally progress for you."

A sliver of sadness passes through Izzy's eyes before she

quickly recovers, brushing it off like it never even happened, but I saw it. It was almost like there was a longing there.

"There's no point in combining two families unless each family is getting something out of it." She offers a relaxed shrug. "And I know that. I've known that my entire life. I was raised to do right by my family, and when my time comes, I will."

Sitting up straighter, she props herself up on the pillows with her legs stretched out and her hands folded in her lap. Pasting that beauty queen smile of hers back on, she puts the focus back on me. "Anyway, enough of that. Now, tell me, what sealed the deal between you two?" Raising a brow at me, she continues. "There's not much my brother needs or *wants*, so you have me intrigued."

I chuckle as I brush a loose strand of hair behind my ear. "I'm surprised Enzo didn't catch you up."

"While he's definitely the gossiping type, he wouldn't tell me a damn thing over dinner. If you ask me, I think he enjoys holding things over my head. He loves knowing information that I want to know. He's kind of an ass like that."

"You know, I can see that," I say, pursing my lips. "He seems like the type that likes a game. Wants to dangle that little piece of information over you like bait for a fish. Just to keep you interested until you're hooked."

"Precisely. Gosh it's so great having some estrogen around this place. I've been stuck with too much testosterone lately. Ever since our . . ."

Before I can ask what she was going to say, a knock comes from my door. I hop off the bed and open the door to Matteo holding a shirt in his hand. His intense gaze pins me in place. Opening the door wider, I gesture for him to come in.

"And that is my cue to go," Izzy says before jumping off the side of the bed. She bumps her hip into mine. "We'll pick up this discussion tomorrow. You have no plans, right?"

"She does, actually," Matteo answers for me.

I raise a brow at him. "That's news to me."

"I thought you might want to get some clothes so you don't have to prance around half naked anymore."

"Half naked is fun, though," I tease.

Cocking an eyebrow, he says, "We're going shopping, and that's the end of that."

"Hold on. *You're* going shopping?" Izzy's brows shoot to her hairline as she points at Matteo. "You don't like shopping. You don't even do it for yourself."

She glances at me, and a sly smile pulls at her lips before she turns her attention back to Matteo. "Why don't you have me take Lux shopping? Seems more up my alley than yours, don't you think?" She gives me a quick wink, and I don't understand why.

"No," he gruffs out, and even I feel the finality in his tone, as it pulls my shoulders back.

Tilting her head, she narrows her gaze up at him, studying him. "Interesting." That's all she offers before turning to me and saying, "I'll see you tomorrow, Lux."

She brushes past Matteo, and before he's able to shut the door, he calls out behind her, "You're staying the night, I presume?"

"Duh. You've left me home for too long by myself. I'm bored," she calls out, her voice getting more and more faint as she walks down the hallway.

"You have another home?" I ask as Matteo shuts the door and turns around to face me.

"Yeah. It's my family's home located about forty minutes out of the city. Some place to call a real home."

A real home. That's something I've never had. My mom

and I moving around so often made that difficult. By the time I finally got comfortable in one town, it was time to pick up and move again. I wonder if I'll ever get a taste of this *real home* of his. Or am I just the wife locked in the confines of the *not real home* penthouse?

"I can see the wheels spinning in that head of yours." He closes the space between us with one long stride and cradles my cheek in his hand, peering into my eyes. "Ask me."

"A-ask you what?" I croak out, my voice hoarse and dry. He's so close to me I can feel the warmth of his breath on my lips. Is he going to kiss me again? Because that kiss we shared earlier, that kiss was nothing but passion. Hot, fiery passion that ignited something within me that has me yearning for more.

"You tell me, Little Lux." And there he goes with that nickname again. It sends a shiver down my spine. A tingle that spreads warmth throughout my body starting at my core and spreading through every ligament and joint.

"I was just thinking about this home of yours."

"And?"

"And if I'll ever be someone that gets to see it or if I'll just be the wife that gets the penthouse version of you."

He feathers my cheek with the pad of his thumb. The caress is so light. So smooth. So endearing. Then he drags his fingers down to my left hand and lifts it between us. Rubbing his finger over my wedding band, he says, "This. This makes you my family." He brings his gaze back to mine. "The penthouse is faster to access when working in the city, and since I've been spending more time here, it's been easier to keep you here. Close to me."

Close to him. It takes a lot for me not to laugh at the statement since he's been doing nothing but avoiding me since I got here.

"I know I haven't been the best husband—"

I scoff.

"But I plan on changing that. Starting with a shopping trip tomorrow to get you whatever you need to make yourself more comfortable."

I glance down to the shirt in his hand. "Is there a reason you're carrying around that shirt?"

He releases a soft chuckle as he steps back and holds it up to me. "I figured you'd need a new shirt to wear. Since you got yours dirty and all."

I laugh so hard a snort escapes my nose, which I try to cover with a cough. I fail so miserably that I just keep laughing. "Is this your way of telling me you don't want me to wear Enzo's shirts anymore?"

His gaze darkens. *"Shirts?"* he says, raising his brows. "He gave you multiple? Of course he fucking did," he grumbles, and I can't help the smile that pulls at my lips. Jealousy isn't a trait I'd find attractive in a man, but Matteo green with envy does something to me. I like knowing his reaction to Enzo is the same reaction I had before I found out Izzy was his sister.

Shaking my head, I say, "No," with a chuckle under my breath. "He just gave me the one. But he did offer me some more if I ever need any." I had to throw that last jab in just to mess with him.

Matteo pulls away from me. "That's it. He's fucking dead."

I wrap my fingers around his wrists. "I'm kidding, I'm kidding!"

He turns back to me. "You were almost responsible for the death of my brother, you know that, right?" he grumbles out.

"I know. I'm sorry. But I couldn't help it. The way you reacted. It just made me want to mess with you a little bit," I say, holding up the little bit of space between my two fingers.

Matteo tosses the shirt onto the bed and pulls me into

his arms. Wrapping his hand into my hair, he tugs it slightly. Not too hard, but just enough for the pressure to force me to look into his eyes. "You better be careful, Little Lux. That mouth of yours is going to get you in trouble one of these days."

I wrap my arms around his neck. "Is that a threat, Matteo?"

"It's a promise," he says before closing the distance between us and taking my lips with his.

He doesn't have to beg for entrance, as I part my lips, eager for his tongue to fill me. The taste of whiskey still lingers on his tongue as he thrusts it into my mouth, searching for mine.

The kiss becomes heated, our mouths becoming one, as he moves his hands to my hips and lifts me up like I'm nothing but a feather. He walks us back toward the bed and sets me down on the comforter, then hovers over me, placing his knee between my legs as he nudges it against my core. I squirm beneath him at the pressure. Excitement runs through my body, fueling me to keep going.

I graze my nails up his back, and he shivers beneath my touch. He moans into my mouth, setting that inferno blazing even hotter inside me. I love that I have the same effect on him as he does on me.

A knock sounds from the door, but we both ignore it, as we can't seem to get enough of each other. I pull him down, forcing him to collapse on top of me, and I welcome the weight.

Another knock sounds on the door, this time accompanied with Enzo's urgent voice. "Teo, we need to get going."

Matteo grunts but doesn't let up on me as he continues thrusting his tongue in and out of my mouth.

Enzo's voice breaks through the imaginary barrier I've put up around us again. "I'm not *trying* to be a cock block, guys, but I'm going to be a cock block. We need to go, Teo. Now.

You can lick Lux's pussy later." He pounds on the door one last time. "Let's go! I'll be by the elevator."

His abrasive comment pulls me out of the moment, forcing me to detach myself from Matteo's lips and look up into his darkened eyes. I'm sure the look of horror is written on my face. "Oh my gosh," I say. The only words that come to mind at that moment.

Matteo lets out a sigh before lifting himself off me and smooths the wrinkles in his shirt. "I'm sorry about that," he grumbles. "You won't have to worry about him again."

Propping myself up on my elbows, a small laugh escapes my lips. That might've been embarrassing, but I'm finding a home in Enzo's comedic, over-the-top personality. "It's fine. Really," I say, brushing it off. "Where are you guys going?" It's late and something tells me this has to do with whatever Enzo told him he found out earlier.

"We have to go and meet a guy," he says. Is this what it's like being married to a Mafia man? Secrets on what he's doing and where he's going?

My shoulders sag and the frown that's found its way onto my face doesn't go unnoticed by Matteo.

"Hey," he says as he climbs back over me. "There isn't much to tell you right now, but if I find anything out about your mother, I *will* let you know."

He presses a delicate kiss to my lips before climbing off me and opening the door. Before exiting, he locks eyes with me. "I won't be back for a while, so don't wait up, okay?"

I'm disappointed but don't let that play out on my face. I fake a smile as I push myself up to a seated position. "I'm exhausted anyway, so I'll just see you whenever I see you."

Something passes in his eyes at my words. At my tone. *Maybe I played that off too cool.* But he nods before shutting the door, and I'm left alone in this room I've gotten far too acquainted with lately.

After taking a shower and brushing my teeth, I get into bed in nothing but my red boy shorts and the plain black tee Matteo brought me.

His woodsy spice scent envelops me as I fall into the abyss of the mattress. I'm tempted to keep myself up until he gets back, but it feels like no more than two minutes passes by before the weight of my eyelids becomes too much, and I'm carried into a deep sleep.

22

MATTEO

The music from the club filters into the night air as Enzo and I pull up. We head down to the basement through the back entrance, making our way to the torture chamber I have set up.

Enzo had the men who roughed up Silvestri's soldier meet Rocco here with the guy after dropping off Luxtyn and me at the penthouse. Rocco's been keeping an eye on him until we were able to show up.

"What's his name?" I ask as I slide my jacket off, placing it on the table that's on the opposite side of the room as this guy. I don't need another suit ruined.

Enzo takes up a spot in the corner of the room, leaning against the wall with a twisted smile on his face as he takes in the bloody situation.

"Luis," Rocco answers. "He's one of Alfredo's guys."

Ahh, Alfredo. One of Silvestris top capos. One of his dirtiest too. He brings in plenty of money for him, but also has the temper of a bomb ready to detonate at any second. Rumor has it his kill number is the highest in the family.

"Luuisss," I say as I walk closer to the nearly unconscious man strapped to the metal chair. *It's like I was just in this situation yesterday . . .*

"I hear you have some information that might be useful to me." I roll the sleeves of my shirt up my forearms. The hairs on my arms stand on end in anticipation, already knowing how this meeting will end.

Luis struggles to lift his head an inch before it lolls to the side. His face is battered, and his eyes are nearly swollen shut. His lip is split in three spots. I wouldn't be able to recognize the guy even if I knew what he looked like.

Luis coughs, spitting blood at his feet as he shifts his head, trying to remain conscious as he mumbles something incoherent.

"Hold up his head," I order Rocco, who does so immediately, pulling the man up by the long dark strands of his greasy hair.

I lean down, balancing myself on the tips of my toes as I prop my elbows on my thighs. Close enough I can taste the blood on the tip of my tongue.

"I'm going to need you to wake the fuck up and tell me what you know about Giuseppe Silvestri, because if you don't, I will kill you. And I'll make it a lot more miserable than it needs to be."

"You're going to kill me anyway, right?" Luis mumbles before coughing a few more times.

"Correct." There's no point in lying. Being brought to me means this guy's time is up. "But I can either make it happen quickly. Or I can take my sweet fucking time." I push myself to a stand and fold my arms across my chest. "It's your choice."

Luis lets out a long sigh. "I heard Giuseppe and Angelo Mancini got into it over the port," he spits out. "Giuseppe partnered with a new source that's been helping him bring in a lot more money through it."

Luis coughs a couple more times before spitting more blood onto the concrete floor. His voice is hoarse and dry as he goes to speak again. "Angelo wants him to pay a larger percentage, but Giuseppe refused."

"That's all you know?" That's the information he felt was worth his life?

"That's all I know. I know it's not much, but I guess the alliance between them is tense right now." He drags in a deep breath, trying to bring oxygen to his lungs before continuing. "I wouldn't be surprised if Angelo decides to go directly to Giuseppe's source and tries to cut him out."

Now that's an interesting interpretation of the situation.

I stand there quietly, pondering that idea before leaning down so I'm directly in front of Luis again. I slap his cheek a couple times, the dried blood on his face cracking against my palm. "Good job. That just earned you a quick death."

Luis drops his head, accepting his fate. I step back and pull the gun that's been strapped to my ankle all night while Rocco steps back from Luis, giving me plenty of room to do what I need to do. I shoot the guy once in the heart and again in his forehead for good measure.

"Clean this up," I order Enzo and Rocco. "Burn the body." I glance over at Rocco. "You're sure his arrival was quiet?" The last thing I need is for anyone to know Luis was here. The whole point of paying off guys that aren't associated with me is to make sure my name stays out of this, but when I heard he had some other information for me, I needed to step in.

"Yeah, Boss. I made sure no eyes were around when we brought him down."

I nod. "Good. You guys take care of this. Enzo, you can get a ride with Rocco back to the penthouse." All I can think about now is getting home to my wife who I'm sure is splayed out on that oversized bed of hers, dark hair fanned across her pillow. Like she's been every night I've snuck in and sat in the corner to watch her.

"Oh sure. Leave all the bitch work to us while you go and get laid. No problem," Enzo says. But I ignore him, leaving the concrete room and opening myself up to the bass of the music coming from the club.

Soundproof rooms. So damn effective for a multitude of reasons.

I get home to a quiet house and go directly to my shower to wash the smell of blood off my body. The information Luis gave us doesn't mean much, but his interpretation of it is what sparked my interest. Mancini cutting out Silvestri, the middleman, is a bold move. Dirty business. Something I don't think Mancini has the balls to do. But it's an interesting hypothesis and would give him one hundred percent of the profits.

And then there's me. He can't cut out the middleman when he doesn't have control of his port anymore. Their business relationship will be null and void when I take over.

After throwing on a pair of black boxer briefs, I wander into Luxtyn's dimly lit room. She's just as I envisioned she would be with her dark hair fanned out on the white pillowcase, contrasting perfectly.

The comforter is down around her waist. The shirt I left for her to wear is bunched up on the side, displaying a sliver of her soft pale skin. She looks fucking *perfect* in my shirt. Pride pours through me at the sight. Her reddish-pink lips are slightly parted, and her chest rises and falls with every breath she takes. My dick awakens as I take her in, imagining what it would be like to have those lips wrapped around it.

I sit in the chair I have positioned in the corner that gives me the perfect view of her. It's where I've fallen asleep every night, making sure to sneak out before she wakes. I sit back and watch her. Quietly. Like a damn creep. What is it with this girl? I've been attracted to women in the past, but never like I am with Luxtyn.

Is it because she didn't show interest in me from the start, unlike the women that find themselves in my bed? She doesn't throw herself at me every second she gets. Hell, I don't think she even knows how to act around me. But our chemistry is unreal, I know that much.

And her strength. The way she's been able to handle everything she's been thrown this past week. I know killers who would break if they had to go through everything she has.

A small whimper escapes Luxtyn's mouth as she rolls onto her side, and I spring from my chair. I find myself at the side of her bed in the next second, wanting to crawl in behind her and wrap her in my arms.

She rolls onto her back once more, turning her head, so it's pointed in my direction. Her wispy hair falls over her face slightly.

Placing a steady hand on the mattress, I lean over and brush her hair out of her face. She's still asleep, but she murmurs something, the incoherent sound bypassing me. I trail my fingers along her cheek as she takes a deep breath in before letting it out, leaning into the movement as if it's the one thing bringing her comfort.

Turning off the dimmed lights, I pull the comforter back and climb into bed with her. It takes everything in me not to pull her body flush against mine and pick up where we left off earlier.

Sliding my arm under her pillow, I place my other hand on her bare stomach. And before I know it, I'm falling asleep to the rise and fall of her shallow breaths.

23

LUXTYN

The scheduled drawing of the blackout shades wakes me abruptly when the sunlight filters through the windows. I swear I could sleep all day if it weren't for those shades being on an automatic timer at 8:00 a.m.

I lie in bed to give myself time to wake up. This morning is different, though. It feels as if there's a space heater aimed directly at my back, and as I shift, there's definitely something hindering my ability to get my morning stretch in.

What is *that?*

I feel around to the weight settled on my side and my hand comes in contact with a hard . . . *arm*?

"It's amazing that the sunlight will wake you up immediately, but you can sleep through a person getting into bed with you." Matteo's low voice rings through my ear as he tightens his arm around my waist.

When did this happen?

Shifting my weight, I go to roll over, but Matteo's hold tightens, locking me in place. "Matteo." His name comes out rough on my lips as my voice gets acclimated to waking up. "What are you doing here? *When* did you get here?"

He chuckles, and the vibration rumbles through his chest straight into me. "Would you rather I be somewhere else?"

"No," I blurt, my tone more desperate than I intended. "I just wasn't expecting to wake up to you this morning."

There's something about being in his arms like this. I feel protected. It's not something I've ever experienced before. When he wraps his arms around me, I want to sink into them, not run away. Keeping people at a distance is what I'm used to, but not with Matteo. He makes me second-guess everything.

"Well, you better get used to it, because you and I will be sharing a bed from here on out."

He pulls me closer to him, and something pokes me in the back. Something hard. Something *big*.

I freeze and my breath hitches, and Matteo's chest rumbles with a low, dark laugh, clearly catching on to what's caught my attention. "Is that . . .?"

"It's first thing in the morning, and you teased me far too much last night." His dick twitches, and he lets out a low groan as he pulls me into his hips. He's not the only one feeling the effects of those scorching hot kisses from last night. The sexual tension is so high between the two of us you can cut it with a knife. If we don't do something about this soon, I swear I'll explode.

The heat from Matteo's lips as he places a gentle kiss on my neck sends a thrill of anticipation to my core. An involuntary whimper escapes me as I lean back, wanting to feel his body wrapped around mine even more.

Before anything else can happen, a pulsing vibration goes off on the nightstand closest to Matteo. Letting it go to voicemail, he continues to place small pecks along my neck, leaving a path of fire in his wake as he reaches up under my shirt. His fingertips graze my skin, making their way up to the curve of my breast before that humming vibration goes off once more.

"Fuck," Matteo groans out as he releases me and rolls onto his back, taking the heat that encompassed me just moments ago and leaving me to feel like a bucket of ice water has been poured on top of me.

I roll over and face his direction just in time to see him pull himself to a seated position on the side of the bed, grabbing his phone off the nightstand.

"Yeah?" he answers.

I focus on the impressive divots his muscles make across his back. The man is shaped like a damn Greek god. Dropping my gaze, I locate the small darkened wound on the lower left side of his back and frown as I realize it's where I stabbed him. In the moment, I felt justified for what I was doing, but now I feel nothing but guilt.

It's hard to believe this wasn't too long ago. How much anger and worry I felt at being kidnapped by him and Enzo to now be here, kissing the man I claimed to not even like.

"Yeah, okay. I'll be there soon," Matteo grumbles back into the phone before hanging up.

Reaching out, I graze my fingers around the tight skin of the wound that has started healing. "I'm sorry," I whisper, and he turns to his side and reaches around to take my hand into his.

"Don't be sorry. I admire that you stabbed me. It shows that you have some fight in you."

"Does it hurt?" I ask.

With a small chuckle, he says, "No. I actually forgot about it until just now."

Standing, he turns to face me, dropping his gaze to mine, and holy, fuck me sideways. The guilt that I had just moments ago is replaced with red hot desire. I've seen this man with his shirt off before, but with his dark hair a ruffled mess and his hooded eyes watching me, I can't help but feel the somersaults race across my stomach.

My eyes are drawn to his bare olive-toned skin painted with ink across his chest, leaving the ripples of his eight-pack abs unmarked. Nothing but a fine line of hair trails from his belly button down to his . . .

"I have to get to this meeting," Matteo grumbles, which draws my attention back up to his eyes. I was spaced out on the deep V-line narrowing its way down his insanely perfect abdomen, which I'm sure he caught onto, as the corners of his mouth pull into a devilish grin and his eyes gleam.

"I shouldn't be gone more than a couple of hours, and then I'll come pick you up and we'll head over to Fifth Avenue to get you a new wardrobe," he says, thankfully not calling me out on ogling him.

"I really don't need much. I can just keep washing the clothes I have and wait until the rest of my stuff gets here. Wait. How *are* the rest of my things getting here?"

"I have a few guys going down to Florida in a couple of days to pack up you and your mother's belongings, and then they'll drive it back up here. I figured it would be nice if she has all of her things when we find her."

The fact he thought about my mom makes my heart swell, but I can't stand the fact we haven't found her yet. What if she's hurt? What if I'm wasting time with Matteo when I could be doing more to find her? And then to tell her I'm married and we've moved all of our belongings up to New York City? This is a lot.

Matteo tucks his thumb under my chin, angling me up toward him. "Hey, stay with me." His gaze locks me in place. "Don't spiral. We'll find her."

I only nod because I somehow believe him. Despite the fact

he extorted me into marrying him, Matteo's the only one who's been willing to keep me in the loop on things from the beginning. I trust what he's saying.

"I still don't need to go shopping, though."

I don't have much money, and I might not know a lot about New York City, but even I've heard of Fifth Avenue. There's no way I can afford anything there.

"I *want* to take you shopping, Little Lux. Let me buy you some things. Even if it's just enough until we get your stuff up here." His voice is so soft. So convincing.

"Fine. But I'm going to pay you back once I get a job."

Matteo laughs a deep throaty laugh like I'm the best damn comedian there ever was. "You're not getting a job."

Pulling back, I say, "Excuse me?"

"You heard me. My wife is not going to work. And you're sure as hell never going to pay me back for anything." That soft voice has been replaced with one of certainty. The rigidness of his tone has me immediately second-guessing the life I've married into.

I've worked my entire life, since before I was even at a legal age. That's the benefit of living in small towns. You work for small businesses that don't mind throwing some cash under the table to a teen trying to make a couple bucks. There's no way I'll never work again. Who the hell does he think he is?

Rolling my eyes, I get my boxing mitts on, prepared to knock some sense into Matteo. "If you think—"

But before another word can escape my lips, Matteo slams his mouth to mine, and while I want to fight him and tell him I'm not some housewife who's going to stay at home all day and spend her husband's money, the words seem to dissipate around us.

He stops the kiss just as quickly, pulling away just enough to gaze back and forth between my eyes. "The next time I see you rolling your eyes at me, it'll be because you're about to come the hardest you've ever come in your damn life. On my fingers. On my tongue. On my dick. It'll be your choice, Little Lux. But the next time you roll those pretty brown eyes of yours into the back of your head, it'll be with my name on your lips while you beg me for more."

Matteo drops his gaze back down to my parted lips and presses a soft kiss to them before swinging himself off the bed and exiting my room without another word. Without even a glance back.

I want to argue with him, but I also want him to do exactly what he said and make my eyes roll into the back of my head as I scream his name in complete and utter bliss.

What is this man doing to me?

24

LUXTYN

The next couple of hours passed by quicker than I thought they would. I decided to spend the first one soaking in the Jacuzzi in my en suite bathroom and the second one eating breakfast with Izzy, who I've decided is my new favorite of the DiMaggio siblings.

She's unlike a lot of the girls I've come across in my life. Although, I'm beginning to wonder if I was always the problem. Never giving anyone a chance since I knew I would be moving soon. I had always adjusted to not making friends because of that reason. Knowing I won't leave New York City anytime soon is making me realize I might need to change my outlook on relationships.

Izzy's bubbly personality is more similar to Enzo's than Matteo's. He seems to be the odd ball out, personality wise, when it comes to the siblings. Although he comes off as cold and calculated at first impression, I'm beginning to realize there are many layers to Matteo.

Since he and Enzo left for that meeting this morning, Rocco was left to babysit me. I also met Izzy's guard, Eddie.

Rocco let me know a few minutes ago that Matteo was on his way back to pick me up to go shopping. It's weird having someone be a messenger for me. If he would give me back my phone, I'd be able to communicate like a normal person. I wonder why he hasn't yet. Does he not trust me?

I finish getting ready in my last pair of clean black leggings and a sweatshirt before slipping on my black combat boots. Maybe it's a good thing Matteo's bringing me to pick up a few things. I still plan on paying him back somehow but need to figure out how to make money here first.

A knock draws my attention to the door. Opening it, I find Matteo on the other side dressed in the same thing he left in, a perfectly fitted black Armani suit with a black shirt unbuttoned at the top, teasing me with the dark ink on his chest.

"You wear a lot of suits," I say.

He smiles while glancing down at his ensemble, like he forgot what he was wearing before taking in my outfit. "You wear a lot of tights and sweatshirts."

Touché.

"Well, you're already wrong. These"—I pull on the fabric of my leggings—"are *leggings*. Not tights. I'm surprised, Matteo. You seem like the kind of guy that would know his way around a woman's wardrobe."

Stepping into me, he wraps his hulking arms around my waist. "Apparently not the *right* woman." It probably shouldn't make my heart skip a beat, but it does. It actually skips several as he plants a peck on my lips, so light it makes me crave so much more.

"C'mon. Let's get you some more of those *leggings* you seem to love so much." I laugh as he pulls me out of my room.

Matteo has Rocco and another guard I just met, Tito, drive us to Fifth Avenue. *How many guys does he have working for him?*

Rocco parks the G-Wagon on a side street, and we all get out. "Keep an acceptable distance back. Make sure you both keep your eyes on *everything*," Matteo orders the two solidly built men. Matteo is jacked, but in a proportional way. His body is that of a Greek god, whereas Rocco and Tito have the bodies of bodybuilders on steroids. Add their height to it and they come off as pretty damn intimidating. They're not quite as tall as Matteo, but they still tower over my five-foot-seven self.

Wrapping his hand around mine, Matteo leads us down the sidewalk, past multiple high-end stores like Louis Vuitton and Chanel. Glancing over my shoulder, I notice Rocco and Tito doing exactly what Matteo ordered. They're following us about twenty-five feet back and have their sights on . . . everything. They scan the road, the sidewalks, even inside the windows of passing stores.

Furrowing my brow, I turn back to Matteo, who also looks like he's scanning the area. "Is there something I should be aware of?"

Without looking at me, he asks, "What do you mean?"

So this is how it's going to be. "Don't play dumb, Matteo. I heard you back there. Why do you need Rocco and Tito to keep an eye on *everything*? And why do you look like you're preparing for an ambush at any second?"

His gaze moves to me, and I divert mine to the sidewalk, taking note of my surroundings so I don't walk into something.

"Elena and Giuliana now know that you and I are married, which means Giuseppe Silvestri knows we're married." He stops us and turns me toward him. "Giuseppe Silvestri doesn't trust my family, so he most likely will not be happy about that information."

I nod. "Because of the port. But you haven't even taken over Angelo's yet. Maybe this Giuseppe guy won't even care."

He breathes out a small laugh as he shakes his head. "That's not how things work. If anything, Giuseppe is probably more skeptical now since I haven't done anything about the port yet."

"And why do you have it out for him again?" I say *again,* as if he's told me before, but he hasn't. All I know is there's some tension between Matteo and Giuseppe Silvestri, but I don't understand why.

He squares his shoulders, straightening his spine as his mouth turns down into a frown. "That's a story for another time. But it's part of the reason I'd prefer you not to work anymore and why I always have guards on you and my sister." He runs a hand through the stubble on his face.

"The world we live in is dangerous, Luxtyn." He continues with a low voice as he conveys the gravity of what he's saying. "Putting a ring on your finger means I've selfishly put a mark on your back. I can protect you, and I *will* protect you, but you have to be willing to let me." He pauses, waiting to see if I'll have a response, but I don't.

"I respect that you want to work, but I have more than enough money for the both of us. Your safety is my concern, and with you having the DiMaggio last name now, I have to make sure you're taken care of. That means working is out of the question. If you want to find things to do, I can help, but please . . ." He releases a drawn-out breath. "Can you let me provide for you and to keep you safe?"

Independence has always been important to me, but the sincerity behind Matteo's words makes me not want to argue. I might not know much about the Mafia world, but from what I've learned, I know it's dangerous. Maybe I should just stop arguing for once.

I give him a small nod, and he lets out a deep breath, as if he'd been holding it while waiting for my response. The sound of a door *swooshing* open behind me pulls his attention over my head.

"Mr. DiMaggio, please come in," the voice of a woman sounds from behind me. Turning around, I take in the blonde who's smiling a little too eagerly at my husband.

"You're not Liana," Matteo grumbles, and if I knew no better, I'd say he's not happy to see this woman who seems to be eye-fucking him directly in front of me.

"Liana had to step out for a client's wardrobe emergency, but she's filled me in on your requests for this visit. I've already pulled some great options for your *wife* here, that I know she's going to love."

The way she called me his *wife* as if she can't believe I am doesn't sit well with me. Everything about this woman gives me the ick. I don't know her, but I know I can't stand her already. And if eye-fucking my husband isn't bad enough, the fact she *thinks* she knows what I'll want to wear irritates me.

Her long blonde hair is perfectly slicked back into a high ponytail, and she's wearing a skintight red dress that cuts off at her knees and a matching blazer and red lipstick. Her nude heels are nearly six inches tall. There's no way this woman picked out anything I'll like.

Matteo mumbles something incoherent under his breath as he lightly pushes me through the door she's holding for us. We walk into the brightly lit store. It's not huge, but there seems to be a front section with meticulously organized racks of clothes and mannequins showcasing different outfit ideas. Farther in the back is a dressing room and tailor area.

I have to admit, the outfits on the mannequins are cute but not so much my style. They're all wearing either dresses or skirts. *Does this place not have any jeans or leggings?*

A black belted trench coat with ribbed sleeves and an oversized shawl collar on a mannequin catches my attention over in the corner, so I slowly walk up to it. I'm drawn to it because it reminds me of a jacket my mom has. She got it when we lived in Colorado, and I borrowed it every time I could. The memory makes me chuckle softly.

"You like that one?" Matteo asks. I hadn't even realized he followed me over here.

"It's nice," I say nonchalantly as I turn to face him. His smirk tells me I didn't play that off as well as I thought.

"We'll take one of these," he orders the blonde. Her eyes widen and her mouth remains in a straight line.

"Oh, we just got that coat in today. There's only *select* sizes available in it for another couple months until the rest of Liana's shipment comes in for the fall season."

Matteo turns to face her. "Well, maybe you should find out if one of those *select* sizes is my wife's size, and if not, then I'll pay extra to have it rushed."

She pauses for a second before pasting on a wide smile, one that I'd consider overly fake, and nods. "Of course, *Matteo*. I'll check after I escort your wife to the dressing room to try on the options I pulled for her."

The way she says his name is too personal. *Too* comfortable. As if she knows him. I do my best to ignore it as she walks up to me, placing her hand on my arm to lead me to the back of the store.

She pulls open the large floor-to-ceiling door with a mirror on the outside with an intricate metal design around it and directs me into the dressing room full of outfits I don't like.

"Why don't you get undressed and try on the first option," she says, pointing to an emerald-green dress suit. "When you're ready to come out, we can see how you like it. Based off your feedback, I can pull some additional options or we can tweak what we have in here. Sound good?" Her chipper voice is too fake for my liking. I just nod in response.

She goes to close the door, but before doing so, she peeks her head back in and says, "I'm Ashley, by the way. Anything you need, please don't hesitate to ask."

Yeah, Ashley. I'll be sure to do just that.

25

MATTEO

The possibility of this saleswoman not remembering who I am flew right out the front door when she opened it. What are the fucking chances that the last woman I let blow me in my club is the salesperson for my wife?

The only reason I came here was because of my cousin, Liana. I believe in supporting my family, and as my favorite cousin, my only cousin, I wanted to bring Luxtyn to her boutique to see if there's anything she might like.

I had no fucking idea Ashley worked here, but why would I? I didn't look into her work history before letting her suck my cock, but I sure as hell wish I had now.

She closes my wife into the dressing room and sashays her way up to me before dropping her hand on my arm, making my stomach churn. "I was excited when Liana informed me you would be coming in today, but I had no idea you got married. And to a different girl than that one that came into the club that night, nonetheless."

I cock a brow at Ashley's hand on my arm before peeling it off me like she's some disease. Because that's what she is. A disease that's come back with a vengeance. Not what I need right now.

She falters slightly as I release her hand. I drop my voice low, making sure only she can hear me. "Listen closely, Ashley. You have one job today, and that's to find some clothes for *my wife*. You and I don't know each other. You and I don't have a history. Do you understand?"

She looks back and forth between my eyes, and I swear I can smell the fear wafting off her. But it's not just fear I smell. It's stupidity. Her overconfidence makes her dense. *She better not do anything fucking stupid.*

The corners of her mouth tick up as she broadens her smile, showcasing her white teeth. "I understand, Matteo," she says with a gleam in her eyes and in a sultry tone that makes my hair stand on end, not in a good way.

Turning on her heel, she walks back toward Luxtyn's dressing room. I decide to check in with Rocco and Tito, who've posted up outside the boutique, ignoring the sixth sense I have that's telling me Ashley's going to be more trouble than her mediocre dick-sucking skills were ever worth.

26

LUXTYN

I've changed into the emerald-green dress suit that has two columns of gold buttons up the front, and shoulder pads. Actual shoulder pads. I laugh as I peer at my unrecognizable self in the mirror.

The dress is actually flattering on me, but it's so far off my style spectrum, there's no way I could have Matteo buy this for me. Ashley nailed the sizing somehow, but this is just *not it.*

A soft knock sounds at my door. "Are you ready to come out?" Ashley's voice chimes through.

Abso-fucking-lutely not.

Plucking at the heavy metal buttons on the front of the dress, I say, "Umm, I think I'm just going to move onto the next option." I glance over at the bright-pink pants suit hanging on the rack next.

That's also not my style.

"How about I just come in there instead?" she offers. I want to say no, but I guess if we're going to get anything done, I'll have to tell her none of these options are really me.

"Okay," I say before she opens the door, pushing herself into the small space.

She takes me in with a bright smile on her face. "That looks *amazing* on you. And the fit. Your husband nailed your size right on the head."

So Matteo's the one who informed her of my size. She is right about that. The fit *is* perfect, but that doesn't negate the fact that I'll never find myself wearing this anywhere.

"Do you love it?" Ashley asks as I slide my hands down the fabric of the dress.

"It's a . . . lovely dress." I make eye contact with her reflection in the mirror. "It's just . . . not *really* my style. At all, actually."

"Really?" she gasps. She walks over to the rack that still has three more options: the pink pantsuit, a navy-blue pencil skirt with a matching suit jacket, and a black and tan lace dress. All of which make me want to melt away onto the floor of this dressing room.

She runs the tips of her perfectly manicured nails over her other choices before turning back to look at me. "Do you like any of these?"

Even though she's rubbed me the wrong way since getting here, I still feel bad telling her I like nothing she chose for me, but I do so anyway. No sense in being unproductive. Shaking my head, I say, "Not really, I'm sorry. I'm just more of a comfy-casual kind of girl."

Ashley folds one arm across her stomach, propping her other elbow on top of it as she rests her chin on her hand. She stands there and rakes her eyes up my body, like she's studying me.

"That's such a shame," she says before dropping her hands back down to her sides. Her ice-blue eyes pierce me with a wicked gleam. "I was really keeping what Matteo likes in mind when picking out these pieces."

There she goes again, speaking about him like she knows him. "Do you know my husband?" I ask, tilting my head at her, intrigued to hear her response.

Her smile brightens a smidge. "You could say we know each other." She lowers her voice as she steps closer. "That's why he brought you in here to see me today."

I narrow my gaze on her. I might have to tilt my head back to keep eye contact, but that's only because she has her damn stripper heels on. "And how well do you know my husband, exactly?" I'm not sure I want to know the answer to this question, but I'm apparently a glutton for punishment.

Her devilish smirk widens more and the gleam in her eye is so bright now, I know I'm not going to like her answer. "Well, he was finishing in my mouth just last week." She offers a loose chuckle that makes me want to punch her in the damn throat. "So, I guess you could say we know each other *very* well." She eyes me up and down. "I wonder if he wants a repeat. You don't really seem like the type that can satisfy a man like him."

My fists clench by my sides as I do my best to keep my anger from boiling over, showing her she's done exactly what she wanted to do—gotten under my skin. The piercing pain of my nails digging into my palm is the only thing keeping me from lashing out on the bitch.

"You can stop trying to make me jealous. You're just embarrassing yourself, and you clearly don't know *my husband* very well." Her eye twitches as I refer to Matteo as my husband.

"Just because you had his dick in your mouth before he even met me means nothing to me. If he wanted you, he would've gone for seconds, and from the way he didn't seem to pay much attention to you out there, I'm going to guess your *skills* were subpar."

Ashley gasps, and if her forehead didn't have the botox it does, I'm sure it would've raised to her hairline at my words. Before she can speak, she's cut off by a hard knock at the door.

"Everything okay in there?" Matteo's deep voice comes through the door.

"Yup," I call out to him. "Everything is perfect." Bringing my voice down to a whisper that only Ashley can hear, I add, "Right, Ashley?"

She lets out a small huff as she responds to Matteo in her disgustingly fake and high-pitched voice that'll no doubt ring in my ears the rest of the day. "Yes, we're just going over her likes and dislikes so I can nail down her looks."

She brings her voice back down, so only I can hear her. "I'll go pull some more options for you. Something more . . . your level," she adds before stepping around me to exit the dressing room.

I'm fuming while I stare at the stupid dress she had me put on in the mirror. I tear it off my body, throw it to the floor in a heap, then stare at my reflection in the mirror.

My chest heaves as I try to control my rage at this chick. Do I even have a right to be annoyed? Who am I even annoyed with? I want to be annoyed with Matteo for bringing me here, prancing me around this high-end boutique, having his high-end boutique employee fuck buddy dress me like what? Someone like her? I struggle to gain control of my shallow breaths as I get more and more frustrated.

Another knock sounds at the door, but I ignore it. If I see that bitch again, I *will* punch her.

Another knock comes through, except this time louder and accompanied with that familiar deep voice. "Luxtyn." *Ugh.* I'm not ready to see him either. I ignore him in hopes that he'll take the hint and leave me alone, but just when I think he's going to knock again, the dressing room door swings open instead, and

Matteo stalks in, making the already tight space more cramped with his broad frame.

I whip around to face him. "What the hell are you doing?" I hiss, keeping my voice as low as I can.

He doesn't answer as he stares at me, slowly dragging his gaze up my body. It's at that moment I remember I'm wearing only my burgundy lace bra and underwear set. It's not insanely sexy, but the delicate lace appliqué on top of the cotton material adds a certain flare.

I move to grab my sweatshirt that's hanging on the back of the chair but am instantly halted in my steps when Matteo growls out, "Don't. Even. Think about it."

My heart feels like it's going to pound out of my chest. My mind yells at me to grab my sweatshirt and cover up, but my body does the opposite, keeping me rooted in place as Matteo continues to watch me like a predator stalking its prey.

He closes the short distance between us, crashing into me and pushing my back up against the cool mirror. I shriek, but it's muffled by his calloused hand. He spreads my thighs with his knee, propping his leg between mine. "Shhh, Little Lux. We don't want the entire store hearing you, now do we?"

I speak, but my words come out muffled under his rough and yet somehow soft hand.

"If I remove my hand, are you going to be a good girl and cooperate?" The heat from his eyes is strong enough to incinerate me in place. I nod in response.

Removing his hand from my mouth, he slides it down my neck, through the valley between my breasts. He follows the movement with his eyes, leaving a trail of fire with each move he makes. "You are so fucking sexy, Lux." He drags his nearly black lust-filled eyes back to mine.

"Don't touch me," I snap. The force of my words come

out stronger than I anticipated. I was worried the electric feel of his body touching mine would make me falter, but the thought of Ashley still fresh on my mind has me ready to fight.

Matteo *tsks* me before wrapping his arm around my back and lowering it down to my ass. He grips a cheek in his hand. It's strong. Rough. Narrowing in on painful, and yet it feels so fucking good. "Is that anyway to speak to your husband, Little Lux?"

"You're my husband on paper, and that's it," I spit back, taking my anger on Ashley out on him. If I'm being sensible, I have no good reason to be mad at him. If what Ashley said is true, then he got together with her before me, and that's fine. We each have our pasts. What's irking me is the fact he brought me here and didn't have the decency to give me a heads-up his ex-fuck buddy would be playing dress-up with me.

Matteo narrows his gaze on mine, and I can see the fire sizzling in his eyes. "I'm going to make you my wife in *every* way possible. Now tell me what happened. Why're you acting like this?"

I narrow my gaze right back at him. "As if you don't know." I try to keep my voice a whisper. "What? You didn't think I'd find out you're parading me around your former fuck buddy and letting her play *Barbie* with me while she dresses me up in some fancy clothing she'd wear? Do you know how humiliating that is? How fucking stupid I feel?" I choke out that last sentence, not because I'm sad but because I'm damn well *livid*.

"You think I'd do that to you?" Matteo asks, as if me questioning his character is so easy for him to roll off his back.

My eyes bounce back and forth between his, attempting to read him for the man he is. *I'm only a business transaction.* His words from our wedding day come back to haunt me. Echoing through the chambers of my mind.

He pushes into me, holding me in place with his body, so I place my hands on his hard chest and push him, but he doesn't budge. He never budges. Wrapping his fingers around my wrists, he drags them over my head, and I'm thrown back to our first kiss in the living room. I almost let out a moan at the memory mixed with the reaction of my body to his, but I keep my mouth clamped shut.

"Let's get a couple things straight, Little Lux," he growls out. "One, that woman out there is by no means my former *fuck buddy*." He thrusts his hips into mine, and this time I can't hold back the moan as he brushes his hardened length into me.

"And two, I would never *prance* you around a former fuck buddy. Not intentionally, at least. Now tell me what Ashley told you."

I shake my head and let out a low, maniacal laugh. "Ashley, huh? Why don't you explain to me how you two are on a first name basis if it's not because you guys have fucked before."

He tightens his grip on my wrists as he shuffles them so they're both being held by just one of his hands. Bringing his free hand down, he grazes my neck before wrapping his fingers around it, giving it a light squeeze. "I'll answer your question once you answer mine."

I open my mouth to argue, but he squeezes my neck harder. Not enough to prevent me from breathing but enough to make me bite my tongue. He feathers the side of my neck with his thumb, sending shivers down my body, making me clench that spot between my legs.

"Are you ready to tell me what Ashley told you?" He drops his gaze to my chest, taking in the rise and fall of my breasts. "Or am I going to have to coerce it out of you, Little Lux?"

I scoff. *This arrogant ass.* "I'm more interested in what *you* have to say, *Teo*." His nickname rolls off my tongue. Snapping his gaze up to mine, I swear I see the fire spread in his eyes, consuming every aspect of his face as it morphs into something primal. Something beyond devilish.

"I love hearing my name roll off your lips, baby."

"Don't *baby* me—"

He increases the pressure around my throat, cutting off my air supply. I try to suck in a sharp breath at the sudden action, but nothing comes through as I squirm in his grasp. This only causes him to push into me harder, his body now encompassing mine.

"I'm going to ask you one more time. What. Did. Ashley. Say. To. You?" He enunciates each word until he releases the tension around my throat. He's starting to make me feel insane. I should feel threatened, scared that he just cut off my air supply, but I don't. As frustrated as I am with the situation, I'm also incredibly turned on. His demands. His rock-hard frame pressed up against mine. It's like he knows exactly how to get my body to beg for his.

He trails his fingers back down that delicate spot between my breasts. I take in a sharp breath as he lowers his fingers even farther down my stomach, past my belly button, hovering over the band of my underwear. I hold my breath as he slides his finger between the fabric, running it along my skin. "Coercion it is. I can work with that, Little Lux."

He pulls the band of my underwear back. "You wouldn't," I say just before he slides his hand under the fabric, down to my core. My eyes widen, and I'm about to say something when Matteo slams his mouth on mine, swallowing down my protests in a heartbeat.

He moves his hand over my pussy. It's as if he's getting acclimated with it, memorizing the most sensitive part of my body inch-by-inch. He finds my clit, and I let out a feral moan that would've been so much louder had his mouth not been there to capture the noise.

Taking a finger, he spreads my slit, finding the warmth of my center. He pulls his mouth from mine, and I whimper at the loss of him. "You're already so fucking wet for me, baby."

My breathing intensifies as he slides a finger inside, my body welcoming him.

"I've thought about this more times than I can count, Little Lux." He slowly moves his finger in and out, stretching me, causing me to let out another moan.

"There's something about you, Luxtyn. You drive me fucking crazy," he says as he picks up the pace of thrusting in and out of me.

A knock sounds at the door. "Are you ready for some more options?" Ashley calls through the door, and I want to tell her to fuck off, but Matteo beats me to it.

"We're fine," he snaps.

"But, I have some—"

"I said we're fucking fine," he growls out, never taking his eyes off mine.

He adds another finger inside of me and continues pumping in and out while pressing his palm against my clit. I have no idea how he's able to do what he's doing with one hand, but it's driving me insane.

I think Ashley says, "Okay," before retreating, but I can't focus on her when Matteo has me feeling like this. He moves his fingers in and out of me even faster, curling them every couple thrusts and hitting that sensitive spot inside of me. I squirm under his grasp as he plays me like a damn fiddle.

"I can feel you're almost there, baby. Squeezing my fingers with that tight pussy of yours. I can't fucking wait until you're squeezing my cock the same way."

His words increase my pleasure. I'm so fucking close I can taste the orgasm on the tip of my tongue, and just when I know I'm about to explode, Matteo does the last thing I expected him to do. He pulls back, releasing the pressure off my clit and removing his fingers so they're barely inside me anymore.

"What the fuck," I hiss out as I try to catch my breath, my orgasm flatlining.

"One more time, Lux. What did she say to you?"

Damn this man. He's doing exactly what he said he would do. I'm so wound up that I need a release, and I need it soon. Matteo's had me on edge lately, and now that I'm finally in his arms, narrowing in on the best orgasm of my life, there's not much I wouldn't do to get that release he has me chasing after.

"All she said was that you guys hooked up recently." The details of him finishing in her mouth don't need to be discussed. The sick image will only dry me up inside.

"That's not all she said." He slowly pushes his fingers into me another inch. As if he's baiting me to keep going, knowing that the pleasure he'll bring me will keep me talking. And he's fucking right.

"And she said that she knows what you like, and that's why you brought me here today. To have her dress me up like the type of woman you want." I hate that she affected me so much. I hate that she's been with Matteo, but what I hate even more is that he felt he had to take me here to turn me into something I'm not. Something that *he* wants. Someone like her.

Pushing his fingers the rest of the way into me, he starts working me up again with shallow thrusts before finding my clit once more with his palm. He leans down into the crook of my neck and whispers, "Don't *ever* think that I would bring you somewhere to dress you like some whore that blew me in my club *one* time before I even met you. That's not what this is."

His fingers build up speed, and my deteriorating orgasm is back with a vengeance. I know it won't take much to push me over the edge, and he knows it too.

"You're squeezing me harder than you were before. You're right there. Come for me, Little Lux. Give me the thing I crave from you the most," he commands, right before biting down on my neck with his teeth.

The pain mixed with the pleasure of his hand and the absolute rawness of it all has me spiraling. I throw my head back against the mirror, and my eyes roll to the back of my head. I cry out, but he moves his mouth from the base of my neck to my mouth, sucking down the sound as he kisses me with absolute fervor, our tongues lashing at each other.

Matteo helps me ride out my orgasm as long as possible as he slows the thrusts of his fingers before finally removing them. Pulling his face from mine, he stares down into my eyes that have finally begun to focus again from the intense climax I just had.

He brings his glistening fingers up to his face and shoves them in his mouth, sucking them clean. Matteo groans. "Fucking delicious."

Holy fuck.

The sight of Matteo licking me off him has me ready to go again, sensitive or not.

When he's done, he grabs my clothes and helps me get dressed. "What're you doing?" I ask.

"We're leaving. We'll go somewhere else to get you some things until we can meet up with my cousin. The only person I wanted you to work with was Liana, and we won't be back again until she's here."

Ahh, so Liana's his cousin. That's why he brought me here. To have his cousin help pick out some clothes for me. Gosh, I feel so freaking stupid that I let Ashley get to me like that.

Matteo and I exit the dressing room to Ashley standing about fifteen feet away with her hand on her hip as she taps her foot. She has a few pieces of clothing in her other hand, and I cringe at her color choices. Neon colors. Green, yellow, and orange. What was this girl's plan? Bring in outfit after outfit that aren't my style and not make a sale? All because she's jealous that I'm married to a man she got on her knees for? I might feel silly for feeling threatened the way I did, but this bitch is an idiot, pathetic, *and* borderline crazy.

She paints on a fake smile when she looks at Matteo and scurries up to us. "I brought some more options—"

"We're done here," Matteo says, his voice stern, unwavering, causing Ashley to retreat into her shell.

"But, I thought—"

"Look, Ashley, I don't know what the hell you thought when you decided to lie to my wife just to try and make her feel inferior to you, but because of your incompetence, you're now going to be unemployed, not to mention blacklisted from ever working in New York City again."

"Matteo—"

He steps into her suddenly, making her jump back into a rack of clothes in shock. "*Don't* fucking say my name. I'm nothing to you. I'm no one." He lets out a dark chuckle. "Except for the man who'll make it his mission to ensure you're never employed in this city again."

Matteo grabs hold of my hand before turning back to Ashley, whose shocked eyes are shimmering with tears, clearly regretting the way she's acted now. "And if you think I don't have connections in all of the major cities in this country, think again. You might want to find a small town where you can work for a souvenir shop making minimum wage, because your career in fashion is now over."

Without another word, he pulls me through the boutique

and out the front door. A smile tugs at my lips. Not only did I have the best orgasm of my life from nothing but Matteo's hand, but he also stuck up for me. I know it sounds stupid, but I've never had anyone stick up for me like that before. And I'd be lying if I said it wasn't the hottest thing I've ever witnessed.

27

MATTEO

After stopping by another store to grab Lux clothes, we head back to the penthouse. We avoid speaking about what happened in the dressing room in front of Rocco and Tito, but I know it's been on her mind almost as much as it's been on mine.

It's all I can think about.

The way she reacted so perfectly to me. The glorious sounds that escaped that mouth of hers. The quivers she made every time I hit each of her spots. The face she made as pleasure took complete control of her body. And her taste. Her sweet fucking taste has permanently marked me, and I don't know if I'll ever be the same.

I order Rocco and Tito to bring Lux's bags up to my room when we get back to the penthouse.

"Oh, I can bring them in," Lux says, attempting to round the SUV to the trunk where her bags remain.

Grabbing a hold of her, I say, "They got it," before guiding her to the elevator.

"I have to speak with Enzo," I say as we get off on our floor.

I've been wasting too much time trying to find her mother, and Mancini has proven to be useless, so while Lux did some shopping, I came up with a plan. One that could put me in the line of fire, but finding Lux's mother makes it worth it. Because she's worth it.

"Okay, I'll go put my clothes away," she says before walking down the hall.

"In my room," I add, reminding her in case she forgot last night was the last night she'd ever be in her own room.

She glances back over her shoulder with that perfect smile of hers that could melt even the coldest of hearts. *I would know.*

I watch as she disappears down the hall, mesmerized by the way she moves. So effortlessly sexy. I swear she doesn't even realize the effect she has on me.

It took everything in me not to rip off my clothes back in that dressing room and swipe her underwear to the side while I filled her with my cock, but that moment was for her. I wanted her pleasure to be the priority there. To show her that Ashley is nothing and she's everything. Hearing myself think that blows my mind. *This girl.*

I find Enzo and Isabella sitting at the island in the kitchen. "We need to talk about Lux's mother," I say, addressing Enzo.

"Oh, well, hello there to you too," Isabella says as she spins on the island stool to face me.

"Lux is putting her newly purchased clothes away in my room. Why don't you go help her?" I suggest. She doesn't need to be here for this conversation.

"Enzo already filled me in on everything, so you might as well tell me what's going on."

I shoot Enzo a glare, to which he holds up his hands and shrugs. "She was annoying the fuck out of me about it."

Rolling her eyes, she hops off the chair. "Fine, I'll leave." She points at me. "Not because you told me to, but because I happen to really like Lux, and sorting through her new clothes sounds way more fun than whatever you two need to talk about."

She doesn't leave, though. She narrows her gaze on me and tilts her head as if she's trying to figure something out. "But if you're planning on talking about Lux's mom, don't you think she should be present for it? Also, since when do you call her Lux? And why the hell won't you call me Izzy?"

I give her a tired look. "That was way too many questions, Isabella." It's not that I don't like calling her Izzy, I just get enjoyment out of how annoyed she gets that I won't. But also, our mother's middle name was Isabella. Even though I was only six, I remember how excited my parents were when they found out Isabella was a girl. Our mother had always wanted to pass her middle name down to a little girl. So I've always called her by her full name, just like our mother did when she was still alive.

"Don't you know the best reaction to something is *no* reaction?" I ask her.

She pops her hip out, propping her hand on it. "So you're saying if I stop asking you to call me Izzy, you'll start calling me Izzy? That's so dumb, Teo. I'm going to go find Lux, but you should think about what I said. If you and Enzo have something to discuss that involves Lux's mom, you should include her in that conversation."

I ignore her suggestion as she walks away, because involving Lux in what I have planned for Enzo and me tonight is out of the question.

"So," Enzo says expectantly. "I'm assuming you've come up with a plan? Or have you heard back from Mancini?"

I scoff. "Of course I haven't heard anything from him. That man is useless, but I do have a plan."

"Let's hear it."

Resting my hands on the edge of the cool marble surface of the counter, I continue. "You and I are going to the strip club."

Enzo spits out the water he just took a sip of, nearly dropping the glass in the process. I laugh because while I didn't do that on purpose, I couldn't have timed telling him more perfectly.

"I'm sorry," he says. "But what the hell are you talking about?" He grabs a towel hanging from one of the drawers and wipes his face before wiping the water off the counter.

"It's exactly what I said. We're going to the strip club." I stretch out my arm so the sleeve of my suit jacket rides up, and glance at the Rolex wrapped around my wrist. "In a couple of hours, actually."

"You know I'm all about going to a strip club, but do you think your wife will be okay with *you* going to one?"

"She doesn't need to know the details right now. Besides, I'm only going to the strip club for her mother."

Enzo raises a brow at me. "You're lying to her now?"

"It's not a lie if she doesn't know to ask about it in the first place."

"Omitting the truth is still a lie." A voice comes from the entrance of the kitchen. I snap my gaze over and see Lux standing there with a look of disappointment on her face. My little deviant sister stands beside her, both hands on her hips as she taps her foot.

Fucking Isabella.

Lux walks in, rounding the island to stand before me. "Care to explain to me why *my husband* thinks going to a strip club is going to help get my mom back?" Her brows are furrowed and her nostrils flared. There's the smallest vein pulsing on her temple.

I let out a sigh of defeat, knowing I'll have to explain myself to her now. "There's a specific strip club that Mauricio likes to hang out at every so often. I have it under good authority that he'll be there in a couple of hours."

Enzo, Lux, and Isabella all look at me with confusion, not knowing where I'm going with this. "I plan on paying off a stripper to get him into a private room to talk a little. After having a few drinks, of course."

Lux narrows her gaze on mine like she's still trying to figure out my plan. "So you're going to have a stripper find out where my mom is?"

"It's actually a damn good idea," Enzo says. "Strippers, bartenders, and barbers are the best listeners. They can get anyone to talk without even talking. It's quite fascinating, really."

"Okay, and what exactly is your plan? Pay off the stripper to get him to talk and then meet up with her after to learn what she finds out? How do you know she's not going to screw you over?"

"The private rooms are decent sized and dark. Very dark. Dark enough for someone like me to hang out in the corner without being noticed. Especially by someone who's going to be too drunk and preoccupied with getting his dick wet."

"Ew, Teo. Must you be so vulgar? It's just creepy when you speak like that," Isabella says from behind Lux.

"Okay . . ." Lux says with a couple nods as if the plan is coming together in her mind. "I like it. When do we leave?"

I release an amused scoff, which takes her by surprise. *Oh, she was serious.* "Absolutely not. You're not coming with us."

Folding her arms across her body, she leans her hip against the island. *She's so damn cute when she gears up to argue with me.* "And why the hell not? It's my mom. I want to help."

"And how the hell do you think you're going to be able to help me at a strip club?" I ask.

"I don't know. What if there are other people there that know about my mom. Maybe I can get them to talk—"

"It's a strip club, Luxtyn," I interject, my voice getting louder. "What the hell do you think you're going to be able to do to get these guys to talk?"

She opens her mouth to answer me, but I hold up my hand, silencing her on the spot. "*Don't* answer that. You're not going to the strip club, and that's the end of that."

"Excuse you," she snaps. "You're not the boss of me, Matteo."

"You're my wife, which means I'm responsible for your safety." We're basically in a yelling match now, and Enzo and Isabella glance back and forth at each other like they don't know if they should leave the room or not. It doesn't fucking matter, though, because I'm about to end this conversation.

"There are men in that club that kill people for a damn living. They're dangerous. You're not going, and that's the end of the fucking story." I storm past her, but of course she has to get the last word in.

"You mean men like you?" Her voice is low, but her tone is unyielding.

I stop, but instead of turning around to acknowledge her remark, I ignore her and walk out of the kitchen toward my office.

I can't argue with what she said. I am a killer. I'm no better than the men who'll be in that strip club tonight, but I don't give a fuck. Lux isn't going, and I refuse to explain it any further to her.

28

LUXTYN

After our argument, I storm back into my room and fall backward onto my bed.

The fact he thinks he can still order me around like he owns me makes me livid. How dare he treat me like that, especially in front of his siblings. It's so damn disrespectful. I should be allowed to go and help, but he treats me like I'm some child who'll get in the way, and that infuriates me.

A knock comes through my door, and I would be inclined to think it's Matteo, but the soft taps tell me it's most likely Izzy.

"Come in," I call out as I bring myself to a seated position on the edge of my bed. If it was Matteo, I'd be telling him to fuck off.

Izzy pushes the door open, letting herself in before closing it behind her. "Are you okay?" she asks softly, the expression on her face displaying remorse.

"Yeah, I'm fine. Your brother's just an asshole . . . no offense."

She lets out a small laugh before climbing onto the bed next to me. "No offense taken. He can definitely be a dick." I let out a humorous scoff because if that isn't the statement of the century, then I don't know what is. "But I'm sorry," she continues. "This is all my fault."

I whip my head in her direction, surprised at her apology. Not *understanding* her apology. She must read the confusion on my face because she continues.

"The only reason that fight happened is because of me. I shouldn't have told you that he was going to speak to Enzo about your mom. I should've let him come to you instead of causing this fight." She fidgets with her fingers in her lap. *She truly believes she's responsible for this.*

I place my hand over hers and give it a light squeeze, attempting to stop her unease. "This is not your fault, Izzy. I appreciate you having my back and telling me when you did. You heard your brother. He wasn't planning on telling me. He was just going to lie to me." And here I thought he was the only one I could trust. The one who *wouldn't* ever lie to me.

"Matteo's a lot of things, but he's not a liar," Izzy says softly. "He might've not come out and told you the way he did, but he would've told you eventually. And had you called him out on it, he wouldn't have lied to your face. He would've been honest with you."

"Great, so you're sticking up for him now?" I snap, and immediately wince at my tone. She rounds her shoulders slightly, lowering her gaze. "I'm sorry, Izzy. You didn't deserve that. I'm just . . . a little tense."

"It's okay. I really am sorry, though. I should've stayed out of it."

Shaking my head, I say, "No more apologizing. I appreciate you for telling me. I truly do. Your brother just knows how to get under my skin, which is even more annoying because he hasn't even known me that long."

I flop myself down onto my back again, letting my legs dangle over the edge of the bed, and let out a long sigh. "I just wish he understood where I was coming from. It's my mom we're talking about, and he thinks it's okay to keep me in the dark. Leave me here to twiddle my damn fingers all day and night while he does whatever it is he's doing."

"I can't imagine what you're going through, but I know if I was in your position, I'd want to do everything in my power to help, too."

"It's a terrible feeling. My mom's my best friend. Whenever I've needed her, she's always there for me, whether that be teaching me how to ride a bike when I was five or teaching me how to do my makeup when I went into high school. And now I'm stuck here feeling helpless, not able to be there for her like she's always been there for me." I let out a long sigh. "I just want to help, Izzy."

A few silent moments pass between us before she gasps. "Wait a second. I might have an idea on how we can help find your mom."

I shoot up, back into a seated position. Bending my knee, I hike my leg onto the bed as I turn to face Izzy, who is mirroring my position. "Please continue."

"Now let me preface this with saying my brother is going to be *furious* if he finds out."

Waving her off with my hand, I encourage her to continue. "If anything, that just makes me want to see this plan of yours out even more."

She chuckles as she shakes her head. "You're lucky my brother has a soft spot for you."

"What do you mean?"

"I mean, if anyone's going to be able to pull this off and *not* get killed by my brother in the process, it's you. He has a soft spot for me because I'm his little sister, but you . . . you, he has a soft spot for a whole other reason. And it'll be the only protection you have in this situation."

A whole other reason.

I want to inquire more, but I'm still too frustrated with Matteo to care right now. Ignoring what she said, I shake my hand, gesturing for her to continue. "Okay, so what's this plan of yours?"

"We're going to the strip club."

"Um, okay . . . how, though? We have a guard watching us. There's no way he's going to just let us leave to go to a strip club."

"Oh, gosh no. But I do know that we can easily evade him, and by the time he realizes we're not in the penthouse anymore, we'll already be long gone and he won't have any idea where we've disappeared to."

Pulling out her phone, Izzy starts typing something. "I know just the person who can help. I'll get us to the strip club," she says, pointing to herself before pointing to me. "You take it from there." She wiggles her brows at me, and the gleam in her eye tells me we're going to be in for an interesting night.

"I take it from there," I repeat, nodding to myself while I think about what that means exactly.

Izzy's phone dings, catching my attention. A smile breaks out on her face. "Perfect! Liana's going to pick us up out front. We just need to get there, and we'll be good. Do you have a plan?"

Not really, but here goes nothing.

"Bear with me, okay? This plan could easily change once we get there, but I'm assuming Mauricio isn't going to be at the strip club by himself, so while Matteo's busy with Mauricio and the stripper"—*which I don't love*—"what if I talk up whoever he's with? This could be a good plan B in case Matteo's stripper doesn't pull through for him. I'm sure whoever's with Mauricio will know *something*."

Izzy slowly nods as she purses her lips and thinks about my plan. It might not be the greatest, but it's the best I can come up with. I want to be useful, and if we're going to be this close to these guys, we need to get some kind of information out of them. The more hands on this, the better.

Reverting to her phone, Izzy quickly types something on it again.

She holds her phone out to me so I can see the screen. She has a website pulled up for The Ruby Lounge, displaying a flier for an amateur night for dancers. I look at her, confused. How did she know—

"I overheard Enzo and Matteo after you stormed out of the kitchen, and they mentioned The Ruby Lounge, so I'm sure that's where they're going tonight. And you're in luck. Looks like The Ruby Lounge has their annual amateur night tonight."

I cock a brow at her. "Okay?"

Dropping her phone back into her lap, she continues. "So this is how we're going to get in. You and I are participating in amateur night, and we're going to blow the socks off whatever men Mauricio has with him. *That's* how we're going to get them to talk."

Oh yeah, Matteo is going to *hate* this plan if he catches us. A sinister grin takes over my face. Pissing him off the way he's pissed me off only makes me want to follow through with this plan even more.

"I'm in," I say. "But I don't have anything to wear. I don't even know what *to* wear to a strip club's amateur night."

"Already on it," she says, typing on her phone. "Also, don't worry about Matteo catching us. Liana has some wigs, so I'll ask her to bring a couple for us. After I do your makeup, even if he does see you, he won't recognize you."

I hope she's right, because the last thing I need is to have him barging in, destroying any chance I have of getting information about my mom.

29

MATTEO

Enzo and I pull up to The Ruby Lounge, and I've already spotted Mauricio's silver Bentley in the parking lot. Looks like my source was correct.

My strip club contact, Frankie, lets us in through a side entrance. The club is owned by Mancini. With Lux and I married, it won't be out of the ordinary for me to be here, but I'm not taking a chance on spooking Mauricio. If he knows about Lux's mother's kidnapping and sees me here, he'll be on guard and even the stripper won't be able to distract him enough to get anything out of him.

I slip some cash to Frankie for his help tonight. He gives me a nod, allowing Enzo and I to pass. Just because he works for Mancini's establishment, doesn't mean he can't be paid off. He's not a made man. He's not even an associate. He has nothing to do with the Mafia. He's simply a bouncer working at a strip club owned by Angelo Mancini.

Enzo and I walk through the narrow hallways lined with dimmed lighting reflecting off the red walls that lead to the main floor. I locate Mauricio immediately. The silver-haired man is sitting front and center with two other men.

Giuseppe Silvestri.

The other one's Niccolò Silvestri, Giuseppe's only son. He hasn't been seen around the city the past few years. Rumor has it Giuseppe sent him to Sicily to train to take over for him. I had no idea he was back.

I pull back so I'm hidden behind the wall. "You see who's out there?" I ask Enzo.

He leans around me, popping his head out to peer into the lounge. "Well, shit. I didn't expect *that*."

"Neither did I. We need to make sure we're fucking discreet. Stay in the shadows and stay alert. Text Rocco and let him know we may need him and Tito for backup in case we end up getting fucked." Enzo nods before taking out his cell phone and sending the message off to Rocco.

I watch the men closely as they guzzle down the drinks the cocktail servers keep bringing, loosening them up effectively. Mauricio already has the stripper on his lap, shoving her bare tits in his face. He whispers something in her ear before she giggles and stands, pulling him up with her. *Looks like we got here just in time.*

I speak to Enzo but keep my eyes trained on Mauricio and the stripper, knowing I need to get to the private room before they do. "Keep an eye out on the Silvestris, but do not approach them by any means. I don't want to scare the fucks before we have the information we need."

"Got it, Boss. Rocco and Tito will be posted up outside shortly."

Looks like the stripper is about to lead Mauricio to the private room any second. "Good. I'll be back as soon as this fucker blows his load."

Enzo lets out a low laugh. "Man, I would not want to be you in this situation."

"That makes two of us. This stripper better get some information out of him, or I'll fucking kill them both back there for putting me through this shit."

I head to the private rooms, staying in the shadows so no one sees me. The stages and poles are lit up for the dancers, but the rest of the club is lit up by red ambiance lighting, making it difficult to see anything unless you're laser focused on it.

I find the farthest private room. This is the one I told Frankie to tell the stripper to use. Typically, the girls use the first one available, so the last one seemed like the safest bet to make sure we end up in the same room.

Slipping into the dimly lit room, I find a spot in the darkened corner.

And now we wait.

30

LUXTYN

Izzy's plan couldn't have worked out more perfectly. The girl knows her guard like the back of her hand. As she said he would, Eddie got up from his seat on the couch in the living room, checked on Izzy and me, then proceeded to do his hourly walk through the penthouse. That's when we took advantage and headed straight for the elevator.

Somehow, someway, we pull it off. I would've put money down that Eddie would've caught us before the elevator doors shut, but that thought escapes my mind as Izzy and I run through the parking garage. The adrenaline has my heart feeling like it's going to explode out of my chest.

Izzy stands before the biometric scanner, placing her hand on the screen and widening her eyes so the retinal scanner can detect her before pulling me through the door of the parking garage.

She glances around before grabbing my wrist. "Come on," Izzy breathes out, dragging me toward the direction of a white Mercedes Benz sedan parked on the side of the street.

After opening the door, Izzy pushes me inside before

sliding in on the dark leather seat beside me. "We did not just pull that off," I gasp out, trying to catch my breath.

"Piece of cake," Izzy laughs out, slamming the door shut behind her. "Thank you so much for getting us, Liana," she calls out to the woman in the driver's seat.

Liana glances back at us over her shoulder, and even under the dimmed lighting brought to us by her tablet-sized car display screen and the city lights, I can see the resemblance. She and Izzy look a lot alike, except where Izzy's hair is a dark-chocolate brown, Liana's is a little lighter, sunkissed by a caramel balayage.

"No problem, but are you going to tell me what's going on now? And why I needed to bring this *particular* choice of clothing, shoes, and wigs?" Sliding her gaze over to mine, she gives me a warm smile and continues speaking before Izzy can answer. "You must be Luxtyn. I'm Liana. It's so nice to finally meet you."

"It's nice to meet you too. And you can call me Lux." *Another DiMaggio I find myself easily opening up to.*

"Lux, now that's a cool name."

"Right?" Izzy chimes in from beside me. "It's edgy."

"Very edgy," Liana agrees, and I giggle at them.

"I want to apologize for not being at the store today, Lux. I assure you Ashley will never be a problem again. Teo already informed me of her disgusting behavior. I let her go immediately."

Heat flushes my cheeks, and I'm immediately thankful for the dimmed lighting as I think about how the inconvenience of having Ashley as my personal shopper led to the most amazing orgasm of my life, and for that, I can't be totally upset by it. I might be annoyed with Teo, but that man knows what to do with those fingers of his.

"It's really okay," I say.

"Alright, as much as I would love to chit-chat it up, we should really get going. Can you bring us to The Ruby Lounge, please?" Izzy says.

Liana narrows her gaze on her. "The Ruby Lounge?"

"You don't want to know," Izzy says.

Liana turns back around in her seat and puts her blinker on to pull out into the busy street. "Oh, yes I do. Start talking, babe."

As we change into the clothes, or should I say scraps of fabric Liana brought us, Izzy explains our plan to her.

We're almost to the club when Izzy finishes applying my makeup, going with a dark smokey-eyed look. Something I would've worn while working at the bar down in Florida. She even applied long fake lashes between the bumps and turns, only using the lights inside the car to see.

Liana brings her car to a stop in the parking lot when I finally get the short blonde balayage wig on she brought me, and Izzy gets her pastel-pink one on.

Turning back around, she gives Izzy and I each a concerned look. "Are you guys sure you should be doing this? I feel like I wouldn't be a very good friend leaving you both here."

"We'll be okay, Liana, I promise," Izzy says. "You know how good I can be at sneaking around."

They exchange a look, and I can tell there's a story there that if we had more time, I would inquire about more.

It's silent for a few moments as they hold each other's gazes before Liana relents with a sigh. "Fine, but I'm staying here in case you guys need me."

"Absolutely not," Izzy says. "If my brothers catch your car out here, we'll all be screwed."

Liana bites the inside of her cheek as she considers that. "Fine, I'll park a couple blocks away then."

"Liana—"

"I'm not leaving you both here like this, Izzy."

Now it's Izzy's turn to relent. "Fine . . . and thank you. That'll actually help us a lot."

Liana nods before we all say our goodbyes and head into the club.

After checking in for amateur night under the pseudonyms, Blondie and Pinky, Izzy and I are brought in the back with the other strippers and given our own vanity spots next to each other to put on the final touches to our looks.

I glance over at Izzy's reflection in the mirror next to mine. I'm still thrown off by the long pink waves cascading around her shoulders and the short blonde ones styled in a cute bob on mine. It gives me a modern *Pretty Woman* vibe that I'm surprised I can pull off.

"Blondie and Pinky?" I whisper to her. "*Those* are the stripper names you decided to go with?"

She shrugs, flashing her teeth in a straight line as she gives me an *oops* look. "I didn't know what else to say when he asked us what our stage names are. I panicked."

"Very original, Izzy."

"Stop calling me that," she hisses. "It's *Pinky*, remember?"

I snort out a chuckle while she glares back at me. "I'm sorry, I just keep thinking of *Pinky and the Brain*, and then I can't take this seriously. You really want me to call you Pinky?"

She turns to face me in the plastic folding chair and pinches my thigh. "Yes, *Blondie*. Now get it together. We need to get our heads in the game."

"Ouch," I say as I rub the tender spot. "Okay, okay. I have it together."

"Did you happen to see who was out there when we got here?"

"*Pinky*, I don't know anyone in the city. So no, I did not happen to see who was out there when we got here."

Izzy pulls me up, and I almost trip over the six-inch black heels Liana brought. They're a tad bit too big for me, so it'll be a miracle if I make it through the rest of the night without eating shit at some point.

Dragging me to the curtains shielding us from the club, she points to a table in the front with three men relaxed in the loungers. "*That* is Giuseppe Silvestri."

Giuseppe Silvestri.

"He's the one in the middle, Mauricio is the one to his left, and then the one on his right is . . ." I turn to see what's caused her to stop in the middle of her sentence.

She's still focused on the table of men, but her dropped jaw and wide eyes have me questioning what's going on in that head of hers. Shaking her shoulder, I ask, "Are you okay?"

As if she's been pulled out of a trance, Izzy quickly averts her gaze to mine. "Yeah, sorry, I totally spaced out there for a second. Um, the other one, next to Giuseppe, that's his son, Niccolò Silvestri. But forget about that. Amateur night starts any minute now, and I bribed the guy to put you on first."

"You did what now?"

I glance back at Mauricio and notice he's being taken by one of the strippers somewhere.

The private room.

That means Matteo should be distracted with Mauricio for however long it takes for the stripper to do her thing back there.

"The faster you get on that stage, the quicker you get off it and onto the floor."

Right. Because I need to get on the floor to get close enough to the guys to talk. "Okay. I can do this," I say, talking myself up.

"Yes you can," Izzy cheers me on. "Now this might not be the best time to bring this up, but do you have *any* kind of dancing experience?" I can tell by her expression that she's expecting me to say no.

"Yes, I know how to work a stripper pole, Pinky."

Izzy's mouth falls open.

"What? Shocked?"

"Um, yes, absolutely."

"My mom introduced me to pole dancing class a few years ago. It's just this thing we do, and the only reason I'm in the shape I'm in."

Izzy checks me out and nods. "That makes sense because your body *is* phenomenal. Short but still banging," she adds with a giggle.

I playfully shove her arm. "I'll be fine out there, but what about you? What're you going to do?"

She waves me off and purses her lips. "Oh, girl. You didn't think you were the only one who's taken pole dancing classes, did you?"

"Seriously?"

"Oh yeah. We even have a pole in the gym at our house. It's the greatest workout of all time."

"I'm pretty sure you might be my spirit animal."

"Thanks," she says with a flattered smile. "I'll take that as a compliment."

"Blondie! Blondie! Has anyone seen Blondie?" a woman shouts from the hair and makeup room.

Izzy shakes my shoulders, reminding me. "That's you, *Blondie*."

Oh shit.

"Right, right," I mutter. *I completely forgot.* "Um, yes. Coming!" I shout back.

Izzy grabs my face between her hands and pulls me to her. "Okay, focus. It's gametime. You have one shot not to mess this up, okay? Now get your hot little ass out there and start seducing those Silvestri men," she says, turning me and smacking me on the ass before pushing me toward the person calling my name.

My heart is thudding so loud as I follow the lady to the side of the stage. "The DJ is going to introduce you and then start the music. Once the music starts playing, I'll cue you, and that's when you can take the stage, got it?"

I nod, in a daze but focused enough to understand. "Got it."

I glance back out into the crowd and find the Silvestris easily. They're right in front of the stage. The pressure of what's about to happen finally hits me, and I do everything in my power to take deep breaths to steady my heart rate. I don't want to go out there and dance for these guys, but I have to find my mom. So, for what it's worth, this one's for you, Mom.

31

LUXTYN

Walking out onto the stage, the bright lights zoom in on me. I focus on being Blondie, my new, hot, badass stripper alter ego, who needs to catch the eye of these guys so I can find out if they kidnapped my mom.

I sway up to the pole at center stage, swinging my hips to the beat of the music, and slide my hands up the sides of my body. The bedazzled black mesh material Liana let me borrow molds to my body and sits perfectly over my black lace pushup bra and matching cheeky underwear.

I know thongs and G-strings are the preferred uniform for a stripper, but there's no way I was going to prance my ass around in that. At least what I have on is sexy, but essentially the same coverage as a bathing suit.

Arching my back against the cool metal pole, I run my hands lightly through my wig, acting as if I'm really feeling myself while stripping off the mesh halter top and matching high-waisted skirt.

Extending my arms over my head, I grab a hold of the bar and hoist myself up, then do a backflip against the pole so my front is now flush with the beam. Catcalls and hollers come from the men, and bills are being thrown in my direction.

I continue to dance and pull myself up onto the bar, adding spins with the beat of the music whenever I see fit. The club is loving it, and I have to admit, it's freeing being up here, showcasing the strength and technique I have. I can see why strippers do what they do.

Before I know it, the song has come to an end and I pinpoint Giuseppe Silvestri, who's standing and clapping, which I'll note as a success since I didn't even completely strip.

Mauricio has returned, taking his spot right next to Giuseppe, which has my stomach bottoming out immediately. *How the hell is he back already?*

I have no idea when he returned, but that means Matteo is no longer being held up in the private room with him. And if Matteo's not in the room, that means . . .

I squint as I scan the room. I'm panicking, but I have no reason to. I look like a different person with my hair and makeup, but I still have this gut wrenching feeling in my stomach that someone's watching me. And I'm not talking about the random patrons here for a good show.

My eyes graze over a familiar hulking figure up against the far wall before quickly snapping back to it.

Matteo.

Time slows, and I freeze as I make eye contact with him. There's no way he recognizes me. *I* barely recognize myself.

I keep telling myself that, but his eyes widen, as if recognition is dawning on him. At that moment, I spin on my heel and nearly fall over but latch onto the pole to remain upright.

Grabbing the two mesh pieces of my outfit off the floor, I hurry off the stage to where Izzy's waiting for me with open arms and all of our things. My eyes widen and I barely choke out the words "Izzy, he's—"

"I know, I saw him. I'm so sorry, Lux." Her worried gaze darts over my head as if she's waiting for someone to show up behind me.

"But he didn't recognize me, right? I mean, I-I'm in a costume. *Everything* about me is different. I barely recognize myself."

She rubs my arms, doing her best to calm me. "I know, I know. I wouldn't recognize you either, but I'm really sorry, Lux. I don't think I can say the same for my brother."

"She absolutely cannot say the fucking same for her brother," a voice growls out from behind me.

My heart stops at the same time as Izzy's eyes widen like she's seen a damn ghost. It wasn't long ago that Izzy and I were sitting on my bed going over this plan, and at that moment, I had zero care in the world if Matteo caught us. But now that we're here, now that I've been caught red-handed, I can't say I feel the same.

I slowly spin and bring my eyes up to meet Matteo's. It's dark back here, but his hardened gaze is cold, sharp, and searing through me.

He stalks toward me, causing me to tilt my head back to keep eye contact with him.

"Teo—" Izzy says.

"Walk toward the back side entrance, Isabella. Enzo's out there waiting for you," he orders with a controlled ferociousness.

"I'm sorry, Lux," she whispers from behind me.

"Now, Isabella!" The anger in his tone sends goose bumps erupting over my body.

Izzy disappears, leaving Matteo and me alone. He slides his coat off and wraps it around my shoulders. The sincere offer lifts a weight off my chest, and I release a deep breath.

"Don't mistake that act for kindness," he snarls before

leaning down to whisper, "I'm going to make you pay for what you just did out there." The threat sends a chill straight to my bones, freezing me on the spot. He pulls away from me, keeping his eyes fixed on mine.

"Matteo—"

"Don't. Fucking. Speak. Luxtyn." He grabs my hand and pulls me toward the exit, not glancing back once as he drags me out into the parking lot.

32

MATTEO

The chilly spring night air is the only thing grounding me as I pull Lux through the parking lot to my Bugatti. I was about to sneak back out of the club after the stripper got the information I needed from Mauricio, but as soon as I walked out into the lounge, something didn't feel right.

A strange pull had me halting my steps and narrowing my gaze on the stripper at the pole. Those dark eyes I would recognize anywhere. Those high cheekbones and full lips with her flawless pale skin that looked soft enough to bite. I knew exactly who that *stripper* was, even with that blonde wig and a face full of makeup on.

I remained rooted in place until Lux was done with her dance, which fortunately for everyone was about twenty seconds later. Had it gone on any longer, eyes would've been shot out by me.

She finished her routine off with a split as she dangled from the pole, showcasing the incredible flexibility I had no idea she had, then a fire ignited within me, consuming me past the point of return. I would make her pay for disobeying me.

I'm practically dragging Lux across the parking lot. She's tripped over those damn sky-high heels more than I can count. She does it again, so I whip around and grab her by her waist and throw her over my shoulder to keep her from face-planting on the asphalt parking lot.

"Matteo—"

Lifting my jacket up, I slap her on her bare ass.

She yelps out. "Ouch! Matteo, what the fu—"

I do it again, but this time harder, causing her to cry out again. "There's a pattern here, Luxtyn. You'd be wise to figure it out now before your ass ends up raw with the imprint of my hand."

She remains silent as I dump her in the passenger seat and reach across her body to buckle her up. I feel her eyes burning into me, but I don't acknowledge her.

Rounding the car, I take out my phone to see Enzo texted a few minutes ago letting me know he and Isabella are on their way back to the penthouse with Rocco and Tito, and that they found Liana parked a couple blocks away and told her to head home.

Where the fuck is her guard?

I shove my phone back into my pocket before opening my car door and dropping into the driver's seat.

The ride home is filled with only my shifting of the gear and the rev of my engine. If I speak now, who knows what I'll say, and I won't be able to take anything back.

My hand tightens around the steering wheel, whitening my knuckles as I take the windy turns to my house.

"Where are we going?" Luxtyn asks.

"Home," I respond, giving her nothing but knowing she'll ask for more.

"This isn't the way to your penthouse. Are we even in the city anymore?"

I sneak a quick glance at her. She has her arms wrapped around her small frame, tightening my jacket around herself. I almost laugh out loud since she was just nearly naked in front of a bunch of disgusting men. All gawking at what's fucking *mine.*

The way she moved on that pole nearly had me as hard as a rock. The only reason I didn't burst through the seams of my pants was the fact she wasn't dancing for me. She was dancing for those other men. Like she was fucking enjoying disobeying a direct order from me to stay the fuck at the penthouse while I handled Mauricio.

"Are you just going to ignore me?" she asks.

Yes.

She releases a sigh and sulks back in her seat when she realizes I'm not going to answer her.

We make it through my gated security, up the long gravel driveway lined with large maple trees that have bloomed. I pull into the ten-car garage attached to my family's home and park.

Rounding the car, Lux has already opened the door and is attempting to pull herself out of the low riding vehicle. Placing my hand on the door, I watch as she struggles with those monstrosities of shoes she decided to wear tonight.

Fine, the black stiletto platforms are fucking sexy, even if they look like they're about to slide off her feet, but now that the image of her working a pole for strangers in them is inscribed in my brain, the shoes need to be burned.

Glaring up at me, she asks, "Are you just going to stand there, or give me a hand?"

Oh, she thinks she can have an attitude with me *now?*

I tilt my head to the side and raise a brow. "You seemed to do just fine when you were working that pole tonight."

Her glare turns into a scowl as her eyebrows draw in and her frown sharpens. She grabs ahold of the arm rest and begins to pull herself up. Her shoes are so loose on her that I'm sure she won't make it three feet without falling over herself.

"You're such an ass," she mutters under her breath as she pulls on my coat and wraps it around her body tighter. Folding her arms across her stomach, she walks a couple feet forward, and buckles like a damn deer.

I shoot my hand out and wrap it under her arm, catching her so she doesn't fall face-first onto the polished concrete floor, and pull her close to me. Close enough to smell her citrus and vanilla scents. It's as intoxicating as ever. "Now, would an *ass* save you from falling on your face?"

She huffs, blowing the short blonde hair out of her face. The blonde looks good on her, but there's nothing like her natural dark locks.

She eyes me as if she's trying to read my expression. Too bad for her I've mastered keeping my face void of emotion. I run my fingers through the short locks that frame her heart-shaped face and flip it up at the ends. It's a gentle gesture. One someone might think may lead to something more.

A kiss.

Something heartfelt.

Something romantic.

But that's not what this is, so I simply release her, shut the car door, and stalk inside.

33

LUXTYN

Matteo leaves me at his car, not even glancing back to see if I'm following him. He's really starting to piss me off now.

Back at the club I felt bad. No, I felt horrible. I didn't think I'd care, but I did. He was mad. He's *still* mad, and rightfully so. I went behind his back and showed up at the place he specifically told me not to go to. And then he found me dancing on stage . . . I know it looked bad.

But now that I've had this forty-minute car ride to think about it, I'm pissed. I'm pissed at his reaction, how he's being an asshole, and that he thinks he can boss me around like a damn child. So now I don't care how he feels, because if he's going to be a dick, then I'll give it right back to him.

Glancing down at my heels, I rip them off with little effort thanks to them being a size too big. And this wig. It's officially making me want to scratch my scalp off. After pulling the bobby pins holding it in place loose, I rip the wig off, and my hair falls in disarray around my shoulders as I stomp toward Matteo.

I walk into what looks to be a large mudroom and notice he didn't even have the decency to wait for me here.

Screw him.

As I make my way through the house, I head down an empty hallway that's dimly lit up by wall sconces. Rounding the corner, I find myself in what seems to be a living room. I can already tell that the house is decorated similarly to his penthouse. Marble flooring, ivory furniture, dark walls, and gold accents. This must be the other house Matteo has. His *home.*

Pictures hanging on the wall grab my attention. The dim lighting makes it difficult to see, but I walk up to them anyway. There's one of three young kids, two boys and one girl: Matteo, Enzo, and Izzy.

Then there's one of the three looking a few years younger than they do now, with an older man and woman. *That must be their parents.* The last picture hanging on the wall looks to be of the same older man and woman on their wedding day.

"Did you get lost?" Matteo startles me, causing me to jump back.

I bring my hand up to my chest and turn to face him. "What the hell, Matteo?"

"I believe I should be directing that question to you."

"Look, I get you're angry—"

"Angry." He releases a devilish laugh. "That doesn't even begin to describe my state of mind, Luxtyn."

He walks away, so I run to catch up with him because he's not getting the last word here. He wants a fight, I'll give him a fight.

I follow him into the kitchen, the dimmed recessed lighting not providing much. He walks around the island and pours himself a glass of what looks to be whiskey. Picking it up, he shoots down the amber liquid before setting it back on the counter and pouring himself another.

"What are we doing here, Matteo?" I ask, my voice impatient.

His nostrils flare and his jaw tics. "Do you have any idea how stupid it was of you to show up to that strip club tonight?" He takes the contents of the glass down again. "You could've gotten us all killed."

"No one knows who I am, and even if they did, I had a disguise on."

He lets out a scoff. "A disguise? That stupid fucking wig you finally decided to take off and some makeup? Please." He pours himself another drink.

I raise a brow at him. "Drinking your feelings now, are we?"

He snaps his predatory gaze up to mine and sets the whiskey bottle down before slowly stalking his way around the island. "Do you know what it was like for me to see you up there on that stage, dancing for those fucking men?"

He runs the tips of his fingers along the countertop as he makes his way toward me. With each step he takes, my heart skips a beat. "If it weren't for having to find your mother, I would've taken my gun and shot the eyes out of each and every one of those men for seeing what belongs to *me*," he seethes.

"Relax, Matteo. I was wearing a bra and underwear. My body was covered." *The important parts.*

He lets out another dark laugh, chilling the blood that courses through my veins. Rounding the corner of the island, he stops directly in front of me. He rakes his eyes over my cleavage, which I didn't realize is now proudly on display as his jacket hangs open.

"You have no idea what seeing you up there did to me," he whispers. "I wanted to punish you for putting yourself in a dangerous fucking situation like that." He looks back and forth between my eyes. "But I also wanted to rip you off that stage and fuck you until you were screaming out my name over and over again."

His words send a current of electricity straight to my core, zapping my spine straight. I hate that I can be so irritated with him, but then he says those words to me and he has me hooked.

He moves around me, forcing me to lean back against the counter while he places a hand on each side of me, boxing me in. "Does that turn you on, Little Lux? Are you thinking about me fucking you raw until you can't take it anymore?"

That jolt finds its way back to my core, making me clench my thighs.

He chuckles deeply. "I can see it in your eyes," he says as he draws a finger down my chest, sending waves of heat through me. "The way they shine so bright when I mention fucking you. The way your body reacts to even my simplest touch." He trails his finger over the fabric that's covering my nipple, and it hardens as he swirls his finger around it.

"Fuck you," I grind out, hoping my voice comes out stronger than I feel, because the truth is, Matteo knows just how to play me. To make me bend at his will. And I hate that I love it.

"That's the plan, baby. You wanted to know why I brought you here? Privacy. Because when I make you scream out my name at the top of your lungs, I'm the only one allowed to hear it," he growls out before slamming his mouth on mine. I part my lips, welcoming him in, which he takes advantage of as he thrusts his tongue into my mouth.

Leaning into him, he wraps his hand around my waist with one hand while kneading my breast with the other. He pulls his mouth from mine and speaks through shallow breaths. "I'm going to make you regret disobeying me, Little Lux."

"Whatever, Teo. Just do something already," I pant out like a desperate bitch in heat. Wrapping my hands around his neck,

I pull him back down and kiss him with so much fervor I struggle to keep track of what's going on.

He tugs the cup of my bra down and pinches my nipple. It's hard, punishing, and I welcome it. Arching my back, I moan into his mouth, needing him to do more.

He rips his mouth from mine again and trails feverish kisses down to my breast before swirling his tongue around my nipple. He teases it while I run my hands through his hair, tugging at the soft waves.

"These tits, Little Lux. You've been hiding them from me for far too long," he growls. Teasing me with the heat of his tongue, he bites down. Hard. I cry out, not in pain, but in pleasure.

Matteo wraps his hands around my waist, then hoists me up onto the counter and pushes on my chest until I'm lying back onto the marble surface. I gasp at the cold countertop against my heated skin, but it doesn't take long for me to adjust.

Standing between my legs, Matteo runs his gaze over my body, taking in every inch of me. "You're so fucking gorgeous, Little Lux."

"Is it safe to say you're not mad at me anymore?"

The gleam in his eyes brightens as he snaps them up to mine, and a devilish grin plays out on his face. "We haven't gotten to the punishment yet, baby."

He tugs on my legs, bringing me closer to him before yanking my underwear off and propping my feet on the edge of the countertop, making sure to keep my legs spread.

A groan escapes his lips as he narrows in on my pussy. "Fucking perfect," he says before kneeling before me and biting the inside of my thigh. I cry out as he runs his tongue over the shallow puncture before moving closer to the part of me that needs him the most.

He's teasing me as he licks and nibbles on my inner thighs before finally moving to the one spot begging to have him. "Look at you, Lux. You're already dripping for me. Who would've thought a little punishment could make you this fucking wet."

"Please, Teo," I breathe out before he slides his tongue over my entrance, which causes me to make a sound I don't think I've ever made before.

He moans into me, the vibration almost too much. "So fucking delicious. Just as sweet as I remember." He trails his tongue up my pussy again before pushing it into my entrance.

Arching my back, I welcome the sensation. *He's going to drive me crazy with that mouth of his.*

Sliding his tongue up to my clit, he sucks on it, making me whimper. "Ahh, fuck, Teo."

He swirls his tongue, applying a perfect amount of pressure before sliding his finger into me. My body welcomes him and begs for more as I clench around him. He gives me exactly what I want, adding another finger. The sensation has me going wild for him, and I know I won't last much longer.

I play with my nipples, rubbing the razor-sharp buds before pinching them hard. The combination of me playing with my tits while Matteo sucks on my clit and thrusts his fingers in and out of me at an inordinate speed has me arching my back, so close to coming.

He twists his fingers and hooks them, hitting the spot he kept hitting in the dressing room earlier today, and just when I'm about to lose all control, he stops and releases his mouth from me. I groan when my orgasm starts to fade.

Propping myself up on my elbows, I stare down at him planted between my legs. "What the hell, Matteo?" I snap.

He lets out a dark chuckle before leaning into my pussy and starting up again, thrusting his fingers in and out of me faster this time. He holds my gaze as he clamps down on my clit and sucks hard, never losing focus, even as I squirm beneath him.

As I start to lose control again, he presses onto my stomach, keeping me from sliding out from underneath him. “I’m almost there,” I pant out through labored breaths, doing my best to remain balanced on my elbows.

Matteo increases the intensity and friction, and just when I’m about to explode, he pulls his fingers out and releases my clit once more. A cry escapes my lips but not in pleasure.

He stands and gives me a smirk before sucking his shiny fingers clean with a moan of approval. The sight nearly does me in. I try to catch my breath as I glare at him. “What the hell is wrong with you?”

He chuckles and says, “You didn’t think I was going to let you come that easily, did you?” Placing his hands on the edge of the counter, he leans in. “This is your punishment, Little Lux. But don’t worry, I’ll let you come eventually, and when I do, you’ll be begging me for more.” He runs his fingers up the side of my leg, causing goose bumps in their wake.

“And when that happens, I’m going to keep making you come so fucking hard and all fucking night, that you’ll beg me to stop.” His gaze darkens. “And when that happens, there’s not a chance in hell I will.”

I should hate what he’s doing to me, but I’m turned on by his words. He’s using sex against me. Punishing me for what I did earlier. And God help me, I’m going to let him.

34

MATTEO

I lift Lux off the counter and slide my coat off her shoulders. She wraps her legs around my waist, so I grip her round ass in one hand while unclasping her bra with the other, then drop it to the floor.

Watching her play with her perky tits as I ate her fucking delectable pussy had my dick throbbing to the point of pain, but the sight of her lying spread out on my counter in only her bra and my jacket was enough to distract me from that discomfort. Now as I walk us through my house to my room while trailing kisses along her jaw and neck, I'm beginning to question if this is her punishment or mine.

Laying her down on my bed, I crawl over her, and she desperately reaches for me. "You're so fucking needy for me, aren't you, baby?"

"Yes," she whimpers as she arches her back, pressing her chest into me. I take advantage and pull her taut nipple into my mouth, tugging before doing the same to the other. A little pain gets my girl going, so a little pain is what she'll get.

Running her hands down my chest, she breathes out, "I

want this off." She starts unbuttoning my shirt. "I want everything off."

Standing up, I shed my shirt and undo my pants before sliding them down my legs, discarding my boxers with them.

"This what you need, baby?" I ask, and her eyes light up as she slides her gaze down my body, pausing on my cock that's standing to attention for her. She nods and licks her lips, and I swear I get impossibly harder.

Flipping on her stomach, she repositions herself on the bed so she's directly in front of me. The warm heat of her breaths caresses the tip of my dick. Grabbing a hold of the back of my thighs, she pulls me toward her, and I swear I almost pass out in anticipation of what she's about to do.

She glances up at me with those big brown eyes and smiles a mischievous grin like she knows exactly what she's doing to me.

She wraps her velvety fingers over my length, and I grunt when my dick twitches from the contact. Moving her full attention back to my dick, she slides her tongue out and licks the glistening bead right off the tip.

"Mmm," she hums out, licking her lips as she glances back up at me before running her tongue along the bottom of my shaft from the base up to the top. A loud groan escapes my lips as I tip my head back at the sight.

Fuck me.

She takes me in her mouth, using her hand at the base to assist. She starts slowly at first, working her way into it, and it's not long before she's bobbing her head in sync with her hand. The sight is fucking incredible.

I wrap my hand in her long hair and help guide her deeper onto my dick. "Look at you, Lux. Taking my cock like a good girl."

She hums a pleasurable response. "You like me calling you a

good girl, don't you, baby?" Her reply is muffled as she takes me deep in her throat, but I know it was a yes.

Her hand moves from the base of my dick to my balls, and she cups them. "Oh, *fuck*," I say as the jolt of ecstasy runs through my heated veins. She uses her other hand to brace herself on the edge of the bed as I control her head, moving faster and causing her to choke on me. "If only you could see yourself right now. You're fucking perfect."

Her lying before me butt ass naked, bobbing her head up and down on my cock while she plays with my balls has me so close to exploding. Too fucking close. The tingling sensation starts in my balls, but this is not how I'm going to come.

I stop Lux, pulling her up to her knees, causing her to cry out in protest. "We'll save you sucking down every drop of me for another time. Right now, I need to be inside you."

Slamming my lips on hers, we go at each other like wild animals impossible to tame. I push her down onto the bed as I climb over her, our lips never leaving each other's.

"I need you, Teo. I need to feel you inside of me."

Reaching down, I grab my throbbing cock and guide it toward her entrance.

"Wait," she says, placing her hands on my chest. "Condom."

"Fuck no," I growl out, and her eyes widen. I let out a breath, already knowing her concern. "When're you expecting your period next?"

Furrowing her brow, she thinks about it for a few seconds before answering. "In a few days. Why?"

"They're regular, I'm assuming?"

"Yes?"

"Then the chances of you getting pregnant tonight are slim." I slide my tip up and down her slit, soaking it in her juices before lining it back up with her entrance.

Before I'm able to push it in, she presses on my chest again. "*Slim* means there's still a chance. And how do you know about a woman's cycle? They *can* be unpredictable, you know."

I let out a chuckle. "If you think I'm going to wear a condom while I fuck my wife, you're sorely mistaken. There will be no barrier between us. Ever, Lux."

There's a twinkle in her eye at my words, and I can tell they're turning her on. I don't give her time to answer because, to be honest, there's nothing she could say that would deter me from doing what I'm about to do.

I push myself into her, and she cries out at the sensation. "You're so fucking tight, Lux." I give her a minute to adjust to my size before I push into her farther, but she freezes and her nails bite into my chest.

Gazing into her eyes, realization dawns on me. "Fuck, you're not a virgin, are you?" That idea never crossed my mind before, but the way she's reacting has me thinking twice now. How could I not consider this before?

She widens her eyes before shaking her head. "No. I just . . . I haven't had *a lot* of sex, and the only orgasms I've had have been self-induced." Her admission does something strange to me. Having sex with a virgin has always been unappealing. I'm not here to show anyone the ropes on how to have a good fuck. But knowing Lux has had sex with other guys before me leaves a bitter taste in my mouth.

"I'm going to need names later," I mutter.

Her brows draw inward. "Excuse me?"

"Names. I'm going to need names of the men you've been with." So I can fucking get rid of them. I will not allow anyone who's been inside my wife to live on this earth.

She rolls her eyes, but before she can argue with me, I silence her with a kiss, not wanting to hear about her previous fucks right now, but happy to know I'm the only one who'll ever make her feel this good. Those fucking guys couldn't even make my girl come.

"I'm going to make you forget about those fucking guys," I say. "But I need you to relax, baby. Take a deep breath and open up for me."

She does just as she's told, taking a deep breath in before exhaling it.

I slide into her another few inches as she releases that long breath. Her walls hug me like we're made for each other. She's perfect. So perfect I've about lost my sense of why I was mad at her.

The tension in her body leaves as she lets out another deep breath, so I take the opportunity to push into her even further. She moans out as she presses her head back into the pillow.

"That's my girl. See what happens when you listen to me?" I thrust in and out of her as she closes her eyes and presses her head into her pillow. "Good girls who listen get to come, Lux. Are you a good girl?"

"Yes," she cries out as she raises her hips to meet mine.

"You sure about that?" I ask as I thrust into her a little harder. Going into Lux raw is the best damn feeling ever. It's something I'll never get sick of. Hell, it's a feeling I'm already becoming addicted to.

She snaps her eyes open, finding mine, and swallows hard. "Yes, Teo," she breathes out. "Please. Just fuck me. Fuck me like I've never been fucked before."

Her words nearly make me lose control, but I don't. I pull out, just leaving the tip inside of her, and hold myself there for a few moments as she whimpers at the loss of me.

"What're you doing?" she asks as she hooks her leg around me and presses her foot down on my ass in hopes of getting me to push back into her. I don't, though.

"Are you going to start listening to me, Little Lux?"

"Yes, Teo, I'll start listening to you." She presses her foot down on my ass again, but I remain hovering just above her pussy. She lets out a frustrated sigh. "I know I messed up tonight, but I promise. I won't do it again. Just please," she begs as she presses her foot harder on my ass. "Fuck me. I need to feel you slam into me over and over."

That does me in, so I push into her, and she cries out, "Oh gosh," throwing her head back into the pillow. I repeat the motion over and over again, getting harder with each thrust. Taking a nipple into my mouth, I suck on it, running my tongue over the tight skin before moving my attention to the other one and doing the same.

Lux drags her nails up my back before settling them in my hair and pulling at my strands. The sensation sends a shiver down my spine as I continue pounding into her.

I can tell she's close, as her walls tighten around me, so I reach down, knowing what will put her over the edge. But before I give her what she wants, there's one more thing I need from her. "Open your eyes." I slow my thrusts.

Lux opens her eyes and takes a few seconds to focus on me. She's so damn pretty with her flushed cheeks and swollen parted lips. Her dark hair fanned against my white sheets makes her fucking perfect.

"I want to hear you say you're mine," I say as I continue my languid thrusts in and out of her.

"W-what are you talking about?"

I stop my movements and brush a lock of hair out of her face. "Those men saw what was mine tonight. I need to know you're not going to do that again unless you want to be responsible for the deaths of every single person who sees you like that. You're mine, Little Lux. You have been since the day I laid eyes on you. You understand?"

She nods.

"I need to hear you say it," I growl out.

"Yes, Teo. I'm yours. I'm all fucking yours."

And with that declaration, I push back into her and find her clit, rubbing circles with the pad of my thumb. It doesn't take long for the combination of sensations to push her over the edge, causing her to cry out my name. The sound of my name on her lips has my balls drawing up and my dick stiffening inside her, and I grunt out a slew of expletives as I pump her full of everything I have.

My thrusts slow to a stop after we ride out our orgasms together. Taking Lux with me, I roll onto my side so I'm not crushing her with my weight. The move is so quick I manage to remain inside of her in the process.

She stares up at me with longing eyes. "I feel like I should be upset with you for how many times you wouldn't let me come earlier. But that . . . that was amazing."

I let out a soft chuckle before giving her a deep kiss on her lips. "You can be mad at me all you want. That just means I'll have to make it up to you all night."

Raising a brow at me, she asks, "All night?"

"*All* night."

"I thought those were just words earlier."

"Oh, you have no idea what you've gotten yourself into, baby. I never make a promise I can't keep."

35

LUXTYN

I learned last night that Matteo is definitely a man of his word. He spent all night reminding me never to doubt him again as he proved himself in every position you can think of: doggy style, cowgirl, *reverse* cowgirl, up against the shower wall, bent over the side of the bed. And just as he said I would, I begged him for more every time.

I'm stretching in bed with Matteo still curled around me when he speaks. "I was wondering when you'd wake up," he mumbles, the sleep still present in his voice as he trails his hand down my bare stomach.

Placing my hand on his, I stop him. "What do you think you're doing?"

He grumbles a low laugh in my ear. "Was last night too much for you, Little Lux?"

"How was it *not* enough for you?" I ask, sincerely shocked at this man's libido. He's seven years older, and *I'm* the one who can't keep up with *him*.

"You drive me crazy." His tone is rough. Needy. "I just want to be inside you twenty-four seven."

"Yeah, well, not today. Maybe not for a few days. I can barely move, my body's so sore. And my vagina?" I let out a humorous scoff. "It feels like it's on fire." I tense up at the joke I made because the realization of the lack of protection we used last night dawns on me. "Oh my gosh."

Matteo freezes. "What?"

"We didn't use *any* protection last night." How could I be so stupid? I remember talking about it, but then I got carried away and . . . *shit*.

Matteo immediately relaxes behind me. "Oh, that's it?"

I roll around in his arms to face him but not without letting out a groan at my aching muscles. "What do you mean, *that's it*? Are you not concerned about that?"

Matteo's eyes remain closed as he lies there with his head on the pillow. "I already told you last night that I'm never going to wear a condom with you."

I jab his chest with my finger. "Matteo, getting pregnant is a real thing. Not to mention STDs. We haven't even had that conversation yet."

Matteo's eyes snap open. "First of all, I like when you call me Teo, so moving forward, that's the only name of mine that I want to hear off your lips. Secondly, you're not going to get pregnant, and even if you do, you're my wife. Having children is inevitable, and if it's sooner rather than later, so be it."

My mouth falls open, and I'm about to tell him I'm not ready to have children, but he continues. "And thirdly, I do *not* have any STDs. I *always* wrapped it up, and I also had Doc draw my blood and run tests on me the night you stabbed me to make sure I was clean." He looks proud as he says that. "And I haven't had sex with anyone else since I met you."

How efficient of him.

"Okay, so what about me? You don't know the guys I had sex with. What if one of them gave me something?"

His expression darkens. "Never speak about having sex with any other man but me again," he growls out. "And I already know you're clean. I had Doc do a full panel test on you when he did your DNA test."

I blink at him. "Why am I not surprised?"

"You didn't think I wouldn't be prepared, did you?"

I roll my eyes and shake my head at how over the top this man can be. "On a serious note, though. This whole baby thing? I'm not ready for that, so I think I should look into some birth control. The pill or something."

My mom talked to me about the pill when I turned sixteen. Since I wasn't having sex, I never went on it, and since I had only had sex a few times before last night, it's just not something I ever bothered myself with. But becoming pregnant in the near future gives me anxiety. I'm not ready for all of that.

He must see the seriousness in my expression and hear it in my tone because he slides his hand under my chin, tilting it up, and says, "I'll schedule an appointment with Doc for you."

"Um, okay?"

"Why are you posing that as a question?"

I think about that for a second before answering. "I don't know. I guess I'm just surprised at how easy of a conversation that was."

Teo laughs and pulls me closer to his chest. I snuggle into him and wrap my leg around his, entangling our bodies together. He places his chin atop my head, and it all feels so . . . comfortable. Normal. Like this is where I'm supposed to be.

We lie here together quietly until our breaths become in sync with one another before it dawns on me that I have to pop this perfect, invisible bubble I've put us in. Pulling myself back, I find Teo's gaze. "So were you able to find anything out about my mom last night?"

My heart beats erratically, like I'm about to have a panic

attack as I wait for his answer. "I did," he says. His tone gives me nothing on what to expect. "Mauricio doesn't know when to shut-up once he's started speaking. The stripper barely had to do any work."

I stare at him expectantly, waiting for him to continue, and when he doesn't, I decide to mess with him. "We prefer being called *dancers*, Teo." He grows still and his eyes narrow in on mine. I shove at his chest. "Hey, I'm just kidding."

Grabbing my hand, he holds it to his chest right above his heart. The thumping of the organ seems to have picked up pace. "You might be kidding, but you should know I was *not* kidding when I told you last night that I'll kill any man that sees you like that again."

"I know. And I'm sorry about last night. I don't think I ever actually said those words to you. I didn't mean to upset you."

Cocking a brow, he looks at me as if he doesn't believe that last bit. "Oh, you had no idea I'd be upset about you stripping?"

I roll my eyes. "Okay, fine. So I knew if you caught me that you'd be upset, but I was pissed at you, so I didn't really care about that at that moment. I just wanted to help find my mom and it felt like you were keeping me from doing that." My voice gets soft because I did just want to help find my mom. "It felt unfair."

Matteo's face softens as if he finally understands where I'm coming from. It's crazy how quickly it's changed from this being his world and me just living in it, to what it is now. I'm not an expert, but this feels like a real relationship. A real marriage. Talking through things. Understanding one another. Yes, we had a hiccup with the strip club last night, but that also led to the most amazing sex of my entire life. And I want to say he felt the same way. It's like we've had a breakthrough in this *business transaction*.

Brushing a strand of hair behind my ear, he says, "It wasn't my intention to make you feel that way. I was trying to protect you. Being around those men is unsafe, and I won't risk anything when it comes to you."

"I know, and now that I've had some time to think about it, I realize it was an impulsive move." I chuckle to myself. "I mean I didn't even get any information out of those Silvestri guys. My plan was . . . not very well thought out."

"It definitely was not. But fortunately for you, mine was."

My eyes light up. "Did you find my mom? Do they have her? Where is she?" My questions come out in rapid fire. Not a beat separating them.

"Woah, woah, woah. Hold on. No, I have not found her yet, but I'm almost certain Silvestri didn't take her."

My brows crinkle. "What does that mean? If they don't have her, then who does? What did Mauricio say?"

"The stripper was doing her thing and Mauricio was drunk. She got him talking about what he does and asked him if he ever kidnaps people. Pretending like it was some turn-on for her. He confirmed that he does, but he hasn't done so in a while. I signaled to her to keep going and when she asked if he's ever had to kidnap a woman before, he had a look of confusion on his face and asked her what woman he would need to kidnap."

"Oh . . . okay. And you believe him?"

Nodding slowly, he says, "I do. But it's not adding up." He stares off in space over my head. "Nothing about this is adding up."

I let out a long sigh. "So now what?" I ask, feeling helpless. I don't know what to do, and I'm losing faith that we'll ever find her. And that's killing me.

"Hey," he says, pulling my attention back to him. "I'm going to call your father and see if he has any leads, okay? I'm going to work with him on finding her. I have to go into the city, but Enzo and Isabella are on their way here from the penthouse. Enzo needs to come with me, but there's plenty of security here already. I figured you and Isabella can hang out, even though I'm beginning to think you're a bad influence on each other."

That tugs a small laugh out of me, which I think was his intention. Reaching up, I wrap my hand around the back of his neck and bring him down to me, placing a light peck on his lips. "Thank you, Teo. I don't know what I would do without you."

"Don't thank me yet. Not until we have you and your mother reunited, which *will* happen." Teo's optimistic attitude is the only thing holding me together. The only thing keeping me grounded and from losing my mind. He'll never understand how much that means to me.

With a small nod, I trace my fingers along his chest tattoos, then notice small writing right above his heart. It's almost as if the tattoo artist had to find it a home among the other intricate ink. The words say *Mother* and *Father* in beautiful calligraphy and are stacked on top of each other with a date from three years ago separating the two.

I've been so worried about my mom that I haven't talked to Teo about his parents. *What the hell is wrong with me?* It's something I've been wondering about ever since he dropped that information at Angelo's house the other night.

He must see the question written all over my face because he says, "Go ahead. Ask me."

I bring my gaze up to meet his as I struggle to ask. "Y-your parents. What happened to them?" I whisper, nervous to hear his answer.

Teo swallows deeply before responding. "They were killed by Giuseppe Silvestri." His words slice through me as I let out a gasp.

"He asked my father to partner with him, so he could have access to his port. Silvestri was already using your father's port, but having access to more ports gives him more income and power."

Teo swallows deeply once more, and his eyes go sullen. "When my father denied him access, Silvestri decided to make an example by having them both killed. He had some guys dump their bodies about a half a mile outside our security gates."

Teo's jaw clenches repeatedly as he struggles with reliving the nightmare of his parents' murders. Cupping his cheek, I brush my thumb along his jawline, and he relaxes.

"I'm so sorry, Teo. You don't have to tell me any more."

"No, I want to. I need to get this out." He clears his throat as I bring my hand back down to his chest. "Enzo and I were the ones that found them. We were on our way back to the house. Those bastards left my parents lying on the ground with bullet holes right in the center of their heads and a note that said, *This is what happens when I'm denied what I want.* I knew immediately it was from Silvestri because the cocky son of a bitch had his family crest on the note. He wanted me to know, so that I wouldn't make the same mistake my father did."

The unshed tears stinging my eyes threaten to spill over at the pain in Teo's voice.

His eyes darken and his expression hardens. "So the reason I want to control your father's port is because I want to dismantle Silvestri's main source of income. I want to take it all away from him until the Silvestri name means nothing anymore. And then when that happens, I'm going to fucking kill him. I want him to go down knowing there will be nothing left of his name. Nothing of his family. His legacy will be void at that point."

His menacing tone should scare me, but it doesn't. Knowing he'll kill someone should scare me, but it doesn't.

"And you haven't been able to carry out your plan because of me," I whisper, staring at the tattoo he got for his parents. He was so adamant about taking over Angelo's port when he married me, but my own problems have overshadowed avenging his parents' deaths.

Placing a finger under my chin, Teo lifts my face so I'm staring deep into his eyes. "Don't do that. Your mother is the priority right now. Nothing will change what happened to my parents, but I can help you not have the same fate with your mother. My revenge will come, but for now it can wait until she's back, safe and sound."

A tear runs down my cheek, but Teo swipes it with his thumb before bringing his mouth down to mine and giving me a long, sweet kiss. I don't know how we ended up the way we are this quickly, but I know with Teo by my side, my mom and I will be reunited.

36

MATTEO

After showering and getting ready to go into the city, I head out to the kitchen where Lux, Isabella, and Enzo are sitting around the island eating breakfast. "Have you given it to her yet?" I ask Enzo, who I caught in the middle of taking a bite of a blueberry scone.

He pulls the pastry from his mouth and furrows his brows. The crumbs hanging off the corner of his mouth really complete the expression. "Have I given who, what?"

"The phone, Enzo. Have you given Lux her phone back yet?"

Lux whips her head toward Enzo. "You have my phone?" she asks before stealing a glance at me. "I'm finally getting my phone back?" She hops off her stool and rounds the island, stopping in front of Enzo with her hand held out. "Can I see it, please? Maybe my mom messaged me. I need to check."

Enzo glances between Lux and me. Giving him a nod, he pulls the little black phone out from his pocket and hands it to her.

"We've made sure to keep it on and charged the entire time

we've had it. I didn't want you missing anything important," I say.

"And did I miss anything important?" Lux asks, her face deep in her phone as she goes through it.

"No. Although your boss called and left you a voicemail, asking when you'd be back. Said something about how you should've been back by now. I texted her letting her know you quit." She didn't like that Lux left her hanging, but I don't give a fuck.

"Okay," Lux says as she continues scanning her phone. Once she's determined she missed nothing important, she glances up at me with a defeated look on her face. "Nothing. Absolutely nothing. I even tried pinging her last location again and it doesn't even register anything anymore."

"I'm so sorry, Lux. My brothers will find her, though. I know they will. And I'll do anything I can do to help, too," Isabella says as she rubs Lux's back.

A tidal wave of emotions overtakes me for a few seconds at the sight of my sister comforting my wife. I want to be the one to comfort her. The only one.

Holy fuck. I'm jealous of my own damn sister.

I love that my sister and wife get along, and it's irrational for me to want to be the only one who gets to comfort Lux, but I can't help the way I feel. That's how I'm wired. What's mine is mine. I'm not going to act on it, but I can sure as hell silently seethe about it.

The disappointment is clear on Lux's face as her eyes gloss over, but before she sheds a tear, she forces them away and puts on her brave face that fools everyone but me. *I have to do something about this.*

"Enzo, let's go," I call out. I need to have a little conversation with Mancini. We've wasted too much time. We need to find her mother.

37

LUXTYN

After Teo gives me a sweet kiss goodbye, he and Enzo head for the city, leaving Izzy and me here with Rocco, who seems to have made himself scarce.

"I'm so sorry about last night," Izzy says as we continue with our pastries and coffee at the kitchen island. "I find myself saying that to you a lot. Especially in the last twenty-four hours."

"That idea was as much mine as it was yours," I say. I don't want her to feel bad. Yes, she had the idea to go to the strip club, but I went along with it, so I'm just as responsible. "Did Eddie end up getting in trouble for letting us sneak out?"

Izzy purses her lips and lets out a long whistle. "Oh yeah. Luckily for him he was just demoted, though. I still can't believe after all of the times I've snuck away from my guards, last night was the night I got caught. Granted, I've never snuck out to a place where my brothers would be."

"Demoted is lucky?" I ask.

"For sure. The Teo I know would've shot him point blank in the head." She tilts her head as she considers that statement.

"Actually, since you and I were involved, he probably would've tortured him first, and then killed him. Draw out the process just to prove a point."

My eyes widen at the visual in my head of my husband murdering someone because of me. "Um, so why doesn't he now?"

"Oh, girl, because of you, duh. My brother's usually wound up a lot more. Not much keeps him from losing it, but with you," she says with a point of her finger. "With you he seems to have calmed down a little bit. He hasn't been so quick to snap. He's *slightly* more rational. No woman has ever had that effect on him. It's actually impressive."

I don't respond, but I can't help the smile that creeps on my face.

"Plus, Eddie is actually very good at his job, I just happen to be better," she adds with a shrug. "He just had Enzo rough him up a little bit and then demoted him. Might be forever or it might just be until he's proven himself to my brother again. Who knows."

Enzo roughing someone up is not something I can picture. He seems like such a teddy bear, but she says this so casually as if it's normal. How does someone get used to this life?

"So, what happened last night?" Izzy asks. "I'm assuming that things went well since you and Teo seem . . . happy." She pops a piece of her blueberry scone in her mouth.

I raise a brow at her. "Do you *really* want to know how last night went?"

She considers that question for a few seconds before shaking her head. "Yeah you're right. Don't give me details. Just answer me this. Is it safe to say he's *not* going to kill me for last night?"

I let out a giggle. "Yes, I'd say it's safe to say you're not going to get in any trouble. I took the brunt of the . . . punishment last night for the both of us."

She eyes me cautiously at my use of the word punishment, and I giggle again.

"Oh my gosh, ew. You're blushing," she says with a point of her finger.

"I'm not blushing!"

"Yes, you are. And you're giggling. You're giggling and you're blushing, and you used the word punishment like a creep. You guys had sex, I get it. But punishment?" She makes a dramatic gagging noise before shivering. "I'm officially grossed out."

Laughing, I say, "If you didn't want to know the answer, why did you ask?"

"I have no idea. I'm nosy and you're kind of my only friend, other than Liana, so I want to talk to you about stuff like this, but I've very quickly realized I cannot. Not when my brother's involved. So, thank you Teo for ruining my breakfast *and* my friendship."

"Okay, from here on out we won't talk about me and your brother."

"I don't necessarily mind talking about you and my brother. It's just the sexual stuff I could do without."

Holding up three fingers like a Boy Scout, I say, "I promise to never speak about Teo and I's sex life ever again. Scouts honor."

She laughs at my theatrics. "Perfect. Now, what about you guys, emotionally?"

"Emotionally?" I ask as I take a bite of my bagel, pretending not to understand the question.

"Yes, like your *emotions*, Lux. As in those things that make us feel things." She pauses, but I continue to give her a blank stare, so she repeats her question in a simplified way as if I didn't understand her the first time. "How do you feel about my brother, Lux?"

I laugh awkwardly. Sex I can talk to Izzy about, even if it is her brother, but feelings? I'm suddenly uncomfortable.

"Oh, well, I, um, uh . . ."

Her hand frozen in the air, holding her scone, she furrows her brow. "You like him."

"Well, of course I like him. He's, you know, cool."

She spits out a laugh. "No, I mean you actually *like* him."

"I mean, sure. Yeah, I guess." I don't know what I'm saying. This is all coming out wrong. Of course I like Matteo, but why is it so difficult to talk to Izzy about?

"Lux, are you uncomfortable talking about your feelings with my brother because he's my brother, or . . ."

I set my bagel down on my plate and wipe my fingers on my napkin before taking a deep breath. "I'm sorry. I just have never had a friend to talk to about my feelings before. I also haven't really had feelings for a guy, like, ever before, so I'm not really sure how to explain them."

Now it's her turn to set her scone down and take a deep breath. "You've never been in a relationship before?"

"Not exactly."

"Wait a second," she says, holding out her hands. "This is going to be the only question I ask about you and my brother's sex lives, but were you a virgin before last night?"

I shake my head and offer another uncomfortable laugh. "Oh no. Not at all. I mean, I haven't had a bunch of sex, but there were a couple guys. I just never dated them or anything. It was never about that."

The tight, cracked feeling on my lips from my nervousness causes me to lick them, offering them some moisture. "My mom and I have moved around a lot, so it made forming relationships with people difficult. I would try when I was younger, but then I started realizing there was no point since I would be leaving soon and would never see them again."

"That's really sad, Lux."

Shaking my head, I brush her off before giving her a smile. "Oh, it's okay. It's not that big of a deal. It's probably why my mom and I are super close. I always had her, so I don't regret a thing about how we lived our lives."

Placing her hand on mine, Izzy says, "Well, now you have us, too. Don't forget that."

We silently finish our breakfast as I think about my feelings for Teo. We're cleaning up our dishes when I finally speak again. "To answer your question, yes. I do like Teo. Like, *really* like him."

Spinning on her heel after throwing away the trash, Izzy gives me a big smile, showcasing those perfect teeth all the DiMaggio siblings have. "I know. I can tell. I just wanted you to admit it."

I roll my eyes. After all of that, she just wanted to rub it in my face.

"You guys are good together. You're both bringing softer sides out of each other that you might've not even known you had. It's pretty cool to witness. If you ever want to talk more about those feelings of yours, I'm all ears. They can be difficult to decipher sometimes, but I think you're beginning to understand yours better than you think."

I roll my eyes again. "Alright, I think that's enough cheese for one day. Let's go watch a movie or something. I'm exhausted and I could use a chill day. Watch a rom-com or something to help keep my mind off everything."

"C'mon," she says, throwing a comforting arm around my shoulder. "I know just the movie."

38

MATTEO

Pulling up to the guard post at Mancini's estate, I roll down the window to speak to one of the burly looking men he has working. Usually I'd have Enzo drive, but since we're showing up to Mancini's unannounced, I figured I should be the one to take the brunt of this decision, should there be any repercussions. It's unheard of to show up at another don's home unannounced, but this concerns his daughter, so I don't fucking care.

"Matteo DiMaggio," the guard says as he approaches my vehicle. "I wasn't informed you'd be coming this morning."

"That's because your boss hasn't been informed either."

He lets out a dismayed grunt. "Mr. Mancini is busy today. Maybe you should call ahead next time and schedule an appointment."

"Maybe you should use that headset of yours to contact *Mr. Mancini* and let him know I'm just dying to see him." My sarcasm doesn't go unnoticed as the guard's gaze turns cold. He steps back into the guard hut, knowing he can't ignore my request.

"You think it was wise not to give Mancini a call to let him know we were heading over? What if he's not even home?" Enzo asks.

"I thought it would be more fun to surprise him. And it's early. Where else would the old man be?"

The guard speaks into his headset, and after a few more seconds, he reaches for something, and the gates in front of us slide open. I hold his stare until he finally gives me a slight nod to drive through.

Enzo chuckles in his seat next to me. "Well, that was easy."

"And you doubted me," I say with a relaxed scoff.

After parking my car right out front, Enzo and I walk up the front steps and are immediately greeted by the same butler who met Lux and me the other night. "Welcome, Mr. and Mr. DiMaggio." *That's weird to hear out loud in a sentence.* "Mr. Mancini wanted me to bring you to his study."

The butler leads us through the foyer, down the hall, and around the corner into the room I was acquainted with the last time I was here.

"He'll be with you both momentarily. Can I get either of you anything? Coffee perhaps?"

"We're okay, thank you," I say before he exits the room with a small nod.

"I could've used a coffee, Teo. Do you know how late our sister kept me up last night worried about how you'd react to seeing Lux working that pole?"

I snap my gaze to his. "Don't speak about my wife working a pole again. And if you tell me you saw her—"

Enzo holds up his hands in defense. "I didn't see shit. Lux on a pole? I don't believe it."

If rolling my eyes was something I did, I would've rolled my eyes so hard they would've gotten stuck in the back of my head. "You watched, didn't you?"

He shoves his hands in the pockets of his slacks and walks along the wall lined with bookshelves, acting as if he's looking at them. "I don't know what you're talking about. I didn't see anyone that looked like Lux on that stage."

Ignoring him, I take a seat on the couch, and Enzo comes over and drops into the spot next to me. "So, how *was* last night?" his nosy ass asks.

Leaving my gaze on the door, I keep my response short and sweet. "Fine."

He sulks into the couch. "That's all you're going to give me?"

"Were you expecting something else?'

"I saw the way you looked at her when you saw her on that stage. You were pissed."

"Of course I was fucking pissed." I finally bring my attention to his.

He holds up a finger. "You didn't let me finish. You were pissed, but also turned the fuck on. You can't tell me seeing your girl up there doing the damn thing didn't twitch that dick of yours." The gleam in his eye and that shit-eating grin on his face tell me all I need to know about what he'll say next. "So that begs the question. Was I right?"

"Right about what, Enzo?"

With a wiggle of his brows, he says, "The sex. Was it fucking amazing like I said it'd be?"

I let out a sigh and keep a blank expression on my face before turning my gaze back toward the door.

Enzo releases a deep laugh that stems from his gut. "I'll take *that* as a yes."

I shake my head.

"Man, you must *really* like Lux." *I can't deny that.* "You used to have no problem telling me about your sex life. But now," he says with another laugh. "Now I can't even get you to admit if you've fucked or not."

"We fucked. It was the best damn sex of my entire life. And yes, I do really like Lux. Any other questions I need to answer, or is this inquisition over?"

His smile broadens as he grabs my shoulder and gives it a shake. "I already knew. I just wanted you to admit it. I'm happy for you, brother."

A smile threatens to break out on my face but is quickly shoved back down when Mancini's voice sounds in the room. "I apologize for keeping you both waiting," he says as he walks in and takes a seat in the chair directly across from us. "To what do I owe this pleasure?" He peers back and forth between Enzo and me before settling on me.

"I wanted to stop by and check in with my favorite father-in-law. See if you've heard anything about Lux's mother," I say, jumping right to it. *No point in wasting time.*

He sits back in his chair, relaxed, sipping the cup of black coffee he walked in with. "I have not, unfortunately. What about you? Any new revelations?"

"No." I lie, not wanting to tell him I ended up at his strip club last night with Mauricio and the Silvestris.

Mancini narrows his eyes slightly before asking, "How's Lux? I'd like to take her out to lunch today or tomorrow."

"I'll check with her to see what her availability looks like, but I have to tell you, Mancini. She's getting more and more torn up over her mother. She's been begging me to let her help find her. I don't think she's going to want to waste her time getting lunch with you when she could be focusing on finding her."

"What does she think she's going to be able to do to help?"

"She's quite the persistent little thing. Very strong-willed.

She'll figure out something to do. Especially since she's typically home alone all day, leaving her ample time to figure something out."

I study Mancini's movements as he brings his coffee mug back up to his mouth and swallows the hot liquid. There's a slight shake in his hand as he lowers the cup back down to his lap.

"Let me see what I can find out. I might know a guy that can help."

"Great," I say before pushing myself off the couch with Enzo following. "Let's reconvene in a couple of days. See what this guy of yours turns up."

"Sure," he says as he rises from his chair. "Let me walk you both out."

"No need. Enzo and I can see ourselves out," I state as I make our way to the door. "We'll talk in a couple of days."

"Can you, please, tell Lux that I've been thinking about her?" he calls out, causing me to spin around. His gaze remains forward, so all I see is the back of his head. "That I miss her, and if she ever needs to get out of the house, she's more than welcome to come here."

"Sure." *But she won't be coming over here unless I'm with her.*

"I'd really like to get to know my daughter, Matteo, so I would appreciate your support with that. I've made mistakes in the past, but I'm trying to make up for them now."

Even though I know he can't see it, I nod before exiting the room. The sincerity in his voice has me almost feeling like I owe it to the man to help him have a relationship with his daughter, but I can't make that decision yet. There's still something off about Lux's mother's disappearance, and until I figure it out, I can't trust anyone.

Mancini's butler meets us as we round the corner and

walks us to the front door. "Mr. and Mr. DiMaggio, you both have a splendid day," he says before opening the front door and letting us out.

Once we're in the G-Wagon, out of earshot from anyone, I say, "We've planted the seed."

"Now let's see what that gets us," Enzo finishes.

39

MATTEO

Enzo and I don't get back to the house until later that afternoon. Walking inside, I hear muffled sounds coming from the TV in the living room. I make my way down the hallway and find Lux and Isabella passed out on the same couch. Leave it to girls to be in a room with multiple couches and decide to use the same one.

I glance over my wife's small frame sunken into the couch. Her dark hair practically covers her face as she sleeps. She hasn't changed since I left her this morning. Still wearing my dark-blue tee and boxer briefs. It's a damn sight to see. One I'll have seared in my brain forever. I'm tempted to throw all of her clothes out just so I can see her in my tee and boxers twenty-four seven.

Turning to Isabella, I decide to wake her up first with a few shakes. She peers up at me through heavy lids. "Hey," I say. "Why don't you and Enzo take off?"

Squinting, she glances around and stretches her arms over her head as her body adjusts to being woken up. "Why can't I just stay here? I'm comfy," she says as she tucks her hands under her head and closes her eyes again.

Lowering my voice, I lean in so only she can hear my threat. "You can stay, but I can't guarantee you'll like what you hear."

Her eyes snap open and she sits up faster than I've ever seen her move before. "Dammit, Teo. That's twice now I've heard about your sex life today. Why do you have to be so gross?" Her voice is louder now, but not enough to wake up Lux, who's by far the heaviest sleeper I've ever met.

"Shh," I hiss out, holding my finger up to my mouth. "Don't wake up, Lux."

She rolls her eyes before getting up and marching around the couch. She grabs a smirking Enzo and drags him to the front door. From Enzo's facial reaction, I'm sure I wasn't as quiet as I thought with my threat. He knows exactly why I wanted them out of here.

Turning my attention back to my sleeping wife, I pull my jacket off and set it on the back of the couch before kneeling at the base of her feet. She's so damn beautiful lying there so peacefully.

I watch her for a few minutes as I flash back to the events of last night when our bodies got well acquainted with one another. The feel of her soft, delicate skin on mine. Her perky tits tracing lines on my chest. I took each chance I could to memorize every single curve of her body. The memory alone has my dick begging to be released from the constraints of my pants.

A soft whimper from Lux pulls me out of my thoughts, drawing my attention straight to her face.

She's still asleep.

She turns her head to the side, which moves her hair from out of her face as she snuggles into the pillow, and moans out, "Teo . . ."

Well, I'll be damned. My Little Lux is dreaming about me.

The sound of my name on her lips has my cock twitching against the zipper of my pants, and now that I know she's dreaming of me . . . *Fuck.*

Leaning over, I slide my hand up her bare leg. She leans into it, but she's still very much asleep. Keeping my movements quick but subtle, I slide my boxers down her legs, with only a slight stir from her, showcasing that beautiful bare pussy of hers.

She lets out another small moan as she shifts on the cushions. I take advantage of the situation by spreading her legs and lowering myself to her.

I kiss my way up her inner thigh. I already smell her sweet arousal and can't help but let out a groan of approval as I take in the glistening sight. "That must be some dream you're having, baby," I mumble. She's sleeping, and yet she's already so wet for me. I fucking love it.

With my tongue, I glide over her entrance, teasing her to see if she'll awaken. She doesn't, so I do it again, applying more pressure this time.

"Mmm," she moans louder. *Good, she's finally waking up.*

I continue stroking her entrance with my tongue before thrusting it inside of her. *She tastes so fucking good.*

Lux stirs, closing her legs, but I place my hands on them, keeping them open. "Teo?" she calls out sleepily.

I let out a low laugh. "Is there really any question about it, baby?"

"W-what are you—*oh fuck,*" she cries out as I slide my tongue up to her clit and draw circles around it.

"Oh, Teo, *yes.*" I tease her clit more as I switch back and forth between drawing circles around it and sucking on it. "That feels so fucking good." She sinks her hands into my hair, holding me in place. "Ahh, yes. Right there."

Bringing my gaze to hers, she's already looking down at me. I shove the shirt up her body as I continue feasting on her, displaying those round tits of hers with their brown nipples already hardened to perfect points. The sight is remarkable, causing me to grind into the couch for any amount of friction.

I reach up and cradle the curve of her boobs in my hands, making sure to keep the pressure with my tongue on her clit as she begins to writhe beneath me. *She's already close.*

I roll the hardened nubs between my fingers, pinching them. "I'm so close, Teo. Keep touching me like that," she pants, her breaths becoming more erratic as I increase my speed and pressure.

She's rolling her hips into me now, keeping her movements in sync with mine as I stroke her clit with the tip of my tongue with so much vigor and force it has her crying out a few seconds later.

"Oh, *yes*. I'm coming, Teo," she screams as she arches her back, holding my head to her pussy as she rides out her orgasm. I lap up everything I can get from her as she comes down from the high.

Pulling myself up to my knees, I wipe my mouth with the back of my hand, which causes her to blush. "That was one hell of a way to wake a girl up," she says.

I drag myself up her body and plant a kiss on each of her breasts before settling in front of her face. "I can arrange to have you woken up like that all of the time, Little Lux. Having you for breakfast every single day would be a damn treat."

She glances back and forth between my eyes, a furrow in her brow. "What're you doing to me?" she whispers.

"The same thing you're doing to me." It's not a direct answer to her question, but it's enough for her to understand that what's happening between us is real. The feelings we're developing for each other are real.

She reaches up and kisses me deeply as she wraps her hands around the back of my neck and into my hair, ruffling the strands. "I want you to fuck me," she says with her lips still on mine, then she swallows the groan that escapes me. "But I'm far too sore for that."

She presses her hands into my chest, causing me to pull back, and slides out from underneath me. I follow suit, sitting up on the couch.

Lux gazes down at me and bites her bottom lip in the sexiest fucking way I've ever seen. My cock throbs so hard, you can see it trying to pitch against my slacks. She kneels on the floor in between my legs and runs her hands up my thighs. "What're you doing, Little Lux?"

"I need your dick inside of me, Teo," she says as she undoes my buckle, unbuttons my pants, and slides the zipper down. "And since my pussy's out of the question right now, I figured my mouth would be the next best thing."

I let out a grunt as she slides my pants and boxers down my legs, then pulls them off and throws them to the side. The devilish gleam in her eyes appears the second my cock springs forth. She places herself back between my legs and slides her hands over my thighs.

I grab one of the throw pillows off the couch. "Stand up for a second, baby."

She uses my knees to push herself up enough for me to slide the pillow underneath her. Settling herself back down, she gets comfortable.

"Better?" I ask.

A sly smile plays on her lips. "Who would've thought that the big tough Mafia boss who kidnapped me and forced me into marrying him would turn out to be a big ol' softie deep down," she teases.

I shake my head while a chuckle vibrates through me. "Less talk, more action, Little Lux."

Doing as she's told, she slides her fingers up my thighs. The movement is so delicate goose bumps form on my skin, and my dick gets impossibly harder. Slipping her tongue out, she moistens her lips as if she's starving for my cock in her mouth.

Leaning over me, she takes my hardened length into her hand and runs her fingers along my shaft. I let my head fall back onto the couch as the sensation consumes me, and my heart picks up pace while wondering what she'll do next.

40

LUXTYN

I trail my fingers up Teo's velvety skin as I get acclimated to it. A sparkly bead surfaces on the head of his cock and a rush of desire shoots straight to my core. Leaning over, I slowly lick his tip, marinating in the salty taste of him.

With his head resting on the back of the couch, and his arms spread out like he's the king of the world, he lets out a low groan of approval.

Bringing my attention back to the throbbing cock in my hands, I run my tongue along the thick vein on his shaft, from the bottom all the way to the top.

"Ahh," Teo hisses as he brings his head forward. "Your tongue feels so fucking good on me, baby."

I take him into my mouth, swirling my tongue around the head while keeping my hand at the base for assistance, knowing I can't take him all at once.

Lowering myself, I slowly bob up and down and attempt to take him in more each time.

"I know you can take more of me, Little Lux," Teo says as

he wraps his hands in my hair, pulling it out of my face. He peers down at me, focused on my lips wrapped around him.

"Just like you did last night when you took my cock in that tight pussy of yours, I want you to relax. Breathe through your nose, baby. Let your throat open up, so we can really see how much of me you can take."

I squeeze my legs together, as his words turn me on, and even though I came not too long ago, he's starting that build up in me all over again.

I inhale deeply through my nose before letting it out as I focus on relaxing my throat. Then I slide my mouth down his thick shaft, and his grip tightens in my hair. Putting a little more pressure on my head, he directs me farther on his cock before allowing me to pop back up. We repeat the motion a few more times.

"You're such a good fucking girl taking orders so well from me. You're almost there, baby."

I take another deep breath before sliding down his cock again, trying to relax my gag reflex even though I know it won't be possible for me to take him all at once. I move my hand to his balls and roll them, causing Teo to involuntarily thrust into me.

"*Fucking hell,* Lux. You keep doing what you're doing and I won't be able to last much longer."

The mouth on this man has me so desperate for another release that I bring my other hand down to my sensitive clit and rub slow circles on it.

Teo's gaze is fiercely on me and what I'm doing to myself. He continues guiding my head up and down his shaft while I play with his balls and myself simultaneously. The look on his face as he tries to track my movements tells me it's beginning to be too much for him. He's going to be a goner any second.

I pickup the speed on my clit, knowing Teo's going to come soon. And to be honest, the combination of knowing I'm turning him on and the friction on my most sensitive spot has me so close to falling over the edge of that cliff as well.

"Little Lux, you better unlatch yourself if you don't want me coming down that throat of yours in two seconds."

I don't respond or slow down. If anything, I increase the pace and pressure on both of us as I hollow out my mouth and swirl my tongue around him.

Matteo responds to my silent answer with a feral groan as he comes, shooting the back of my throat with everything he has. His eyes remain glued to mine, and it's only a few more seconds until I'm coming again. My moans are muffled by my husband's cock stuffed in my mouth. The logistics of the entire situation haven't computed in my head yet, and I have no idea how any of this even happened. It was all so . . . intense. Something I've never experienced before in my life.

Matteo's hand finally loosens enough in my hair where I can pull myself off him. I wipe the sides of my mouth with my finger, cleaning up any trails of him before sucking my finger into my mouth.

Leaning forward, he grabs my arms and pulls me up to him, maneuvering us so we're now lying down on the couch with his back against the cushions and me facing him.

"You keep doing what you do to me, Lux, and I'm going to end up being a fucking goner for you before you know it."

Raising a brow at him, I playfully say, "I'm pretty sure you already are."

A deep grumble stems from his chest as he pulls me into him and whispers, "You might be right about that, Little Lux. You might be right."

We lie there quietly, just holding each other for a bit, and before I know it, Matteo's breaths are evening out and his arm grows heavy around my waist as he falls asleep. It's not long after that I'm doing the same thing, finding warmth and comfort in him I've never felt in anyone before.

41

LUXTYN

I'm woken up to light circles being drawn on my back, the sensation sending a tingle straight up my spine. "Mmm, is it already morning?" I've lost all sense of time now that my sleep schedule is thrown off.

Teo grumbles out a small laugh. "It's 9:00 p.m. You've only been asleep for an hour or so."

I pull back and look at him, but not before placing a sweet kiss on his lips. The short hairs on his chin tickle mine as I pull away. "Weren't you sleeping too?"

"I was, but only for about twenty minutes. Naps aren't usually in my schedule, so my body doesn't care to have them. I'm surprised I even fell asleep in the first place."

"It's because you're just *so* comfortable around me, you can't help but relax and fall asleep in my arms," I say playfully.

"I think you're right about that," he mumbles as he takes my face in his hand and lowers his mouth to mine. His kiss is sweet and lingers on my lips after he pulls away. With my leg wrapped around his waist, I'm able to feel his cock stir at my bare entrance.

"You have no idea how badly I want to sink back into you," he murmurs as he brings his hand between us. I gasp as he cups me. He made me so sore last night fucking me raw, I'm pretty sure I'd cry out in pain if he slid into me right now. But I also want him so badly that the tears might be worth it.

"This pussy is mine," he says, not making a move to enter me with his fingers or is dick. He continues holding me, and the heat emanating off him feels so damn good. "And I love that you're reminded of that anytime you walk or sit."

His words should probably have me smacking him on his chest, but I can't help but be turned on by them. The pleasure I feel at belonging to him supersedes any pain I could ever feel. Knowing what I know now, I still wouldn't change a damn thing he did to me last night. I could walk stupid for the next week, and I wouldn't care.

My phone dings with a message, which causes me to jump because only two people have my number, and since I'm no longer an employee at Snide's Dive Bar, that could only mean . . .

My widened eyes find Teo's immediately. Pulling his hand out from between us, he sits up, helping me do the same. I grab my phone off the ottoman and close my eyes as I take a deep breath before looking at it.

A text notification from my mom has my heart sinking. My hands are shaking, and I can't seem to process what I need to do next, as my mind is racing a million miles a minute at what the message could be. My phone goes off again, indicating another text has come through, but I find myself in a frozen state. One I can't seem to get myself out of.

I stare at my phone as I grip it in my hands for I don't know how long before Teo slides his hand over mine, giving it a light squeeze. "Here, let me help," he says. The warmth in his eyes is the only thing that brings me back to reality.

My mom.

I shake my head. "No, it's okay. I-I got it."

"Are you sure?"

"Yeah, yeah, I'm sure. I just . . . panicked there for a second. I don't know what to expect when I unlock my phone, and to be honest, I'm scared. I'm scared of the unexpected."

Teo sitting so close, his leg rubbed up against mine, gives the physical support I need, and the softness in his eyes gives me the emotional support. I know that whatever is in these messages I'll get through with him next to me.

Unlocking my phone, I tap on my mom's name to bring up our message thread. My heart drops immediately as I choke out a gasp.

"Oh my gosh."

"Lux . . ." I hear Teo's concerned voice next to me, but I don't respond as I stare at the picture of my mom with her hands tied behind her back and duct tape over her mouth with a newspaper propped up against her. A bruise has formed on her cheek right under her eye, and a wave of nausea crashes into me as I read an address and time that was sent with the picture.

Another picture comes through and it's the same picture, except this time zoomed in to where the newspaper is, showing today's date before another message pops up.

She's alive now, but she won't be unless you show up tomorrow night.

My eyes sting as tears form, and I nearly drop my phone, but Teo grasps it before I do, taking it from me.

He wraps his arm around my body and places a hand on my leg. "It's going to be okay, Lux. But you need to take a deep breath," he says, trying to calm the intense breathing I hadn't even realized took over my body. His tone comes off soft but commanding. As if he's taking charge of the situation but giving me the support I need to figure this out all at once.

Teo peers over the screen with a hardened look. "Giuseppe Silvestri," he mutters.

"What?" I ask, whipping my gaze over to him.

"The address that was sent is one of Giuseppe Silvestri's newest warehouses. I know exactly where it is."

"Giuseppe Silvestri. That's who we assumed did this, right?"

"Yes," he answers, still staring at my phone as if he doesn't believe it. He rises from the couch and pulls on his boxers and pants before pulling his phone out of his pocket. "I'm going to call Enzo over."

Teo paces back and forth while on the phone with his brother. There's something unsettling about his reaction to this. He's normally so collected that nothing could throw him off kilter.

I try to pay attention to what Teo is saying to his brother, but all I can think about is that picture of my mom. Dropping my head between my legs, I take a few deep breaths before letting them out, trying to slow my racing heart and keep the tears at bay. But it does no good as a sob breaks free from my lips and I begin to shake uncontrollably.

All of my emotions hit me at once, causing me to break down as if I'm finally coming to terms with what's happened to my mom and the absolute helplessness I feel from it.

42

MATTEO

I slide my phone back into my pocket. Enzo's gathering a team before heading over here so we can come up with a plan for tomorrow night. As I stand here and watch Lux breakdown, I can't shake the feeling of needing to comfort her.

Resuming my seat back on the couch next to her, I pull her onto my lap, and she comes willingly. I wrap my arms around her and hold her to my chest as she cries.

After a few minutes, her sobs begin to lighten, but the sniffles are still there. She pulls back and peers up at me through her glazed over, bloodshot eyes that send a kick to my gut.

"I'm s-sorry," she murmurs before breaking eye contact. Her puffy eyes and broken tone nearly break my soul.

"You have nothing to be sorry for, Lux. *I'm* sorry you had to see that picture, but we're going to get her back. I promise you. I'll do whatever it takes to get your mother back."

She readjusts herself so she's straddling me. Wrapping her hands in my hair, she places a soft peck on my lips before pulling away.

I gaze into her eyes. The eyes of a fighter. She's been strong.

Too strong. Having to deal with this: her mother's kidnapping, finding her father, being forced into a marriage to a man who's from a different world than hers. It's a miracle she's been able to hold it together for as long as she has.

"The emotions that I'm feeling right now. They're too much. Please, Teo. Can you just hold me?"

"Anything you want," I say before I reposition us on the couch with her leg draped over mine and hold her as she breaks down again. Her sobs are like torture, but I do my best to be here for her.

Comforting her.

Letting her know I'll always be here no matter what.

43

MATTEO

Lux eventually fell asleep in my arms, so I moved her to our bed and left her there, knowing she needs the rest.

I walk down the hall and hear voices coming from my office. “Gentlemen,” I greet as I walk in. Everyone quiets down immediately. “I’m sure Enzo filled you all in on what’s going on,” I say as I look at four of my best men, one of them being the idiot I demoted for letting Lux and Isabella slip out while under his watch. But when it comes to men I trust and the skill set they hold, I know I’ll need him for this, even after the beating he took from Enzo. He’s lucky I told my brother to go easy on him or else he wouldn’t be here at all. Eddie was too comfortable as Isabella’s guard, so I need to get him back on his toes. This mission will do the job.

Enzo nods. “I informed them about the text that Lux received, and that we’re going to be infiltrating the Silvestris warehouse off forty-ninth tomorrow night. They’ll each lead a team of their own. We’ll make sure to have enough manpower to deal with whatever Silvestri sends our way.”

"I called you here to discuss a plan of attack. You all need to be wearing your tactical gear tomorrow night. That goes for the guys on your teams too. We need to be prepared. Silvestri sending that text means the start of a war, and I don't plan on losing any of you because of it." My men nod in unison.

"So the Silvestri's *did* kidnap her?" Enzo asks, confusion laced in his voice. *I don't blame him.*

"It seems so."

"It just doesn't make sense. None of this adds up."

I run my hand through my hair. "I know. I don't know why we haven't been able to find any evidence that points their way."

Enzo shakes his head. "So what's the plan, Boss?"

"We move forward with the evidence that we do have. We need to be smart about this," I say, giving him a knowing look.

We spend the next hour going over the blueprints I got of the warehouse and going over our plan before I dismiss my men to go round up their teams.

While they leave, Enzo hangs back. "This isn't making sense, Teo. Mauricio would've been in on this information. You and I both know that. He didn't mention a damn thing at the strip club."

"I know it doesn't, which is why we need to take precautions in case this is a setup."

I run my hands through my hair and start pacing, knowing the decision I have to make goes against everything my brother and I have been working toward. Bringing myself to a halt, my eyes settle on Enzo and by the look on his face, he already knows the next words I'm going to speak.

"I'm willing to do whatever it takes to get Lux's mother back, Enzo. Even if that means making a deal with our enemy."

44

LUXTYN

I somehow slept through the entire night, even with everything I have on my mind. I woke up to an empty bed but am informed by Izzy that Teo is with Enzo and they're figuring out a plan for tonight. By the time they get back to the house, it's already nearing 8:00 p.m.

Teo walks into the living room, where Izzy and I have spent most of the day. She tried putting on a rom-com to distract me, but all I've done is trap myself in my mind, thinking about what's going to happen tonight. The only thing that's kept me from plummeting into a dark abyss with no return, is knowing my mom is alive. Teo's assured me multiple times that he'll get her back, and it might sound crazy, but I fully trust him.

Wrapping his hand in my hair, Teo softly tilts my head back over the couch and leans down, giving me a kiss on the lips. "I see you found your clothes," he says as he pulls away.

"I did," I say with a small smile, probably the first one I've given all day. "Thank you for bringing them. Wearing your clothes was going to get old pretty quickly."

"That's a shame. I'd be happy to see you in nothing but my clothes, ever."

"What is with you men and your possessive need to see a woman wearing your baggy ass t-shirts and stuff?" Izzy asks before taking a sip of her water.

"What isn't sexy about your girl wearing your clothes with that fully fucked and satisfied look on her face?" Enzo asks as he flops himself onto the couch next to Izzy.

Izzy playfully hits her brother, but I've learned her playful hits come with a serious kick. One I wouldn't want to be on the receiving end of.

"Fuck, Izzy. Must you?" he asks, rubbing his chest where she hit him.

"Must *you*?" she rebuttals.

Ignoring them, I turn back to Teo who's still standing behind the couch. "Are you guys ready for tonight?"

"We are." His voice is calm, which helps to settle my nerves somewhat.

"When are you leaving?"

"Soon. We just stopped by to change into our gear and grab some weapons."

Weapons. Right. Because they're going to go save my mom from people who could actually kill them. My husband and my mom could die tonight.

Matteo must notice the expression change on my face because he rounds the couch to sit next to me. "You do not need to worry. My men and I have been through this type of thing before."

"You've had to rescue kidnapped victims before?"

"Yes, we have. Tactical gear is part of the territory when you do what we do. It's just a safety precaution. I promise we will be fine, and we'll get your mother out of there."

"This seems like it's all a setup. What if she's not even there and you're walking into a trap? What if Silvestri kills you? What if my mom's already dead?" My voice gets higher and more desperate as each question comes out.

"Nothing will happen to me or your mother, Lux. You have my word." He brushes some loose strands behind my ear and cups my cheek. "After tonight, you'll finally be able to put this nightmare behind you."

"But how do you know?" My voice is desperately searching for any kind of reassurance I can get.

"Because in the end I have something that Silvestri wants, and that's how I know he won't do anything to your mother. I promise, Lux. Your mother and I will both be back tonight." He drops his hand and pulls himself back before heading in the direction of our bedroom.

Teo and Enzo return a few minutes later, bodies covered in black, looking like they're part of the SWAT team. Black cargo pants, black long sleeve shirts, black gloves, and black boots. They're each carrying black helmets, and their black vests have numerous weapons, including multiple rounds of ammo for the guns they're carrying.

"Alright, we're going to get going," Teo says as he stands before me. "I won't be able to access my phone once we're in there." I nod even though I don't like that I won't know what's going on in real time. I'm not sure my anxiety can take much more, but I need to hold on just a little bit longer.

"I'm assuming you won't let me come with you?" I ask Teo even though I already know the answer to that question.

His face hardens as he stares down at me. "Absolutely not. I don't want you anywhere near that warehouse, Luxtyn." His voice is sharp, and I see the flinch in his jaw when he grinds his teeth.

Holding up my hands, I mutter, "Okay, okay. I just figured I'd throw it out there in case you need help." Deep down I know I'd be useless in this situation, but being there to help save my mom would put my mind at ease just a little bit. I had to try.

Teo gives me an incredulous look as if he can't believe those words came out of my mouth. Closing his eyes, he takes a deep breath before releasing it. Then he locks his gaze on mine, and I swear a hint of anxiety flashes in them. "Lux, please do not try to sneak out of this house. The last thing I need to do is worry about you when I'm trying to rescue your mother and keep my men and I alive. Please, just stay put."

"I know," I say, suddenly feeling ashamed for even suggesting such a dumb idea. "I know. I promise I won't leave." The last thing I want to do is be a distraction.

"*We* won't leave," Izzy says, coming up behind me and throwing her arm around my shoulder. "I know I can be a bad influence sometimes, but I promise, Teo. We will stay put. Getting Lux's mom back—getting all of you back—is what's important here, and we don't want to mess that up for you guys."

I give her a small smile, agreeing with what she said, and so thankful I have her by my side right now.

Teo lets out a sigh of relief before saying, "There's something I want to give you before we head out." He pulls a velvety black box out of one of the pockets of his cargo pants, and my heart skips a beat at the sight.

What is he doing?

He reads my widened eyes and frozen stature. "Relax. We're already married, so it can't be what you think," he says with a chuckle. "Although, you do deserve an engagement ring, so we'll be taking a trip to my jeweler once all of this is over. But that has nothing to do with this." He pops open the box and inside is a dainty silver chain with a beautiful round emerald pendant in the middle.

Izzy's arm falls from my shoulders when I move forward, the gorgeous piece of jewelry pulling me in. "Oh my gosh, Teo. What is this for?" The necklace is so simple but stunning.

"You didn't think I'd forget your birthday, did you?"

My gaze gets pulled to his, and I swear everything else in the world melts away for a second. It's just him and me, and we're in this perfect little bubble.

Pulling the necklace out of its box, Teo gestures for me to turn around. "May I?" he asks, which I silently answer by turning around and pulling my hair up so it's not in his way.

After clasping the necklace, I turn back around and glance down at the pendant, holding it in my hand. "Thank you, Teo. It's absolutely beautiful."

"Hold on a second. It's your birthday?" Izzy asks from behind me, surprise in her tone. "I can't believe I didn't know it was your birthday. Teo, why didn't you tell me? I didn't get you anything, Lux. You know what, it's okay. After this is all over, you and I are going shopping. And your mom, of course. Ooh or a spa day!"

Izzy's words come out frantic and rushed, but all I can focus on is the fact Teo knew today was my birthday and surprised me with this beautiful gift. *I* didn't even remember today was my birthday, so call me shocked when he knew after everything else he has going on.

"Yes, I like that idea." Izzy continues, mostly speaking to herself. "I think a spa day after all of this is one hundred percent necessary."

"Thank you, Teo. This is the most beautiful gift I've ever received. I don't know what to say."

He pulls me into his arms, wrapping them around my waist. I press up on my tippy toes and throw my arms around his neck while giving him a kiss. "How can I ever thank you for this? It means more than you know."

"Just promise me you'll never take it off," he whispers. He gazes into my eyes and I nod.

"I'll call you once she's out and safe in one of our vehicles," he says while backing up. "Don't worry, Lux. This is all about to come to an end. That was my promise to you, and as you've seen, I always keep my promises." With that, he turns on his heel and walks away, risking his life to rescue my mom. For me.

45

MATTEO

We pull up a few blocks away from the warehouse with over an hour to spare. The text from Lux's mother's phone might've said 10:00 p.m., but we weren't going to come in blind.

Eddie stops our car while Rocco pulls up next to us with Tito and Gianni. Lowering my window, I gesture for him to do the same. "Rocco, I want your team stationed far enough away where you have eyes on the warehouse at all times. I don't want us all going in and then we're ambushed by even more of Silvestri's men from the outside. If or when we need the extra hands, we'll call you over the mic, but make sure to keep us updated on the surroundings."

"Yes, Boss."

"If Lux's mother isn't in plain sight once we get in, I want Tito's and Gianni's teams to cover the bottom floor while I take the second floor with Enzo's and Eddie's teams."

I point to two abandoned buildings, each a block away from Silvestri's warehouse. One on the Northeast end and one on the Southwest end. Each positioned well enough to give us visuals of all four sides of the building.

"Rocco, Tito, and Gianni will take their teams to the Northeast building, and I'll take the Southwest building with Enzo's and Eddie's teams for the next hour. Keep your eyes on Silvestri's warehouse at all times. Every fucking person that enters and exits, I want to know about. You see a homeless person loitering, I want to fucking know. Understand?"

"Yes, Boss," the five of them say in unison.

"Let's do this then," I say before breaking off with our teams.

46

LUXTYN

"You need to stop pacing," Izzy says as she sits on the couch and watches me walk back and forth against the far wall. "You're going to burn a hole into the hardwood floors if you keep going at the rate you are."

I turn toward her and cross my arms in front of my chest and bring one hand up and start biting my thumbnail. "I know. I'm just so anxious and I can't think about anything other than what's going on at the warehouse right now."

Izzy jumps up from the couch and marches over to me with determination. *She actually looks like she's going to slap me.* I'm about to brace myself when she yanks my thumb out of my mouth.

"Stop biting your nails. You're going to destroy them." Weaving her arm through mine, she leads me to the couch where she pushes me down before taking a seat beside me.

"They're going to get your mom. Trust me, Lux. My brothers have had to deal with kidnappings before and they've never lost one man from it."

"Really? I guess that makes me feel a little better," I mumble.

"It should. Having grown up in this world, you get acclimated to the dark side very quickly. They're professionals."

"It's a quarter to ten," I say, glancing down at my phone. "Do you think it'll take long? What happens if thirty minutes goes by and they still haven't contacted us?" I throw my head back into the couch cushion. "Shit, I should've asked when was an appropriate amount of time to start panicking if I haven't heard back from him."

"I don't think whatever he would've told you would have helped. The panic is already full on."

My phone rings, causing my head to snap up, but I don't recognize the number. Matteo already entered the necessary numbers I need, so who could this be?

"Hello?" I answer.

"Luxtyn, it's me, Angelo."

Izzy eyes me warily. I mouth, *Angelo*, letting her know who I'm speaking to.

"Oh, hi," I say.

"I hope it's okay that your husband gave me your number."

"Oh, of course. Yes. I'm sorry. I didn't mean to come off cold, I just have a lot on my mind right now."

"Understandably so. Matteo updated me on Char. I wanted to come over and make sure you have support."

"Izzy's here, so I have support." I wince at how abrasive that comes off, realizing he might think I'm rejecting him. I need to start working on things with him because he is my dad and I want us to have a relationship. It's not something I ever thought I'd have. It's not something I ever thought I'd need. But now that I've been given the opportunity to have it, I don't want to squander it.

"But if you're already on your way over, then I could definitely use another person," I add.

I swear I can hear the smile in his voice. "I'm almost there, actually. I'll be pulling up to the gates in a couple of minutes. If you could let the guards know I'm coming, I'd appreciate it."

"Of course. Yes. I'll do just that. Um, I guess we'll see you soon, then."

"You will. Talk to you in a bit, Luxtyn."

Izzy's brows are furrowed.

"Angelo's almost here," I say. "He wants to be here for support. That's okay, right?"

"Um, yeah. I guess."

"Are you sure? If you're uncomfortable with him being here, I can just tell him I'll see him tomorrow or something."

She shakes her head and puts on a smile. "No, no. Of course he can be here. He should be here. He's your dad."

I let out a sigh. "Okay, cool, thanks. How do I tell the guards?"

"I can do that for you," she says, and pulls her phone out from her hoodie pocket. Putting her phone on speaker, she calls down to the guard post and lets them know Angelo will be arriving soon.

"Ms. DiMaggio, your brother never informed us that Angelo Mancini would be coming tonight. He specifically ordered us not to let anyone in or out," the guard on the other end says.

"That's because he didn't know. But Angelo Mancini is the don's wife's dad. You'll let him through when he shows up, please." This isn't something I've ever realized before, but Izzy can be intimidating when she wants to be. The rigid tone in her voice as she told the guard to let Angelo through was the closest I've ever seen her act like Teo. I guess the similarities between them don't just lie in their looks.

The guard on the other end pauses for a moment before caving in with a sigh. "Of course, Ms. DiMaggio. We'll call once we've let him through the gates."

"Thank you," she says before hanging up. "Sometimes being a female in this world is hard. You have to be stern. Put your foot down. Make sure they know you're not one to fuck with, because if you don't, you'll never get the respect you deserve."

"Females aren't treated with the same amount of respect as the men are?"

"Not really." Izzy shrugs. "It depends. The women in our world are typically supposed to be more submissive and obedient. I don't know if you can tell, but that's not me," she says with a small laugh. "So while my brothers are used to it and allow me to be who I am, that doesn't mean it's the same for everyone else. Sometimes you have to be domineering to prove a point. Force them to respect you. Let them know that you're not one to fuck with."

Izzy's phone rings, snapping our attentions to it. "Hello?" she answers.

"Ms. DiMaggio, Angelo Mancini has just been let through the gates. He should be arriving shortly," the guard says.

"Great, thank you so much!" she says in her bubbly voice before hanging up.

"C'mon," she says as she climbs off the couch, "let's go meet him at the door. He'll probably be there any second now."

We make our way to the front door, and just as she suspected, by the time we open it, Angelo's walking up the front steps with a smile on his face. He immediately gives me a hug, which I reciprocate before he greets Izzy with a hello.

"You really didn't have to come tonight, but I appreciate that you did," I say as we make our way into the living room.

"I wouldn't leave you to deal with this alone." He glances over to Izzy who's wearing a blank expression. I've never seen her be so . . . cold.

"Although, it seems I jumped the gun on that assumption. Looks like you already have company. You're a good friend, Isabella. I'm glad my daughter has someone like you in her life."

Izzy's gaze darts between Angelo and me. "I'm going to go grab something to drink from the kitchen. Give you two a moment alone to catch up. Do you guys want me to bring you anything back?"

"I'm okay, thank you. And I appreciate you giving Luxtyn and I a moment." He reaches out and places a hand on mine. I think it's supposed to be comforting, but something feels off about it. "I have a lot of time to make up for, so take your time in the kitchen."

The smallest twitch in Izzy's temple grabs my attention, but before I can think anymore of it, she gives Angelo a tight smile and turns on her heel to head for the kitchen, leaving the two of us alone.

The energy in the room feels strange. Unlike the other times I've been with Angelo, this is the first time I've been alone with him, and my mind blanks on what to say.

"Well, Luxtyn," Angelo says, and turns to face me. "Since I was unprepared for Isabella to be here with you, it looks like I'm going to have to take advantage of our time alone and speed up this process."

"What're you talking about?"

"You're going to have to come with me," he says, his tone unwavering and a smile still on his face.

"Come with you where?" Confusion laces my tone. "Teo asked me to stay here, so I can't just leave with you right now." I check the time on my phone and see it's a little after 10:00

p.m. "He should be calling me any minute to let me know he has my mom."

Angelo releases an amused scoff. "*Teo,*" he repeats. "That boy's lost all of his common sense since you came around. Who'd thought he'd be so easy to crack?"

I take a couple small steps back because that feeling in my gut telling me something is off is taking over.

"Stop backing away from me, Luxtyn. This can all be very easy for you. All you need to do is walk out of this house with me before your sister-in-law comes back." This time, his voice comes out harsh and the rigid lines in his face flatten as his smile thins out. Like he's changed the person he is.

I'm about to call out for Izzy but think otherwise. I don't know what Angelo wants with me, but the darkness in his tone tells me that Izzy shouldn't be here. If anything were to happen to her, I would never forgive myself.

"Don't do anything stupid, Luxtyn." Angelo holds his hand out towards me. "You're going to come with me, and you're going to keep quiet. Or else I'll kill Isabella with one shot to the head. You got it?"

His words confirm my suspicions. I slowly nod, and before I can move my hand into his, he grabs me and drags me toward the front door.

"What're you doing, Angelo?"

"Quiet," he hisses as he pulls me out the front door, down the steps, and to the trunk of his silver Bentley, popping it open. Zip ties and duct tape lie on the floorboard, and I freeze. "Now, are you going to cooperate, or do I need to use those things on you?" he asks, and nods to the trunk.

Shaking my head, I say, "No. I'll cooperate. Just, please. Don't hurt Izzy."

The frown on Angelo's face turns up into a cruel and twisted smile, and the wicked gleam in his eyes shines bright under the moonlight. "Give me your phone, and then get in the trunk, Luxtyn."

Doing as I'm told, I fumble to pull my phone from my sweatshirt pocket and hand it to him before getting into the trunk. I lie on my side and watch as he chucks my phone somewhere into the night.

"Now keep quiet. We're leaving and I can't have the guards questioning why you're coming with me. You make a sound, and I kill every single person who matters to you. Including your mother," he threatens before shutting the door, making everything go black.

47

MATTEO

We've held up in this abandoned brick building, conducting surveillance of Silvestri's warehouse for the past hour, and nothing notable has come up. A buyer showed up at 9:30 p.m., loaded his merchandise, and left with his crew, leaving Silvestri and his ten men in the building. I don't know why the fuck he would plan this when he had a buyer coming.

"Are we going in?" Enzo asks as we peer from one of the top floors of the abandoned building we've posted up in. "It's past our mark time. What's the plan?"

I let out a sigh because none of this makes sense. My gut is telling me Lux's mother isn't in there, but I have to check, for her sake. In case I'm wrong.

I'm about to give the go ahead to Enzo, but my phone vibrating in my pocket stops me. Seeing it's Isabella calling, I freeze as a dreadful feeling consumes my body. She knows this is a bad time to call me, so the only reason she would is if . . .

"Isabella?" I answer, my tone sharp, desperate to hear why she's calling.

"Teo"—her voice is frantic—"she's gone! She's gone! I don't know what happened, but she was here one minute with him and now she's gone! They're both gone!"

"Isabella, what are you talking about? Who's gone and who the fuck is *him*?"

I hear her try to control her breaths before saying the one thing I hoped she wouldn't say. "Lux and Angelo Mancini were here, and now they're not. He took her, Teo." Her voice comes through unsteady, and she sniffles as if she's been crying.

"I need you to tell me everything that happened," I order, trying to control my ragged breaths as I realize this entire thing was a fucking setup.

"Angelo came here saying he wanted to support Lux while you were rescuing her mom, but now they're gone. I called down to the guard post and they said he left about ten minutes ago and that she wasn't in the car, but she's not here. She's not here, Teo!"

"*Fuck*!" I slam my fist onto the brick windowsill of the abandoned building we've been keeping watch from for no fucking reason.

Enzo eyes me cautiously. "What's going on?"

"Isabella, I'm sending some guys to stay with you in the house, but once they're in, shut it down and don't let anyone in unless you hear from me."

"Teo—"

"Isabella, lock it down and keep it that way until I'm back."

"O-okay. Just, please find her. I'm so sorry." She hangs up, and I snap my attention to Enzo.

"Mancini took Lux."

"Fucking hell," he breathes out as we make our way toward the stairs, Eddie falling in line with us.

"Alert Rocco, Tito, and Gianni and let them know there's been a change in plans. Send some soldiers to my house to guard Izzy. The rest of them I want to follow us. I have no idea what we're walking into," I tell Enzo as I bring up my tracking app.

Enzo shouts some commands before he asks, "Where are we going?"

"We're forty fucking minutes away from where her tracker is pinging and they're going in the opposite direction as us," I say as we run toward the stairs of the abandoned building.

I focus on the area on the map, trying to figure out where Mancini could be taking her while trying not to trip down the stairs.

Rocco, Tito, and Gianni are parked out front by the time we make it down the stairs. Enzo jumps in the driver seat of our SUV while I climb into the passenger seat and Eddie slides in the back with two other soldiers.

Giving my phone to Enzo, I say, "Here. Get us to her location as fast as you can." Directing my attention to Eddie, I tell him to call Rocco and have him follow us with some of the guys while the others head back to Izzy. I stare out the window while Enzo speeds toward the highway.

We're coming for you, baby. Just hang on. I won't let anything happen to you.

48

LUXTYN

You make a sound, and I kill every single person who matters to you. Including your mother.

Angelo's threat rings through my ears as I lie here in the dark. I can tell we're on a windy gravel road, as my body bounces up and down and jolts from side to side.

He kidnapped me.

He has my mom.

And he sent Matteo to that warehouse. But for what? To get to me? None of the pieces of the puzzle are fitting together in my mind, and the realization that this entire thing has been set-up by Angelo has me sick to my stomach.

The car comes to a stop, and I hear him get out and speak to someone. Their muffled voices make it too difficult to decipher what they're saying, but I know it's another man.

The trunk door clicks, indicating it's been unlocked, and my heart picks up speed even though my body freezes.

The door swings up, displaying Angelo and another older gentleman I don't recognize. He's wearing a gray suit, and his long dark hair, peppered with strands of silver, is slicked back into a low ponytail. When I make eye contact with him, he displays a grim smile, showcasing a fake gold tooth. My stomach hollows out at the sight.

"Fausto, why don't you help her inside," Angelo orders.

"Wait," I cry out, and scramble deeper into the trunk, wanting to get as far away from these men as possible.

"Tsk, tsk, tsk. You said you were going to cooperate, Lux."

"Don't call me that," I grumble.

"You're my daughter. I should be allowed to call you by your nickname, don't you think?"

"I'm not your daughter."

Angelo lets out an unenthused sigh. "I had a feeling you'd act this way. Fausto," he snaps, and keeps his eyes coolly on mine. "Get her inside now. With force if you must. It seems she hasn't learned her manners quite yet."

Turning on his heel, Angelo stalks off. I let out a scream when Fausto wraps his calloused hands around my wrists and tightens his grip as I try to pull away from him.

"Get your hands off me," I screech while sliding my legs in front of me to kick him in the stomach before he's able to pull me out. His grip loosens and he heels over, coughing from the sharp contact.

Yanking myself free from his grasp, I try to jump out of the trunk, but he takes up the majority of space and I trip over him, falling to the ground. The jagged rocks send a sharp pain through my palms, but I ignore it as I push myself up to a stand.

I'm about to take off running but quickly plummet to the ground once more, except this time with the weight of a grown man on top of me. The side of my face slams onto the rocks, and I let out a cry as I endure the weight of Fausto on top of me.

"Lux, sweetie!" I hear a frantic cry from somewhere behind me. "Get off her!"

Sliding my face across the gravel, I lift my head as best as I can to see my mom standing on a cabin porch not too far away. Angelo's standing behind her with a gun to her side. She's wearing a dark blouse and a pair of jeans, similar to what she was wearing in the picture I received of her yesterday. Her hair hangs down in their usual loose waves that end just below her shoulders. My stomach sinks as I take in the dark shadow around her right eye and the split in her upper lip.

"Mom," I cry out. Fausto lifts himself off me but drops his knee into my spine, putting enough pressure on it to know it's a threat and to stop moving.

"If you don't get inside the cabin right this second, Lux, I will make you watch me kill your mother in one clean shot," Angelo threatens as he holds my mom against his chest. A whimper falls from her lips when he shoves the gun deeper into her rib cage.

"Fine," I grind out.

"I'm sorry, what was that?" he calls out to me.

Huffing out a breath, I repeat louder this time. "Fine, I said."

"Good. Fausto, get her up and inside the damn cabin now." Angelo pushes my mom back inside, and I swear, even from this far away, I see tears form in her eyes. I do my best to keep it together as Fausto lifts me and clamps my hands behind my back.

"I'll make you pay for that kick to the stomach, *cara mia*," Fausto threatens in my ear. I don't know what he called me, but the way the Italian words slipped off his tongue doesn't resonate well with me. It sends a disturbed shiver up my spine.

He pushes me to start walking, and I do so, making my way up the small steps, then entering the cabin. I quickly scan the room, locating my mom on the couch while Angelo stands off to the side a few feet away. Now that I can see her clearly in the light, I take in the dark circles under her eyes that have aged her since we last saw one another.

Her eyes widen as she takes me in, but before she can say anything, I throw myself down onto the couch and wrap her in a hug, squeezing her hard as if she's going to disappear again and this is the only way I can keep her here with me.

"I-I'm so s-sorry, sweetie," she chokes out between sobs.

"You have nothing to be sorry about, Mom. This isn't your fault."

She rubs my back before pulling away to look at me. Wiping the tears that I hadn't realized shed from my eyes, she narrows in on the side of my face. "Look at what he did to you," she says softly.

I lift my hand to my face and wince at the burning sensation. I suck in a breath, realizing the gravel must've pierced my skin when Fausto had my head buried in it.

"Fausto wouldn't have had to get physical had Lux cooperated," Angelo says as he takes a seat in the loveseat across from us.

I observe my surroundings to see if there's anything I can use to our advantage to get out of here.

The front door of the cabin opens up to the living room on the left and the kitchen on the right with a small circular dining room table placed directly in front of a large window that overlooks the front porch. The living room is small with only two loveseats positioned on both sides of a brown coffee table and the armchair at the head, facing the wood burning fireplace surrounded by stone. The cabin seems fully furnished, as if someone was living here.

Glancing straight ahead, my attention is pulled to picture frames hanging on the wall. There are a few of me growing up and a couple with my mom and me. The one in the center is what throws me off the most. It's a recent picture of my mom and me on a beach down in Florida, but we're not the only ones in the picture. Angelo's in the picture. It looks so real you'd have no idea it was photoshopped unless you were there.

What the hell is this place supposed to be?

Bringing my attention back to my mom, I ask, "Has he had you here this entire time?"

My mom nods.

"You said you weren't going to hurt her." She addresses Angelo who's sitting comfortably in the loveseat with one leg crossed over the other and an arm draped across the back cushion.

"It's fine, Mom."

"I need the first aid kit. Her face needs to be cleaned up. I can see specks of dirt in the cuts. It'll surely cause an infection if I don't get them out."

With a flick of his hand, Angelo directs Fausto with a silent command. He takes off down the short hallway, and it's not long before I hear him open a cabinet and ruffle through some things. We sit in silence for a few moments before Fausto returns with a first aid kit and hands it to my mom.

She opens it and sifts through the contents as I peer over, looking to see if there's anything in there of use.

"There's nothing in there that you can use against us, Lux."

Snapping my gaze to Angelo's, I give him a cold, dead look, to which he chuckles.

"I learned that lesson when your mother stabbed me with the small scissors that were in there." He lifts the sleeve of his suit jacket and points to a small mark on his forearm that looks like it's mostly healed now. "Seems like you two have that in common, huh?" His smirk delves deep into my skin and makes me want to wrap the gauze from the first aid kit around his throat and listen as he takes his last breaths.

"Why are you doing this? What was the point of kidnapping my mom and I? What is this place?"

My mom attempts to bring the alcohol wipe up to my face, but I shake her off. She sighs but retracts her hand.

"I did this for you, Lux. You and your mother, of course."

I scoff. "What the hell are you talking about, Angelo?"

"Don't you think it's about time you start calling me dad?"

I tilt my head and small lines form on my forehead as my brows shoot up while I come to the realization that this man is delusional. "You're a fucking psychopath," I spit out. His spine straightens and he squares his shoulders.

He brings himself to the edge of his seat as if he's ready to pounce. There's a cold, cunning glint in his eyes. The sinister look is a complete one-eighty from where he was. "Watch your damn language when you're speaking to me."

"Why did you do this?" I grind out, needing to have answers. "And Matteo. Why did you send him to that warehouse?"

"Matteo needs to be eliminated," Angelo says. His words are like a punch to the gut, taking away my breath. "Just as much as Giuseppe Silvestri."

"What did you do, Angelo?" My voice is barely a whisper.

"I'm tired of Giuseppe using my port. He thinks he has all of the power and control, but he needs to understand that the only reason he's been able to do all of his trafficking is because of *my* port. My port has given him the power and money he has now." He shakes his head. "But not for long."

Shifting his wrist, he glances down at his watch. "Right about now, Giuseppe shouldn't be a problem anymore. And neither should that husband of yours. Then guess who'll have full access to both ports in the city," he says, subtly glancing down to my ring finger. I subconsciously take the sleeve of my sweatshirt and cover my hand.

"Me. I'll be the one with all of the power here. The biggest player in the city."

I rack my brain as I begin to put the pieces of this fucked-up puzzle together. "So the whole point of sending Matteo to that warehouse was to have him and Giuseppe kill each other."

"Precisely. I knew Giuseppe was going to be at that warehouse because he had a weapons deal with the Russians tonight, so sending Matteo in there immediately on the offense, shooting up the place in an attempt to rescue your mother, would cause an all-out war between the two, resulting in them killing each other."

Matteo can't be dead. He's stronger than that. He's smarter than that. I refuse to believe it. He's not dead. He can't be.

"Why not just kill them yourself if you're so adamant about it? Why go through all of this hassle?"

Angelo simply sits back in his chair and crosses his leg over the other. And that's when realization dawns on me. This fucking bastard.

"Wow. Hiding away in this cabin while Giuseppe and Matteo take each other out so you can reap the benefits of both of their deaths? You're a damn coward."

Angelo's face hardens. "I'm not a coward, Luxtyn. I'm thinking smarter. Not harder. Why would I get my hands dirty if I can just let them take each other out?"

"Your hands are as dirty as they come."

"Lux, sweetie—" My mom's gentle voice comes from beside me as she places her hand on my arm.

I turn my attention to her. "No, Mom. He needs to hear what a sorry excuse of a man he is." I focus back on the slimy bastard sitting across from me. "I'll kill you if anything happens to Matteo." He waves me off as if he doesn't believe I'll do it, but that's where he's wrong. I'll end him for this. "Why did you need to create this elaborate plan? Why did you need to kidnap us both?" I have a feeling I know the answer to this question. The furnished house and the photoshopped picture are my answer, but I need this psychopath to tell me the truth.

His face softens. "I wanted to have a relationship with you, Lux. I wanted to have a relationship with you and your mother."

My mom gives my arm a light squeeze, reminding me she's right there with me.

"You claim you want a relationship with us, yet you put your hands on my mom and allow Fausto to put his on me. What the hell kind of relationship do you expect?" I spit out.

"Your mother was being disobedient. She took you away from me. She hid you from me. All because she thought the life I live is too dangerous. Don't you think that's unreasonable? A father should never be separated from his child, so she deserves the punishment she's received."

"That's enough, Angelo," my mom utters.

"You don't speak to me like that," he roars. He moves faster than my brain can process and stalks over to my mom, back-handing her across the face and splitting the cut on her lip open again.

I scream and throw myself on him, running off survival mode. After finding the slickness of his eyes with my thumbs, I press them in, and a roar tears out of him before I'm being ripped off and thrown to the floor like a rag doll.

My back slams into something sharp, and it takes me a moment to realize it's the edge of the stone fireplace hearth. I try to push myself up, but before I'm able to, there's a grip in my hair, angling my face up. My gaze is strained, but I see Angelo standing a few feet away, rubbing his eyes.

"Luxtyn," he warns. "That was not a very smart thing to

do." He blinks a few times. I didn't do much damage because I barely got to push my fingers in before I was torn off him.

Fausto pulls me up to my feet by my hair, and I wince, not knowing at this point where most of the pain on my body is emanating from. Angelo does the same to my mom, pulling her up by the strands of her hair.

"Let go of her," I grit out.

He pulls his gun from behind his back and holds it up to her temple. "Tell her the truth, Char. Tell her how you took her away from me. How you never told me about her. How you took away my chance to be her father before I even knew about her."

I flail my arms and start kicking at anything I can get my feet on. It's not until I feel a gun jammed into my ribs that I stop moving. "Keep it up, *cara mia*, and you won't like what happens next," Fausto whispers into my ear.

"Tell her, Char. Go on," Angelo barks out.

My mom's shimmering eyes roam over to mine. "I'm so sorry, sweetie."

I shake my head. "No, I'm sorry." The vision of my mom becomes blurry as tears fill my eyes.

"Angelo's r-right." She takes a deep breath. "I found out I was pregnant with you after he got engaged to another woman. I didn't tell him because I knew what it would mean. Either he'd take you from me or he'd kill us both. So I ran. I ran and never looked back. I'm so sorry," she cries out.

"This isn't your fault, Mom. You were only doing what you had to do to protect us both."

"She wasn't protecting you, Luxtyn, she was being a thief!" Angelo yells as he presses the barrel of the gun harder into her temple. She winces and attempts to pull away, but his hold on her is too firm. "And now she's going to pay for taking away over two decades of your life from me. I was hoping time would get her on my side, but she's proving to be more difficult than she's worth. But don't worry, Lux, you and I are going to be a happy family together. You'll see."

Holding my breath, I watch as Angelo goes to pull the trigger. The loud sound of a gunshot goes off before my mom and Angelo fall to the floor in a heap. Nothing but her cries echo in my ears.

It's as if I've been caught in my own terrible version of the matrix, as everything slows to a near stop. I have no idea what's going on when Fausto pulls me in front of him and moves the barrel of the gun from my ribs up to the side of my head as he frantically tries to reposition himself behind me. And that's when another gunshot goes off, then we're both falling.

I'm lying facedown on the hardwood floor with the weight of Fausto on me when I see blood drip down my shoulder.

I've been shot.

I can't feel anything. My body is frozen. Muffled voices slowly come through before I hear another loud noise. I want to move. I want to get up. But I can't. I just lie here as the blood continues to drip down, pooling on the floor beneath us.

49

MATTEO

I never should've trusted Angelo Mancini. Once a snake, always a fucking snake. The signs were there, and I overlooked them like a damn idiot. My fucking gut *told me*, but I ignored it, and now my wife is in danger.

This is all my fault.

All my fucking fault.

My mind races as situation after situation play out in my head of what we could be driving up to as Gianni speeds along the windy road, following Lux's tracker. If anything happens to my girl, I'll dismember Mancini's body limb by limb and anyone else who's touched a hair on her head. I'll fucking burn this city down for her.

I can't lose her. I fucking can't.

Enzo must feel my internal struggle from the driver's seat because he says, "We're going to get her back, Teo. You just have to hold it together a little bit longer. For her."

The strain on my heart is still there. It's painful, but I take a deep breath as I attempt to keep myself from losing my mind.

I can't lose her. I won't *fucking lose her.*

"Cut the lights," I tell Enzo as we get closer. I look over my shoulder, and Rocco turns off his lights a few moments later, following our lead.

"Pull off over there," I say, pointing to a turn-off on the road.

We jump out of the G-Wagon as Rocco comes to a stop behind us, then meet them at their car. Turning to my side, I point to the light shining a few hundred feet away. "See that light?" I ask in a hushed tone. "According to Lux's tracker, *that's* where she is. We need to get closer before I make a plan. I need to see what we're dealing with first."

I give my guys a silent gesture, and we make our way toward the light, keeping our rifles up and ready to fire at any moment. I have no idea what we're walking into, but we use the night vision mode on our scopes to scan the surrounding woods as we make our way up.

We're still a couple hundred feet away from a wooden cabin when I raise my fist, halting my men immediately. We're far enough away where the light doesn't shine on us but close enough to get a better view of what we're working with. The only car in the driveway is Mancini's silver Bentley. The trunk is still open, and it makes me wonder if that's because Lux put up a fight when she was taken out of it. My stomach churns thinking about her having to fight anyone.

I quickly scan the area, confirming no one else is in sight. There's no guard, no other vehicles, no one. Pointing, I signal to my men to flank the sides of the house while Enzo and I approach the cabin. The only noise is the crunching gravel beneath our boots.

As we approach the cabin, a scream breaks through the night air, so loud and sharp it forces me to break out into a sprint, not even thinking about anything other than my wife and needing to get to her immediately.

I can't be too late. I can't be too fucking late!

As I race up to the cabin, I get a good enough view of the inside of the house through a window, then slide to a stop. Enzo skids next to me. My heart stops, but I don't think, I just act on instinct and lift my rifle. Enzo, always being so in tune with what I'm doing, does the same thing. I locate Fausto who has his gun pointed at Lux, and Angelo with the barrel of his jammed into Lux's mother's temple.

"Fuck," I hiss out.

I can tell the tension is high in the room when Angelo jams the gun into Lux's mother's head, and that's when I make the decision.

I don't give any orders to Enzo.

I can't even breathe, let alone speak.

There's no time.

I act on instinct, and I just shoot.

The bullet slices through the window, and Angelo and Lux's mother fall to the ground. Before my brain can process anything, I aim my rifle at Fausto, who now has Lux positioned directly in front of him with a frantic look in his eye, and take my shot, knowing I wouldn't have much time to do so.

Another bullet flies through the window, and Fausto and Lux fall to the ground before I take off into another sprint, using my long legs to jump the three front steps and barrel through the door. All I hear are the muffled hollers of Enzo and my men as they follow suit.

My gaze locks in on Lux's body when I enter the cabin. She's lying still on the floor under Fausto. "Check on her mother," I tell Enzo before jumping over the small coffee table to reach Lux.

"Lux, Lux baby," I call out as I lift Fausto's dead body off her. The blood from the shot I took to his forehead ran down her shoulder and pooled on the floor beneath her. I move to her other side to get a better view of her face.

Kneeling, I brush the dark strands of hair out of her face, revealing dried blood that runs from the top of her cheekbone down to her jawline. I almost lose my mind at the sight, but when I'm met with those beautiful brown eyes of hers, the rage seems to disappear. Nothing else matters but her.

"T-Teo?" she whimpers out, and relief floods her face as her eyes widen and her lips part. It's as if she can't believe I'm standing here before her.

"I'm here, baby."

She attempts to push herself up but winces, which sets alarm bells off inside my head. I reach for her. "What hurts?" I run my hands over her body as softly as I can while trying to locate the source of her pain.

"I-I think I'm okay," she whispers, but I hear the pain in her strained voice.

She pushes herself up again, releasing small grunts with her slow movements. "Easy now," I say but am immediately caught off guard when she throws herself into my arms, and I stumble back.

I'm worried I'll hurt her, but when she tightens her grip around my neck, I cave, embracing her in what feels like the longest hug of my life. I never want to let her go, because I'm afraid she'll disappear on me again if I do.

Her body quivers and a sob breaks free from her lips. The sound seeps into my chest and wraps its way around my heart, squeezing it tightly.

"Y-you came," she cries out.

My hand finds its way into her hair as I cradle her, rocking us back and forth in subtle movements. "I'll always come for you, Little Lux. I'd go to the ends of the earth and back to find you. Never giving up until you're back in my arms," I whisper.

"I'm so fucking sorry, baby. No one will ever take you away from me again. I promise you."

Her cries lighten, then she freezes, tensing in my arms as if she's just noticed something. "Mom!" she calls out over my shoulder.

I help Lux up, and her mother rushes over to us from around the coffee table. "Oh, sweetie," she cries out, and they embrace each other, tears falling down their faces.

"Tell Doc to meet us at the house," I say to Enzo who's already on his phone, typing out a message.

"Already ahead of you, Boss. He's heading over there now."

"Are you hurt?" Luxtyn asks her mother, concern piercing through the air while she runs her hands along her body like I did with her just moments ago. "I thought you got shot. I-I thought we both got shot," she says, grabbing her shoulder where Fausto's wet blood remains.

She looks at her soiled hand with wide eyes, and I rush to her side. "It's not yours," I say, taking her hand in mine, doing my best to hide the harrowing memories. "It's from the gunshot I left in Fausto's head. You and your mother weren't shot."

Her eyes raise to mine. "You shot him?"

I nod.

Her eyes move to Mancini's dead body before quickly returning to mine. "And Angelo?"

I nod once more and study her, waiting to see what reaction she'll have to knowing how easy it is for me to kill people. I have to remember she's not from this world, and while Fausto and Mancini deserved the bullets they received, that doesn't mean she'll be okay with it.

Lux reaches up, taking my face between her soft hands. "Thank you," she breathes out. Her eyes glisten as more tears threaten to break free. "You saved me. You saved us." Leaning in, she raises herself on her tippy toes and kisses me. The sound of someone clearing their throat causes her to pull away.

"Dammit, Teo. Where are your manners?" Enzo reprimands. "Luxtyn's mom is *right* here." He tilts his head towards her. "At least introduce yourself before you maul her daughter."

Fucking Enzo.

Although, I can't say he's wrong. But the adrenaline coursing through my veins mixed with the need to feel Lux had me distracted.

Giving my attention to Lux's mother, I extend my hand to her while pulling Lux into my side. "My apologies, Ms. Stockwell. My name is Matteo DiMaggio. I wish we could've met under better circumstances, but it's an honor to finally meet you." I want to introduce myself as Lux's husband, but after everything that's happened tonight, I know the best thing would be for Lux and her mother to catch up on everything.

Lux's mother eyes me suspiciously before dropping her gaze to my left hand. She quickly shifts it to Lux's before sliding it back to mine. It's a quick and subtle movement I know Lux didn't notice. It's not something anyone would notice unless they were studying a person.

Taking my hand in hers, she smiles. It's warm, not fake. A mother's smile. "It's nice to meet you, Matteo. Please, call me Char," she says as she pulls her hand away. "I can't thank you enough for saving our lives." She rubs Lux's back in an endearing way, but it causes her to wince, and Char retracts her hand quickly.

Moving behind Lux, I lift her sweatshirt to get a look at her back, immediately spotting the root of the pain. She has a line that extends from one side of her narrow back to the other. It's about a quarter of an inch thick and is red, with the markings of a bruise already forming around it. The tender skin is broken throughout, spilling bits of blood along her pale skin. I curse under my breath, pissed off at not getting here sooner, and pull her sweatshirt back down.

"I was thrown against the edge of that stone," Lux says, pointing to the fireplace.

"You have a bruise, some swelling, and a few small lacerations." She had to have been thrown hard for it to break her skin through her sweatshirt. "Come on. We should get you both home so Doc can take a look at you two."

We exit the cabin, and the SUVs are already here. Enzo helps Char into the back of ours while I help Lux. Closing them in, I turn to my men. "Enzo and I are going to take Char and Lux back to the house so Doc can check on them. Clean this up. Save the bodies and have them sent to the family. Let them know why the fuck exactly they're dead."

Enzo walks around to the driver's side, and I hop in on the passenger side. Then we quietly make our way back to our house, doing our best to give Lux and her mother some privacy as they hold one another in the back seat.

50

LUXTYN

I wake before my mom this morning and lay in bed thinking about last night.

When we got back home, the doctor cleared us after cleaning up the cuts on our faces, the ones I had on my back, and a couple shallow ones I hadn't realized were on my palm. I'm just so thankful nothing worse happened to my mom during the time she was at that cabin.

With it being so late and the absolute exhaustion from the night, my mom and I fell asleep in one of the spare rooms. I didn't want her to be alone.

She begins to stir, and my heart tightens as I take in the purple, blue, and yellow of her bruised cheek. Snapping her eyes open, her frantic look tells me she thinks she's still in that cabin in the woods.

I reach for her hand, placing mine on top of hers. "It's okay, Mom. You're safe. I'm here."

Pulling her gaze to mine, the emotion washes over her face as she realizes where she is. "Oh, Lux, sweetie. I'm sorry."

"You have nothing to apologize for, Mom. *I'm* sorry."

She pushes herself up to a seated position, and I follow suit, sitting across from her with my legs crossed as she sits up against the tufted headboard with her legs outstretched in front of her.

We sit in silence for a few minutes before she lets out a long, drawn-out breath. "I was just trying to protect you," she says, her voice soft as she stares directly ahead. "When Angelo and I met, we were young, and I thought I was in love. When his father arranged for him and Elena to get married, he ended things with me. I voiced my dismay with Angelo, but he didn't care. It was his duty as the next don of the Mancini family to get married and complete their alliance with Elena's family."

She brings her gaze to mine. "I'd explain to you what a don is," she says before glancing around the ridiculously oversized spare bedroom we're in before landing her eyes back on mine, "but something tells me you already know."

"Mom, I—"

She places her hand on top of mine and gives it a small squeeze, silencing me. "Let me get this out about Angelo first. Then we can talk about everything else." I nod as she pulls her hand back.

"It was when I expressed how upset I was about the marriage that Angelo began to show his true colors. He was cold, not caring about my feelings one bit. That wasn't who he was before."

Tears form in her eyes. "And then I found out I was pregnant with you. It was the happiest and yet scariest moment of my life. I had no one. No family. Only a couple friends I couldn't confide in because I knew it couldn't get back to Angelo. I wasn't one hundred percent certain what he would do, but I knew his family was capable of dangerous things."

Her words tear through my heart. Knowing what she had

to endure back then, all by herself. No one to help. No one to even talk to.

"So I did the only thing I could think to do, I ran. I ran and I never looked back." She chuckles under her breath as a tear slides down her cheek before she brushes it away.

"I was worried they'd come after us. It's why I moved us around so often and kept us away from large cities. I wanted to keep you safe."

Rising up on my knees, I lean forward and give my mom a hug. My tender back yells at me for the movement, but I ignore it, knowing my mom needs me right now. "I'm so sorry, Mom. I can't begin to understand what you've gone through. I'm just so sorry."

I pull away and sit on the heels of my feet. "And thank you. Thank you for always being there for me. And for saving me before I was even born."

"I'd do everything all over again for you. I'll always protect you, sweetie." She gives my forearm a squeeze. "Even if you don't need it anymore." I take in the look in her eye and know she's talking about Teo.

"Don't think I didn't notice that ring on your finger last night." She holds up her left hand and wiggles her ring finger as she raises her eyebrows at me. I'm not sure if I should interpret it as support or not, though.

"Or the way you and Matteo embraced one another like you were each other's lifelines." I bring my gaze to hers and recognize the solemn look, then prepare myself for the hard conversation ahead. "He's in the Mafia, Lux. I don't want to see you go down a dangerous path like I did."

"Mom, Teo's not like that."

"But . . ." she continues, holding up her finger. I keep my mouth shut, not realizing she wasn't done speaking. "I know you're an adult, so I'm not going to tell you what to do. I just want to be here for you. So tell me what I've missed out on."

I spend the next fifteen minutes catching my mom up on everything that's happened. The contract, the marriage, how Teo and I started off hating each other, and how it somehow turned into something else.

"Do you love him?" she asks.

The question lingers in the air between us for a few moments as I try to figure out how to answer it. Glancing down, I fidget with the hem of my pajama bottoms before returning my gaze up to my mom who gives me a knowing look. Regardless of what she thinks, I answer her the best way I know how. "We haven't known each other for long, and I know it's going to sound nuts, but I do. I really do."

Brushing my hair back behind my ear, my mom cups my cheek, focusing on me. "Sometimes it doesn't take long for us to develop deep feelings for another person, sweetie. Especially when we're put into dire situations that force us together."

"You don't think I sound crazy?"

She pulls back from me and laughs. "Oh, no. You definitely sound crazy. But I'm here to support you in any way you need me to."

"Okay, Mom." I chuckle as I roll my eyes and change the subject. "Are you hungry? Maybe we should go get some food to eat."

"I could go for some coffee," she says, and we climb off the bed.

"Oh, these people have french presses and grind their own coffee beans here. Just wait until you try it. The coffee is far stronger than the stuff we're used to. You'll think you've been drinking dirty water your entire life."

"I do remember the coffee being better when I lived in the

city," she laughs out as she follows me through the already open bedroom door and down the hallway to the kitchen.

It's not long after I make each of us a cup of coffee that Teo comes strolling into the kitchen, dressed in a dark-blue suit and a white button-up that's top buttons are undone, showcasing that beautiful olive skin like he always does. Only he can make a different version of the same outfit look better and better every day.

He halts in his step as he rakes his eyes over me in my new silk pajama set I got when we went shopping the other day.

"Teo," I breathe out, realizing just how much I missed him last night. How I hated not waking up in his warm arms. It's insane to think I've developed these feelings for him so quickly, but I can't deny it.

My mom must notice the shift in the room because she hops off the stool at the island and picks up her coffee cup. "I think I'm going to make myself disappear for a little bit. You know how I've always enjoyed my morning coffee outside."

"Mom," I scold, snapping my attention to hers. "It's way too soon for a disappearance joke."

"Oh, sweetie, I promise I didn't mean anything by that. I didn't even realize." She holds up her hand to her chest as if she's flabbergasted herself.

"Keep making jokes like that and you'll get along great with Enzo," I mutter before pointing down the hallway. "If you go down that hall, you'll run straight into the living room. You can access the back deck from there."

Once my mom leaves the kitchen, Teo walks toward me, and I feel like there's a barrier between us. Like there's an elephant in the room that I'm not privy to.

He leans his back against the counter as I spin on the stool to face him, and folds his arms across his broad chest, tightening his suit jacket around his shoulders. “I guess we should talk, huh?”

51

MATTEO

I hated not sleeping next to Lux last night, but I knew she needed to be with her mother, so I respected her wishes. That's not to say I didn't sneak into the spare bedroom during the night to check on her. It might've been the worst decision I could've possibly made, as all I wanted to do after seeing her lying there was take her back into our room, wrap my arms around her, hold her tight, and never let go.

Leaving their bedroom door open was the only thing that kept me sane, but when I went to check on them this morning, I could hear them talking.

He's in the Mafia, Lux.

I don't want to see you go down a dangerous path like I did.

Char's words seared through me like a heated knife lit by the flames of hell. I didn't stay a second longer, wanting to give Lux and her mother some privacy, but also needing time to cool off. Someone coming between us, especially someone so important to Lux, was pushing me to the point of insanity.

As I rest my back against the counter, I turn my head to

look at Lux, and *damn*. She's still absolutely stunning, even with the cuts that fucker Fausto left on the side of her face. When she explained to Doc how she got her injuries last night, all I could see was red and I nearly had to leave to go find someone or something to take my anger out on. The only thing that grounded me was Lux's hand on my thigh and the look she gave me that told me she needed me there for support.

"I missed you last night," she says with a smile as she slides off the stool and wraps her arms around me.

Unfolding my arms, I wrap them around her, making room for her to snuggle into my chest. I take in a deep breath, allowing her scent to consume me.

"I missed you, too, Little Lux," I murmur into the soft silk of her hair.

Pulling her head back she gazes up at me, studying my face with a crinkle in her brow. "What's wrong?" she asks.

I hate what I'm about to say next, but Lux's mother is right. This world is no place for her, and as much as I want to be selfish and keep her to myself, I have to at least give her the option to get away from this life. No matter how much it breaks me or tears at my heart, shredding it into a million little pieces with no chance at repair.

Cupping her cheek in my hand, she leans into it while her eyes remain focused on mine. "My life is constantly full of danger, Lux. That's not something that will ever change." The crinkle in her brow sharpens as her confusion grows.

"I forced you into a marriage with me." She opens her mouth to speak, but I stop her with a quick move of my finger, placing it lightly on her lips. "I forced you to say yes to a world you should have no part of. And now . . ." I gaze back and forth between her eyes and can see the vulnerability behind them as I speak. It's as if I'm seeing a direct reflection of the heartache I'm feeling within myself. "Now I'm giving you the chance to say no. To walk away from the dangers of this place. To walk away from me."

Lux brings her hand up to my chest, pressing on it lightly. "You want a divorce?" The surprise in her voice lingers in the air between us for a few moments.

I keep quiet, not able to let the words fall from my lips because this isn't what I want. I want to keep Lux to myself for the rest of our lives, but I can't be selfish.

"I want you to say it," she says, her voice growing louder. More urgent. "I want you to tell me that you want a divorce."

I drop my head and shake it as my voice remains low. "I can't."

"Then what is this all about?" she demands. Her hand pressed against my chest gets firmer. I lift my gaze back up to hers and cover her hand with mine.

"I'm trying to keep you away from a dangerous life. To give you a reason to get out."

"So you're saying you're not able to protect me? To keep me safe?"

"Of course I can protect you," I growl out. "I'd put my life on the line to keep you safe. I'd do fucking anything for you, Lux."

"Then I'm not going to say no. I'm not going to say no to being part of this world that you live in." She wraps her other hand around the back of my neck. "Because a world without you is a world I want no part of. I'm in this with you, Teo. I'm *choosing* to stay married to you for the rest of my life."

Her words set off an explosion of warmth in my chest, and I get lost in her eyes, not wanting to fight her on this because I need this woman like the air I breathe. She *wants* to stay with me. I've given her the choice, and she chose me. Like I would choose her every damn day.

I let out a long sigh of relief, knowing I've done the right thing. Knowing she refuses to leave me is the greatest fucking joy I could receive. "I swear I'll live every single day making you the happiest woman in the world."

A smile breaks out on her face. "You already do, Teo. You already do." She pulls my face down to hers, and I close the distance between us with a deep kiss full of meaning and emotion. I've fallen for this woman with everything that I have.

Sliding my hands up from under the sleek fabric of her pajama shorts, I grip the curve of her ass, lifting her into my arms. With a giggle, Lux instinctively wraps her legs around me, locking them in place behind my back as I continue to kiss her.

"What exactly do you think you're doing, *Mr. DiMaggio*?" Lux asks before pressing her lips back to mine.

"*Mr. DiMaggio*, huh?" I mumble against the heat of her mouth. "I could get used to you calling me that."

Tangling my fingers in her soft hair, I bring her closer and crash my lips back on hers as I walk us to our bedroom.

"Mmm, Teo. I want to feel you inside me," she murmurs as I set her down on the edge of the bed before stepping back to look at her—her flushed cheeks and swollen lips that beg to have mine back on them.

"In due time, baby, but right now I need to taste you. Not having you in my bed last night starved me of that pleasure," I say as I strip my jacket and dress shirt off. "Undress. Now." It comes off as a command and she responds immediately. I fucking love it.

She shimmies out of her pajama bottoms, letting her black lace underwear fall to the floor with the black shorts while I kick off my shoes. She watches me through hooded eyes as I push down my pants, letting my boxer briefs go with them, releasing my strained length from its confined space.

Lux's eyes light up when they fall to my dick. An involuntary twitch pulls from me as she licks her lips, but that's not what right now is for. Right now the only thing that matters is me tasting her.

She lifts her arms to pull her top over her head, but the movement has her stopping and sucking in a sharp breath.

Her back.

Closing the small distance between us, I place my hand on hers, pushing it back down to her lap. "Let me," I say as I unbutton her silk top. My fingers graze the valley between her breasts as I work my way down the buttons, and the heat from her skin sends a spark through my entire body.

Shedding the fabric off her shoulders, I step back and relish in her naked body. The piece of artwork it is. How it's something I know I'll always look at in absolute awe and never take for granted.

"I don't know what I did to deserve you, Little Lux, but I'm going to spend every day for the rest of our lives worshiping you the way you deserve."

I move around her to climb onto the bed and lie down, positioning my head at the base of the headboard before directing her. "Climb on top of me."

With a smile on her face, she crawls over me and straddles my hips. I let out a groan as her slick heat rubs against my hardened length. Grabbing a hold of her hips, I say, "Not there, baby. Climb on top of my *face.*"

Lux's eyes widen before a smirk pulls at the corner of her mouth. "Yes, *Mr. DiMaggio,*" she says in a sexy-as-sin voice. I almost force her to stay put, wanting to slam my cock so deep inside of her at the way she calls me *Mr. DiMaggio*, but I let her crawl up to my face, positioning herself right where I want her. Right where I *need* her.

The wet heat from her core drips on my face as she hovers over me. "Already so wet for me, baby?"

"I'm always wet for you, Teo," she breathes out as I grab her ass and pull her down onto my mouth, forcing her to drop her weight onto me.

"Teo," she cries out as she grabs ahold of the headboard and tries to offset her weight on my face, but I don't let her. I want to feel everything she has to give me.

Gripping her ass harder, a silent warning to her not to move off me, I mumble, "That's right, Little Lux. Brace yourself on that headboard while I eat this delicious pussy of yours. You're going to need it."

Her body quivers while I move my tongue along her slit, drinking in her sweet juices I crave day in and day out now. I let out a low groan at the same time she lets out her own voice of approval before I increase my speed.

Finding her clit, I rub it with my tongue and press her harder to me, not able to get enough of her.

"Oh fuck, Teo. Oh gosh, yes," she moans as she grips the headboard with both of her hands. The view of the curve of her tits hanging above me as she leans over will forever be inscribed in my brain.

As if they're calling my name, I move my hands to cradle her boobs, rubbing the hard peaks between my fingers. She lets out another feral moan as she grinds into me, and the rawness of it all has my throbbing cock standing on end. I won't last long at this rate.

Lux picks up her speed on my face as I keep the pressure of my tongue on her pussy, and a few seconds later, she's crying out in pleasure as she rides her orgasm out on me.

Her labored breaths come out uneven as she settles down from her high. "That was fucking amazing," she pants out.

I mumble out a chuckle when I wrap my hands around her

waist and lift her. "We're not done yet, baby," I say as I help position her over my cock that might combust as soon as I enter her wet heat.

Lux wraps her hand around my dick and runs it along her slit, coating it in her juices before lining up with her entrance. I let her take control, and she eases herself onto me, but the little minx messes with me by pulling herself up so just my tip remains inside of her.

"What exactly do you think you're doing, Little Lux?" I growl out with a raise of a brow.

A devilish smirk forms on her face. "This is kind of fun being in control," she says. "Seeing just how far I can push you."

I let out a tortured laugh as she repeats the movement. "Oh, you think you're in control, do you?" I ask, but before she's able to respond, I grip her hips once more and slam her onto me while thrusting my hips forward, her slickness allowing me to fully impale her tight hole.

She lets out a cry as she leans forward, resting her hands on my chest. "*Holy fuck*, Teo."

"Ride me, baby. Use me like the good girl you are."

She feels so fucking phenomenal as she clenches her walls around me and grinds her hips into mine. Her hair falls forward, draping against my chest before I brush it out of the way. Wrapping my hand around her head, I bring her face down to mine and crash my mouth against hers, thrusting my tongue into her mouth as it seeks the comfort of her own.

Lux's sharp moans mix with my low groans as I push myself up to a seated position. Feathering kisses down her neck, I make my way to her tit as she bounces up and down on my cock. "Oh yeah, baby. Keep bouncing on me just like that," I growl out, loving the sensation of her on top of me.

I suck her nipple into my mouth and caress her other boob.

She runs her fingers through my hair, pulling on the strands as she lets out another moan of pleasure.

Grabbing her ass, I lift her slightly, and as if we're on the same wavelength, she readjusts her legs from straddling my sides to wrapping them around my back, giving me a new angle so I can get deeper inside of her.

Bringing my mouth back up to hers, I mumble, "I can't get enough of you, Little Lux. I don't think I'll ever get enough of you."

She increases her pace, squeezing me with everything she has, and I meet each of her thrusts with my own. "You feel so fucking good, Teo," she pants out before thrusting her tongue back into my mouth.

Her walls tighten as I brace myself with my hand, extending it behind me so I can get more leverage as I lean back. Knowing I'm hitting that sweet spot, her moans become more in sync with my thrusts, so I pick up my pace while she does the same until she pulls her lips off mine and cries out my name while throwing her head back.

After a few more hard thrusts, her orgasm pulsing around my cock sends a tingling sensation to my balls and has me exploding like none other inside of her, giving her every drop of me as her name passes on my lips.

Our movements slow before coming to a stop, and there's nothing but the sounds of our rhythmic breathing as we come down from our highs.

I wrap my fingers in her hair and rest my forehead against hers as I close my eyes and marinate in this feeling. "You're everything, Lux," I breathe out. "I'm so fucking honored to call you my wife. I love you, baby."

Lux stares at me with parted lips before a smile breaks out on her face. "I love you too, Teo," she whispers. "And I'd choose this life over and over again if it meant choosing you."

She snuggles into me and I've never felt so satisfied in my life. I know it's wild that we haven't known each other long, but we've fallen in love with each other, and I can't imagine a stronger woman than Lux standing by my side, becoming the mother to my children, keeping me on my toes each of every day.

52

MATTEO

Three Months Later

"You ready to do this, Teo?" Enzo asks as we stand in Brooklyn Bridge Park, the home of the best view of the New York City skyline, and where I took Lux on our first date. *Who knew I could be so fucking cheesy.*

"That depends," I say as I fidget with the lapels of my suit jacket. "Did you remember the rings like I asked you to?" Enzo's eyes widen as he pats the pockets of his slacks and jacket.

"I swear, Enzo, I will fu—"

"Oh, here they are!" he yells, pulling the small black ring box out of the inside pocket of his suit jacket. He gives me a wink before laughing. "Man, you should see your face right now." Patting me on the shoulder, he adds, "Lighten up, Teo. You're getting married! Well, remarried, I guess. What do they call these things again?"

"Vow renewal, Enzo," I grit out, my anxiety getting to me, knowing Lux will be here any minute. "And if you had lost the ring that Lux chose, I really would've fucking killed you." Since the wedding band Lux has is a family heirloom, I had her pick out an engagement ring to go with it. We decided to stick with the band I already have, but I had it inscribed with our vow renewal date without her knowledge. She thought I left it with our jeweler to have it cleaned.

The past few months have been filled with her and I getting to know each other, inside and out, the old fashion way of dates and, well . . . having the best sex of my entire fucking life. I had no idea it could get better every single time we're together.

Having the relationship I do with Lux is something I never thought I'd have. My wife was always meant to be a business transaction, but Lux is so much more than I could have ever imagined. She might've started as an arrangement between that psychopath of a father she had and me, but she quickly became the most important person in my life.

Not only are Lux and I doing well, but Char and I have developed a good relationship too, and I have to admit, it's nice having a mother figure back in my life again. After we got her back from Mancini, I made it my mission to win her over and prove to her I'm nothing like that fucking man. My efforts are proving to be working well in that department.

I feel the vibration from my phone go off. Pulling it out from my pocket, I see it's a text from Char.

> Char: We're pulling up to the park now. The dress fit Lux perfectly. Izzy had to threaten her to keep her from crying and ruining her makeup.

A smile breaks out on my face, knowing that my beautiful wife will be here any minute.

Me: Tears of joy or tears of anger with wanting to kill her husband for keeping her in the dark about her own wedding for so many weeks now?

Char: Tears of joy, and possibly embarrassment. She has no idea how she never caught on to what you've been planning.

I had to be sneaky when planning this vow renewal. With how things started between the two of us, I wanted to make our marriage ceremony special for her. I wanted it to mean something instead of just being words repeated back and forth to each other for the sake of it.

I had Isabella and Char bring Lux to Liana's boutique to get her measurements done for a dress Liana is making for an event we have to go to in a few months. I could not have planned it to go any better than it did, because while Liana was taking down her measurements, she gave Lux her portfolio of designs, which included a line of wedding dresses she's been working on, to see if there was anything that caught her eye.

Falling right into the trap, Lux voiced how much she loved a particular wedding dress design, and then it was a cake walk from there. Char and Isabella surprised her with the dress and doing her hair and makeup a couple hours ago, and now they're all almost here. I'm about to get married to my wife all over again, and I can't fucking wait.

One of my G-Wagons pulls up, and my heart skips a beat knowing that on the other side of those tinted windows sits the woman I've fallen madly in love with.

Isabella and Char hop out in their dusty-blue dresses and round the SUV to help Lux out. After what feels like an eternity, my breath catches as I finally get the first glimpse of the love of my life as she walks toward Enzo and me with her mother and my sister flanking her sides.

She's a damn vision with her dark hair in a fancy updo and some strands hanging loose around her face. Her smile stretches wide from ear to ear as she makes her way toward me in an elegant and modern strapless satin gown with a slit high enough to give me a tease of what I'll have wrapped around my waist tonight. Or sooner, if I'm lucky.

Holding out my hands, Lux comes to me willingly, excitement radiating off her. "I can't believe you kept all of this from me. I feel so dumb for not putting it together," she says as I line her up in our spots.

"I wanted this to be a surprise for you and to make it as memorable as I could," I say while Char walks around us and takes her spot where an officiant would.

Lux glances over at her mother in confusion. "You're doing the ceremony for us?"

Smiling at her daughter like she's the greatest joy in her life, Char says, "Since you're already married, anyone can conduct the ceremony. But Teo, knowing you as well as he does, knew you'd want it to be private, so I volunteered to perform the ceremony so you truly are just surrounded by the people who love you most."

Letting go of my hands, Lux throws her arms around her mother and hugs her before pulling back. "We've really come full circle, haven't we, Mom. New York City was the reason we had to constantly move." Lux takes a second to look around at me, Enzo, and Isabella before turning back to her mother. "And now it's the reason we're finally able to settle down."

Rubbing her arm, Char says, "Yes, sweetie, and I'm so proud of you."

"Okay, stop. That's enough of the mushy gushiness. You're going to ruin her makeup, and I will *not* stand for that,"

Isabella calls out from behind Lux, and we can't all help but chuckle at how high strung she is about it.

"You look stunning, Little Lux." I take her hands in mine once more. "I don't know what I did to deserve you in my life, but I can't wait to say *I do* to you all over again."

A tear escapes her eye, rolling down her cheek.

"Ooh, she's crying, Izzy," Enzo says from behind me in his little shit starting way.

"I swear, Teo. I worked hard on her makeup!" my sister yells.

We all laugh, and I can't help but pull Lux into my arms and lightly wipe the tear from her cheek. "I love you, Little Lux," I say before jumping ahead to the part where I get to kiss my wife, giving her one so full of emotion I could get lost in it and never find my way out.

Finally pulling away, I gaze down into Lux's sparkling eyes as she says, "I love you too, Teo. More than life itself," before a playful smile breaks out on her face. "Now let's do the damn thing."

EPILOGUE

LUXTYN

"I would like to make a toast to the birthday girl," I announce, raising my champagne flute in the air to toast Izzy. Teo, Enzo, and Izzy raise theirs to join me before continuing.

"I know we haven't known each other long, but you quickly became not only my sister-in-law, but also my best friend. You're one of the greatest people I've come across in my life, and I'm so happy to be here with you celebrating your special day. Here's to a freaking fantastic year. I have a feeling twenty-four is going to be your best one yet." We all clink our glasses in cheers before taking a sip of our champagne.

We're at Izzy's favorite Italian restaurant celebrating her birthday. It's a tradition her parents started when she was young, and a tradition that Teo's continued to uphold even after they passed.

Izzy mouths, *I love you* to me as she sets her champagne flute down, and I blow a kiss back to her.

Life in New York City has been nothing short of amazing. After the vow renewal Teo surprised me with last month, he's been able to focus on the transition of taking over Angelo's territory. To my surprise, there wasn't much backlash when he returned the dead bodies of Angelo and Fausto to the Mancini family, informing them of the consequence of his actions for kidnapping my mom and me.

There's not much they could do. Angelo's territory is now Teo's, which makes him their new don. Many of Angelo's men had caught onto his crazed behavior and his lack of leadership prior to his death, so they had no issues with Teo stepping in. He gained the respect and obedience from most of his men quickly.

There were some that went back to the Silvestri family, like Elena and Giuliana, along with the men with previous loyalties to Giuseppe Silvestri, like Mauricio. There weren't many, but there were some, and Teo let it happen, knowing he wants none of those men working for him.

A warm hand finds its way on my thigh, rising slowly past the hem of my sweater dress. Clasping it in my own, I give Teo a playful side-eye. "And what exactly do you think you're doing?" I ask, bringing my gaze to his already darkened one. I can tell by that devilish grin that he's ready for this night to be over so he can take me to bed.

Leaning in, he whispers, "I'm ready to take my wife home and spend all night worshipping her perfect fucking body."

I clench my core at his words, which I'm sure will have me dripping in seconds if he continues. "We haven't even finished our main course yet, Teo. You're going to have to practice some patience tonight."

"Or how 'bout I take you in the back of the restaurant somewhere and enjoy my dessert first?" he rumbles in my ear. The vibrations quake through my entire body, and I swear I'm about to melt for him right here in my seat.

I'm about to take him up on his offer when our private room is invaded by unwelcome people. I recognize the three men from the strip club: Giuseppe and Niccolò Silvestri followed by Mauricio.

Just when I fear this will be one of those scenes you'd see in a Mafia movie, where everyone draws their guns, Teo and Enzo surprise me by acknowledging their presence with unimpressed facial expressions and by merely leaning back in their seats.

Pointing his finger at Teo in a threatening way, Giuseppe snarls, "What the hell do you think you're doing denying me access to Angelo's port?"

"Giuseppe, now is not the time nor place to speak business," my husband says coolly. His disinterest in this conversation only adds gas to the flames in Giuseppe's eyes as he steps closer, looking like the predatory monster he is.

"Matteo, you either give me access back to that port immediately, or—"

"Or what?" Matteo spits out. "You'll kill me like you did my parents?"

Giuseppe's jaw twitches. "You're asking for a war if you do this, kid. I'd think twice before entering that dangerous territory. You might've gotten lucky with taking out Angelo, but I promise you it won't be the same with me."

Teo leans forward, pushing back his plate before interlacing his fingers and setting them down on the table before him. "I've had a few years to think about this, and if a war is what you want, then a war is what you'll get."

The tension rises in the room as Giuseppe stares down at Matteo, his gaze dripping in anger. Glancing over at Niccolò, I notice he's focused on something else. When I locate the source of his attention and see it's Izzy, whose dropped gaze remains in her lap, my mind shoots me back in time to that night at the strip club at her reaction to seeing Niccolò beside his father. That falter in her step as if she'd seen a ghost.

It's not something I would've paid much attention to, but seeing the way he takes her in, waiting for her to give him the same attention he's giving her, tells me this is something else entirely.

I hear the deep rumble of a dark, maniacal laugh. "You're nothing but a child still, Matteo. You think I'm worried about some twenty-nine-year-old who's on a power trip coming after me? I've been in this game far longer than you have."

The vein on Giuseppe's temple throbs. It's something you can see even under the dimmed lighting of the room.

"I'm going to do you a favor and give you some time to rethink this decision of yours. I made Angelo Mancini a very rich man. You'd be wise to choose the same path he did."

Matteo leans back in his chair, looking as confident and disinterested as can be. But I know that look in his eye. It's calculated. Smart. He knows exactly what he's doing. "I assure you, Giuseppe. I will not be changing my mind."

Giuseppe cocks a brow, and we all feel the shift in the room. I glance behind him at Niccolò whose focus is brought back to his dad and Teo. I try to read his expression, but it's empty.

Giuseppe's jaw tics as he tenses, knowing Matteo's not going to give him what he wants right now. "This is the last leniency I'm willing to offer you. I'll give you a couple weeks to make the proper decision." He finally glances around at the rest of the table before looking back at Matteo and adds, "Enjoy whatever the hell this is, Matteo. Because if you don't make the right decision, this'll be the last little family outing you have." Without another word, Giuseppe turns on his heel and stalks away with Mauricio following suit.

Niccolò remains rooted in place, and I can see the curiosity in Teo's eyes as he stares at him, waiting for him to speak.

I glance back at Izzy who's now focused on Niccolò. Bouncing my gaze back to him, I watch as his eyes slide over to Izzy, narrowing in on her before saying, "Enjoy the rest of your birthday, Isabella." And without another word, not even enough time for Izzy to respond, he turns on his heel, leaving us to get back to our dinner.

Izzy's mouth drops slightly as he exits, like she wants to call out something to him but thinks twice before doing it. Teo and Enzo share a questioning look.

"How did he know it's your birthday?" Enzo asks, glancing over at Izzy.

Teo eyes his sister, waiting for her answer, as if he suspects it might be something he doesn't like. And if what I've come to think is correct, Teo will absolutely not like this.

Izzy's gaze falls to the side of her plate. "It's not rocket science, Enzo. The cards and gifts you guys got me are right here," she answers, placing a hand on the small pile of gifts she has. "It was probably to reiterate that threat his dad just made. Letting us know this will be the last family celebration we'll have if Teo doesn't give Giuseppe access back to the port."

Her answer seems to taper off any more suspicions from her brothers, but I continue to watch Izzy closely as Teo and Enzo envelop themselves deep in conversation. She seems to be lost in her own thoughts as she shifts her pasta around on her plate with the tip of her fork. I can tell she's trying to keep her expression neutral, but there's something else there. And with the threat Giuseppe left lingering in the air, I'm worried about the path we're about to go down and what that could mean for us all—what it could mean for Izzy.

THE END

SWIPE FOR AN EXCLUSIVE BONUS SCENE!

What's next?

Preorder The Snowed In Collection now!
Preorder The Bonetti Crime Family Book Two now!

BONUS SCENE

Want more Teo and Lux?

Sign up for my newsletter and receive an exclusive bonus scene now!

GET YOUR FREE BONUS HERE!

ALSO BY T. PRICETON

The DiMaggio Crime Family

Matteo: A Forced Marriage Mafia Romance (The DiMaggio Crime Family Book One)

Available on Amazon, Kindle Unlimited, and Audiobook

Isabella: A Second Chance Forbidden Mafia Romance (The DiMaggio Crime Family Book Two)

Available on Amazon, Kindle Unlimited, and Audiobook

Vincenzo: An Enemies to Lovers Mafia Romance (The DiMaggio Crime Family Book Three)

Available on Amazon, Kindle Unlimited, and Audiobook

The Bonetti Crime Family

Massimo: A Forced Marriage Mafia Romance (The Bonetti Crime Family Book One)

Available on Amazon and Kindle Unlimited

LET'S CONNECT!

Check out my links below to stay up to date on the latest from me!

https://linktr.ee/tpriceton

ACKNOWLEDGMENTS

I want to start off by saying thank you to all of the amazing readers who took a chance on my debut. Having so many people in my corner made this release so much more exciting for me, so thank you!

A big thank you to my editors and beta readers for helping me fine tune this story.

Melissa, thank you for being a cheerleader for me, and for helping me figure out this process. I'm so lucky to have you as part of my support system.

Lane, thank you for always being there to answer my tech questions and for supporting me throughout writing and publishing this debut.

J, not only were you a beta reader for me, but you rallied behind me throughout the rest of this project. Whether that be through emotional support as I overthought every word I wrote, or by holding me accountable during our editing sprints. Thank you so much. I truly value our friendship.

Thank you to my girl, Natalia—my ride or die. There really aren't any words that I can use to describe how appreciative I am of you. You stuck around through my roller coaster of emotions and helped give me the confidence I needed to follow through with publishing Matteo. I will always be grateful for you.

And last, but not least, thank you to my husband, Mr. Priceton. You've been so incredibly supportive since the day I finally caved and told you my crazy dreams of becoming a self-published author. You've lifted my spirits when I was feeling down and you helped with the boys and around the house any time I needed to clock in some words. I'm so lucky to have such an amazing spouse. Without you, Matteo would've never come about. I love you so much!

xoxo,

T

Printed in Dunstable, United Kingdom

80677386R00190